CATRIONA CHILD was born in 1980 in Dundee and spent a great deal of her youth ploughing up and down swimming pools. She has a degree in English from the University of Aberdeen and an MA with distinction in Creative Writing from Lancaster University. She won the Sunday Herald Blog competition in 2007, was shortlisted for the National Library of Scotland/The Scotsman Crime short story competition in 2008, and has been published in the Scottish Book Trust *Family Legends* anthology and in *Northwords Now*. Her first novel, *Trackman*, 2012, was described by *The Herald* as having 'all the makings of a cult hit'. She lives in Edinburgh with her husband Allan and children Corrie and Alasdair.

Swim Until You Can't See Land

CATRIONA CHILD

Leabharlanna Poiblí Chathair Baile Átha Cliath
Dublin City Public Libraries

Luath Press Limited
EDINBURGH
www.luath.co.uk

Hardback edition 2014
This edition 2020

ISBN: 978-1-912147-02-1

The publisher acknowledges the support of

ALBA | CHRUTHACHAIL

towards the publication of this volume.

The paper used in this book is recyclable. It is made from low-chlorine pulps
produced in a low-energy, low-emissions manner from renewable forests.

Printed and bound by
Ashford Colour Press, Gosport

Typeset in 10 point Sabon by Main Point Books, Edinburgh

For Corrie

Acknowledgements

Thanks go to –

Gavin and everyone at Luath Press for their continued support and encouragement.
Jennie Renton for, once again, putting up with my many fonts.
Grant for his help with the German, and Fred and Sarah for their help with the French.
Ossian for his medical knowledge.
Sue for reading the initial drafts and for her editing advice.
James for his continued support, and for giving me the chance to try out an early draft of chapter one on an unsuspecting audience.
The Yahoo group 'Photo History' who confirmed that I had not imagined the idea of 'street photographers.'
Dr Juliette Pattinson from the University of Strathclyde, who helped with my questions on coded messages.
My local library who made the research involved in this book so much easier.
Mum, Dad, Jamie, Iona and Eilidh for being the best family in the world. Dad, especially for his constant nagging – 'How's the book coming along?'
Also my extended family and friends – Childs, Elders and Irvines, and my Grandparents (Connel and Dundee), especially Granny Dundee's stories about ww2.
Speckled Jim, gone but not forgotten, and the inspiration for the fish character.
Allan, for always being there and making things easy.
Finally, to Corrie – our beautiful wee girl. Thank you for sleeping on my tummy while I looked at edits.

If you are a person who is drowning,
you put all your efforts into trying to swim.
Eileen Nearne

Hannah's Got The Wright Stuff!
Local swimmer takes four golds

Perth City Amateur Swim Club have a new swimming sensation in Hannah Wright, after she dominated the Midland District championships in Dundee this weekend. Hannah, aged only 11 and competing against girls two years older than her in the U13 category, stormed to victory in all four stroke disciplines.

She won the 100m Backstroke and Breaststroke on Saturday then followed this up with wins in the 100m Butterfly and Freestyle on the Sunday.

Coach, Greg Candy, said he was thrilled at how well Hannah had done but wasn't surprised at her success. 'I knew from the moment I saw her that she had a natural ability for the sport. I've never seen a swimmer like her in the 35 years I've been a coach.'

NO DIVING.

I curl my toes around the edge of the pool and adjust my goggles, push on them till they suck at my eyeballs. Bend forward, tap my painted toenails, then

I dive.

Streamline, I skim just below the surface of the water, catch a flash of yellow t-shirt as I enter the pool. Chris, the lifeguard, leans against the wall, eyes closed, hair sticking up. His whistle dangles from his shorts pocket. When he first started working here, he called me up for diving. Now he doesn't bother. He knows who I am.

(who I was)

He knows I'm not about to go breaking my neck.

'Will you keep an eye on things while I go to Bayne's,' Shirley asks.

'Yeah, no problem.'

'You want anything? Filled roll? Donut? Need to get there before the school's out or there'll be nothing left.'

'Eh, cheese and tomato roll, if you don't mind.'

'Cake?'

'Go on then, a custard slice.'

The door goes and I look up, expecting it to be Shirley, back again with another question.

You want a drink?

Bottle or can?

Butter on your filled roll?

(on top or doggy style?)

It's not her though, some old woman I don't recognise.

She puts a bag of Revels on the counter, then rummages through her handbag, lifts out her purse and slides a piece of paper from it.

'And a lottery ticket, please,' she says and hands me the paper.

Six numbers scrawled in that spidery handwriting that all old people seem to have.

5   16   21   26   32   44

Her accent's strange: Scottish, but with a twang of something else. I print the lottery ticket, put it down next to the Revels.

'£1.57, please.'

The woman doesn't answer, doesn't hand me any money, doesn't move.

I follow her gaze. She's looking at something behind my head. Does she want cigarettes?

'Anything else?' I ask.

Her face has gone a dirty silver colour, like the Brasso polish Gran used to buff on my swimming trophies.

It's a dumb rule anyway, no diving. Diving is the only way to enter a pool.

None of this descending down a flimsy, metal staircase while it rattles off the tiled walls.

None of this lowering yourself feet first from the edge, the cold water chilling you from the toes up.

No, that just gives the water the advantage, gives it the power. If you don't dive in, then you struggle to get your shoulders under. You have to bounce, bounce, bounce, try to plunge yourself deeper, deeeper, deeeeper, until you finally build up the courage to submerge completely.

You're beaten before you've even managed to dunk your head under. Game over. Back to the showers with you.

Diving gives you the upper hand, puts you in control.

The woman doesn't speak, although her lips keep moving. Vibrating, quivering. Dark, like she's wearing purple lipstick.

'Are you okay?'

Her fingers spread and the purse falls from her hand. Change spills, rolling and clattering off the counter and onto the floor.

I move out from behind the till but before I can get to her she crumples. There's a thud as she hits her chin on the glass-fronted counter.

Shit, that was loud.

A crack runs out along the glass, slicing the reflection of Panini stickers, Rizla papers and mix-up sweets beneath it.

My heart's pounding as I move towards her. She's lying on her side, blood dripping from her chin. Her false teeth have fallen out. I accidentally kick them in my haste and they spin away across the floor.

I kneel beside her, knock a display of chewing gum off the edge of the counter. It falls, showering us with packets of Extra.

'Sorry, sorry,' I say.

She doesn't look well, not well at all. She gasps for breath, fumbles with the buttons on the collar of her blouse, blood pours down onto her hands but I don't think she's noticed she's bleeding.

'I'll get that,' I say and undo her top button. Her hands grab at mine, clammy and damp.

She's wearing a silk scarf tied around her neck so I lift it, press it against the cut. The blood, warm and sticky, seeps into it, turns the pale silk dark.

Shit, what do I do? What the hell do I do?

Shirley's the first aider, not me. Where is she?

The chlorine, the wet, the chill, it hits you all at once but it doesn't matter. Because you're straight into your stroke and the cold's gone before you're halfway down your first length.

I know how to work the water with my hands, with my feet. I know the shapes to make with my arms, my legs. Keyhole, figure of eight, breakout, pull through. My hands are paddles, the roll of my shoulders, the froth at my toes.

Push me on, propel me forward. Push me on, propel me forward.

Stroke, stroke, stroke, breathe, stroke, stroke, stroke, breathe.

My hands shake as I squeeze the scarf. Blood oozes, dribbles between my knuckles.

'Don't worry, you'll be alright,' I say, but my voice is different from how it normally sounds.

Her eyes roll backwards, eyelids fluttering. She looks worse now, if that's even possible. There's no colour in her face, drained away with the blood through her chin.

Shit, I think she's dying. She's dying and I'm just sitting here letting it happen. I need to do something. Come on, Hannah.

I let go of the scarf. My hands are covered in blood and I wipe them on the woman's jacket before digging my mobile out of my jeans pocket.

999

'Hello, you're through to emergency services, what service do you require?'

My brain has stopped working. Service? What service do I require?

Ambulance, ambulance, ambulance, ambulance.

'Sorry, ambulance, please.'

'That's alright. Can you tell me what's happened and the address?'

'It's Shop Better, on the High Street in Kinross. I'm sorry, I can't remember the exact number, next to the Post Office. An old woman's collapsed, she's bleeding.'

'Is she breathing?'

The door opens.

Thank fuck for that.

It's Shirley, back from Bayne's with the filled rolls and the custard slices.

'Hells bells, what's happened?' She drops the paper bag and box of cakes onto the floor.

'She went all funny, then she just fell.'

'Hello, can you hear me? Can you hear me? What's your name?' Shirley asks, as she grips the woman under the armpits and tries to prop her up against the counter.

'Get an ambulance, Hannah, I think she might be having a heart attack or something. It's not good, whatever the hell it is.'

I'm not sure Shirley should be saying stuff like that in front of the old woman, but I doubt she's aware of what's going on.

'I've already done that,' I say and hold the phone up to my ear again. The woman is still there asking questions.

'There's a first aider here now,' I say. My hands are shaking so much I can't hold the phone still. I hear the phrase 'the ambulance is on its way' and I hang up.

I'm out of breath and all I've done is make a phone call.

Shirley's still trying to prop the woman up, but she's lifeless and falls to one side.

'She's bloody heavy for such a wee thing,' Shirley says, her face flushed, 'pass me some aspirin, will you?'

'What?' I reply.

'Aspirin.'

It's not a sore head, Shirley, I feel like saying, but I grab a box from behind the counter, pass it to her. She pulls the foil packet out of the box, presses out a white aspirin.

'Crunch and chew, crunch and chew.'

I think Shirley's lost it. She's trying to force the Aspirin into the woman's mouth. My eyes are drawn to a circle of silver foil from the Aspirin packet which lingers in the air before landing in a pool of blood on the floor. It floats, rippling from side to side; the whole surface shimmers, even the blood has a glossy sheen to it.

'Crunch and chew.'

I notice something lying to the side of the blood, grab Shirley's arm.

'Her teeth, Shirl.'

Shirley picks up the aspirin, now pink, which has fallen from the woman's mouth, tries to pop it back in. The woman's eyes are rolling in her head, backwards, forwards, side to side.

'Her teeth fell out.'

'What?'

'Her false teeth fell out.'

'Oh Jesus.'

'Shall I get them, they're just here?'

'I think she's stopped breathing, Hannah.'

Shirley grabs the woman by her ankles, pulls her forward until she lies flat. There's a thud as the back of her head hits the floor.

Shirley sees me flinch.

'That's the least of her problems, tell them she's stopped breathing.'

'Tell who?'

'The ambulance, where are they? They should be here by now.'

Cap tight against my skull, costume a size too small, slick against shaved skin. Bubbles rise to the surface from my nose, my mouth.

Stroke, stroke, stroke, breathe, stroke, stroke, stroke, breathe.

The water slides off me, gathers like pearls on my nails, my bare skin. I'm impervious. Silky and varnished.

Stroke, stroke, stroke, breathe, stroke, stroke, stroke, breathe.

Shirley starts to do CPR. My eyes are drawn to her tits as they bounce up and down.

'One and two and three and four and five and six and seven and eight and nine and ten and eleven...'

Stroke, stroke, stroke, breathe, stroke, stroke, stroke, breathe.

Breathe, come on, breathe. You can't die, not here, not on the floor of Shirley's shop.

Shirley lifts the woman's blouse, uses it to clean her chin. I see her bra, her bare stomach; the skin saggy and stretch-marked, off-white like porridge. Shirley presses the woman's nose, tilts her head back, blows into her mouth, then she's bouncing again.

'One and two and three and four and five and six and seven and eight and nine...'

I try to stop it, but my brain keeps saying inappropriate things, things I'm ashamed to be thinking of at a time like this. Hell, at any time.

Shirley could do with a decent bra.

I never realised how big her tits were before.

I wonder if she did that to my dad?

Bounced up and down on him, her tits smacking him in the face.

Jesus, Hannah, stop it.

Her face is red, hair stuck to her sweaty forehead.
'I   need   help   can   you   breathe for   me?'
I know it's a horrible thing to think but I don't want to go near that
old woman. I don't want to touch her. Her chin's stained with blood,
seeped into the wrinkles, paint filling in the cracks.
'I don't know how.'
'I'll   show   you.'
I shuffle forward so I'm on the other side of the woman.
'Pinch   her   nose,   form   a   seal.'
I lean forward. She smells. It's so strong, meaty.
I put my lips over her mouth, slowly, willing the ambulance to show.
I try not to think about what I'm doing. Think about anything else, even
Shirley doing Dad is preferable to this. Shirley's tits, Shirley's tits,
Shirley's tits.
The woman's face is cold, clammy. I can taste salt. I close my eyes,
blow, but I'm barely touching her, not forming the seal that Shirley's so
keen on. My hair's covering her face, it makes it easier. I press down
harder, blow again. Pretend I'm kissing a mermaid.
'Well   done, one   and   two   and   t h r e e
and   four   and   five   and   six...'
Shirley's counting's getting slower, her chest heaving.
Stroke, stroke, stroke, breathe, stroke, stroke, stroke, breathe.
'...twenty-six and   twenty-seven and   t w e n t y - e i g h t
and twenty-nine   and   thirty.'
Mermaid kiss, mermaid kiss.
'One and   two   and   three   and   four...'

Dark tiles, T-shaped on the bottom of the pool tell me the wall's coming.
I don't need the reminder though, I know exactly where I am.

I know the number of strokes, the number of breaths. I close my eyes
and I still know where the wall is. I can't gauge distance on dry land, but
in the pool I have an inbuilt GPS system.

I stretch with my arm, a flash of red fingernails. Then my hand pulls
me down, flips me over into a tumble turn. My feet plant on the wall,
firm, no sliding on wet tiles. Knees bend, I thrust myself forward, arms
out in front, head down. Streamline. A short breakout, hips undulating,
dolphin kick, then I'm back into my stroke.

I hear the sirens, in the distance, then louder and louder as they approach
the shop. An excuse to get away.
My legs may be wobbly but they want me as far away from this as

possible. They propel me up and towards the door. I stumble, kick a packet of chewing gum as I go. It spins across the floor, hits the front door as I open it. I pick up the packet, fall out onto the pavement. Fresh air, glorious fresh air. I suck it in as I wave down the ambulance.

Two paramedics jump out, doors slam. They run past, nod at me but don't stop to talk. I stick two bits of chewing gum in my mouth.

Crunch and chew. Crunch and chew.

I think I'm going to puke. I can feel warm saliva collect in my mouth, a pulse in my gut.

I lean against the shop window, inhale through my nose. I try to breathe the gum, let the mint cleanse me, push out the rich, metallic taste of the old woman. I don't want to see what they're doing to her in there. Using defibrillators. Making her back arch and legs quiver.

Shirley and Dad having sex, Shirley and Dad having sex, Shirley and Dad fucking.

My knees buckle and I sit down on the pavement. People walk past, stare at the ambulance, at me, try to peer in the shop window. Nosy bastards. I can see the kids from the High School, getting closer, closer. Girls and boys in blazers and ties and black shoes, pounding along the pavement towards me. Laughing and joking and bumping into each other. After their crisps and their Irn-Bru and their donuts and their ten pee mix-ups.

I spit the gum out into the gutter. Everything's spinning and there's black spots in front of my eyes. I think I might pass out. Shirley would never survive another cycle of CPR.

I close my eyes, lean forward and put my head between my knees. I don't care that the kids are getting closer, that they can see me sitting on the pavement. If I keep my head down and my eyes shut, they'll go straight past and it won't matter.

I won't see them, they won't see me.

Like being underwater, everything muffled.

Stroke, stroke, stroke, breathe, stroke, stroke, stroke, breathe.

With each length, I loosen off. Shoulders, hips, wrists, ankles, neck. Heart pumps. Lungs swell.

Stroke, stroke, stroke, breathe, stroke, stroke, stroke, breathe.

I've got the lane to myself. Not many people can be bothered getting up this early to swim.

(late compared to when I used to get up)

The Daybreak Dip.

One of the reasons why I like this time so much. I'm free to power up and down the pool, nobody in my way as I count the metres before work.

400m.

800m.

1200m.

I hear footsteps and hurried voices, then the ambulance doors slam. I jump as the sirens come on again, can see the blue flashing lights behind my closed eyelids. Was she dead? Did they just carry a dead body past me?

No, they wouldn't bother with the sirens if she was dead.

The noise fades as the ambulance moves further away and I allow myself to break the surface of the water. Open my eyes, everything's clear and in focus again. The kids are walking past me now, looking down at me, hesitating, staring in the shop window.

'What happened?'

'Did somebody die?'

'That girl's got blood on her.'

I get to my feet, force myself back inside the shop.

I glance at the clock as I turn to breathe.

Time to get out.

I finish the length, pull my goggles and cap off.

My hair flows out behind me as I float on my back, watch the rise and fall of my chest as my breathing slows, goes back to normal.

'That you for today?' Chris asks, still leaning against the wall, arms folded.

'Yeah, need to get to work.'

'I'm tired just watching you.' He yawns, his eyes fill with tears and he wipes them away.

I laugh, even though he makes the same joke every morning.

In the showers, I close my eyes, let the water wash away what it can of the chlorine.

Never powerful enough.

Never hot enough.

I like it hot.

Hot enough to pink my skin.

Taste salt and shampoo as the water drizzles the back of my head, my shoulders.

You can lather, rinse, repeat as much as you want, the chlorine never truly washes off.

(you stink of swimming pool)
I tilt my head back, let the water pour over my face, into my mouth, enjoy the taste, comforting, like sucking bath water through a sponge.

Shirley's sitting on the floor.
I move the sign on the door.
CLOSED.

2

'MENTEUSE! TELL US the truth.'

A hand gripped the back of her head, plunged her face into the water.

She'd never felt cold like it, not even paddling in the North Sea. The water clamped at her head.

How long was he going to hold her under? Was this it? End of interrogation? They were just going to drown her. Leave her face down in this marble trough.

Lungs tight, she breathed out. Air flushed from her nose and mouth, she felt it whoosh past her face on the way to the surface. She only had so long now before she'd have to breathe in. Then it would be water, rushing and flooding her.

She shook from side to side. The man was too strong though. The more she struggled, the firmer his grip. His hand fixed on the back of her head, her skull nestled in it like an egg in an eggcup. Her fingers flexed, useless, her wrists bound. She dug her fingernails into the palms of her hands, drew blood.

Then she was pulled backwards by her hair. Face out of the trough like a plunger with a suck of air. She shivered as the water ran down her neck, her back, her shoulders. Another man stood opposite the trough, watching. He moved aside to avoid getting his boots wet.

'Tell us the truth. *Dis-nous la vérité.*'

The German accent was unmistakeable, despite the French words coming from his mouth. He wouldn't last five minutes trying to blend in as a native.

The accent has to be just right, or the locals will spot you a mile away. And you can't trust anyone. There are collaborators who will hand you over to the Boche in a flash if they think it will get them a loaf of bread.

Her lips trembled as she tried to speak.

'*Je vous en prie*, I am telling you the truth, my name is...'

Before she could continue, the man opposite nodded and she felt the force on the back of her head again. Plunged under, too quick to take a proper breath. Bubbles escaped from her nose and mouth. Less air than last time, less air. She'd been speaking when he pushed her forward. That wasn't fair.

'You are a British spy, admit it and we will stop.'

She heard the man speak as she was lifted out of the water. She didn't try to answer, just took a deep breath. Air, beautiful air, filling her up.

Her head felt delineated, the skin tight, smooth like a pebble. Hair hung wet over her forehead, irritating, she wanted to push it out of her eyes.

They warned you about this. They trained you for this. They told you how ruthless the Gestapo would be if you were caught.

Training, God, that seemed so long ago now.

Dates, names, addresses rushed through her head. She tried to remember. She had to remember.

.. / .- -- / .... .- -... .. -. . / ...- .- .-.. --- .. ...

It was very important she got everything right. She listed it all in her head, tried to ignore the burning in her chest, the pain in her lungs. Tried to push away that other voice. The scared part of her. The part screaming. Oh, God, just tell them the truth. They already know anyway.

She didn't think she'd get caught. Even when they told her the averages.

The average lifespan between arrival and capture for a w/t operator in France is six weeks.

Remember the story.

Your name is Sabine Valois.

You are from Paris.

You have been ill, suffering from Rheumatic Fever.

You have been staying with your aunt while you recover.

Your name is Sabine Valois.

Sabine Valois.

She was going to die.

Malade. Rheumatic fever.

Paris.

Aunt's house in the country.

Sabine.

She was going to die. Face down in the bloody baignoire.

Sabine Valois.

Your name is Sabine Valois.

She was going to die.

Going to die.

Sabine.

Die.

Sabine.

Die.

How many times had she been ducked? It was never-ending. A relentless cycle of submersion then air, submersion then air, submersion then air. She could see shapes in the water, dark behind her closed eyelids, dots, dashes, dots, dashes, dots, dashes.

'*Tu parleras.*'

'*Je m'appelle Sabine Valois.*'

'*Tu parleras.*'

'I am Sabine Valois.'

He wore a dark suit, a revolver slung at his side, his hair slick, in a side parting.

'*Tu parleras.*'

'*Je suis Française.*'

'You are a British spy.'

'*Non, je suis Française.*'

'*Lügner.*'

'*Je ne parle pas allemand.* I can't speak German.'

'You are a British spy, tell the truth.'

'*Je m'appelle Sabine Valois.*'

'*Lügner.*'

She'd been taught to expect this kind of brutal treatment at the hands of the Gestapo. Trained for it. They picked her because she was good, because she was brave, because she was strong. She couldn't let them down.

Wake up, *wach auf, wach auf.*

Shaken awake at two in the morning, three men wearing German uniforms standing over her. Dragged to a cellar, tied to a chair. She knew she was still in Britain. They were so brutal though, so convincing. They shone a lamp into her eyes, slapped her, forced her to answer questions about who she was, what she was doing.

Je m'appelle Sabine Valois.

They kept her there for hours before finally revealing it was all a test. A practice run for the real thing. The Gestapo would be worse than this, they told her, as they unbuttoned their tunics, took her for cocoa and scrambled eggs, gave her feedback.

As if it was a job interview, nothing more.

I am Sabine Valois.

British.

I live in Paris.

British spy.

This was real. There was real hatred, venom behind the questions. Nobody would smile at her. Give her cocoa and scrambled eggs. They would keep going until she spoke or until she died.

Sabine Valois.

Liar.

They didn't believe her. They knew she was a spy. Maybe she should just come clean?

No. If she admitted they were right, even in her head, then they had her. She was not a spy. She was Sabine Valois. She had never been to London.

Oh God, but the water was so cold and she didn't want to die, she didn't want to die.

'We will stop if you tell the truth.'

She'd wet herself. Could feel the contrast of the warm water as it trickled down her thighs under her skirt.

What if they saw, if they noticed? She couldn't help it. Hadn't even realised it was happening until it ran down her legs.

I am Sabine Valois.

Lügner.

She had nothing to be ashamed of. They were trying to bloody drown her and she was worried because she'd wet her pants. Of all the stupid, bloody things to worry about now. God, she hoped they saw it. Hoped they were disgusted by it. She wanted to disgust them.

They disgusted her, after all.

Pigs.

Good, this was good. Anger was good. It kept you fighting, made you strong.

'Talk and we'll stop.'

'*Je dis la vérité.*'

'Liar.'

If you are able to withstand the first quarter of torture, then you probably won't talk.

How long had it been? Was she a quarter into it yet? How was she supposed to know what a bloody quarter was unless she knew what the total was.

She felt the silver crucifix nestled under her blouse.

God

(George)

Please keep me strong.

Her chest spasmed, her mouth opening and closing. A reflex action, like a fish on the deck of a boat.

(a felucca)

She'd stopped struggling so much now, not a conscious decision. She just couldn't fight. She was so tired. The crucifix rocked against her chest.

'*Lügner.*'

'*Je ne parle pas allemand. Je suis Française.*'

She slumped over the edge of the trough, her bosom crushed against the cold marble. Water sloshed over the top, soaked her. If he let go of her hair, she wouldn't have the strength to lift her head.

'Talk.'

'*Je vous en prie, je m'appelle Sabine Valois.*'

She had to stick to the story, no matter how weak her body was. She would die knowing she hadn't let anyone down.

'*Vous êtes un espionne Britannique.*'

'Non!'

'Liar. *Tu parleras.*'

The longest he'd held her under yet. This was the end. They didn't care if she was guilty or innocent. She was just another French girl, soon to be another dead French girl. She wanted to die with her eyes open but it was too painful. Dot. Dash. Dot. Dash. Dot. Dash. Dot. Dash.

Her shoulders bucked and rolled, she could feel her legs trying to kick. Her faithful little body, trying to keep going, trying to ground her soul even though it was too late now.

The hand on the back of her head was too strong.

She suck, suck, sucked as she was pulled free of the water; the air no longer sweet and pure, but painful. Pin pricks up and down her windpipe and inside her chest.

The man standing opposite swung an arm. His   hand   in slow   motion   came   towards   her   and the slap when it hit wasn't sore.

She saw him connect with her face but she didn't feel it. It was happening to someone else. The hand holding her hair let go and she fell backwards away from the trough. God, the irony, if she died down here in a puddle on the floor.

She could hear them speaking German now. Did they believe her? They sounded far away, at the other end of a long corridor. She could still feel the hand gripping her head.

The ghost of it.

She watched two pairs of boots as they walked away from her, leaving wet footprints.

She was alone.

The concrete, damp against her cheeks.

She was alive.

She closed her eyes, lay still on the wet floor.

It's All'wright For Local Swimmer!

Local swimming prodigy Hannah Wright had a successful weekend at the Scottish Schools Swimming Championships in Edinburgh, winning the 50m Butterfly in a new meet record of 31.16.

Hannah, who qualified for the event after winning the local Midlands District School Championships, beat off competitors from all over Scotland to claim the title.

It was the first time Hannah had competed in a long course event, but she took it all in her stride.

'I usually train in a 25m pool, so it was different from what I'm normally used to,' said Hannah after the event. 'It was fine though, I just pretended it was still 25m when I dived in!'

3

'I DON'T KNOW about you, but I need some tea before we start trying to sort this out.' Shirley says, gesturing to the mess on the shop floor.

She's still out of breath, hair matted, clothes crumpled.

I nod, not sure I can speak right now.

The floor's covered in stuff, fallen from the counter and knocked over by the paramedics in their rush.

There's a clear space in the middle of it all, like someone's come along with an old woman-shaped cookie cutter. If I close my eyes, I can still see her lying there.

I swallow down sick, feel it burn my throat.

'You okay, sweetheart? You're really pale.'

I nod again, scared to open my mouth in case I puke.

'Sure?'

'Feel a bit queasy.'

'Come on. Let's just go and sit down for half an hour. It's the adrenaline you know, it's fine once it's pumping round you, but when it leaves you...'

Shirley puts an arm around me, leads me into the staff room. I turn my face away from her bloody hand on my shoulder.

(use the adrenaline, Hannah, use the nerves to your own advantage)

I could work it in the pool, but not today.

I stand at the sink and scrub my hands, smother them in soap, turn the tap up full so the hot water splutters out. My red fingernails flash at me through the foam.

'God, Hannah, that water's burning,' Shirley says as she takes over from me at the sink.

The smell of cheap soap makes my stomach turn.

'Look at that,' Shirley says, holding out her hand, 'can't stop it from shaking.'

She squeezes her hand into a fist then stretches her fingers out again. Still shaking.

'You were brilliant,' I reply, 'If you hadn't come back when you did...'

'When I went on that first aid course, I never thought I'd have to use it,' she says as she flicks the kettle on.

Bang! Bang! Bang!

We both jump.

Bang! Bang! Bang!

'What is it?' I ask.

'I think it's someone at the door, can't they see we're closed?'

Bang! Bang! Bang! Bang!

'Just ignore it, they'll go away,' Shirley drops teabags into two mugs.

I want to get out of here, go home, get out of these clothes. Shirley can deal with all this, it's her shop.

'Oh, I'm vibrating.'

'What?'

'My phone,' Shirley replies.

I can't help it though, my mind conjures up dildo. Maybe that's what she uses now she and Dad aren't shagging?

Maybe they used one together?

Fuck sake, what's wrong with me?

Shirley pulls her mobile out of her cardigan pocket.

'It's Calum,' she says, before answering.

'Hi love.'

'What? No, I'm okay.'

'How do you know we're shut?'

'Oh, is that you? Hang on, I'll let you in.'

'Calum's outside,' she says, hanging up.

She leaves the staff room and I relish the few seconds of calm, of being on my own.

'Hey, Hannah,' Calum says as he follows Shirley back through, 'you alright?'

'Yeah, feel a bit weird, but I'm okay. You want tea?' I hold up a spare mug.

'Aye, thanks. Mum was just telling me what happened, fuck sake, eh?'

'Language,' Shirley smacks him on the back of the head.

He sits at the table, smoothes his hair down. He's in his school uniform, tie hangs loose, fraying, the top button of his shirt undone.

The old woman's hands, grasping for the top button of her blouse.

I grip the counter, unsteady.

'I was heading to Bayne's when I noticed you were shut,' Calum says. 'I got a real fright when I looked in and saw the mess.'

'Oh, you just reminded me,' Shirley goes back out into the shop and returns with the Bayne's bag. It seems like ages ago since she asked me what I wanted from the bakers. I can't believe she's still hungry.

I finish making the tea, carry the mugs one at a time over to the table.

Even that's a struggle.

I sit opposite Shirley and Calum.

'Not sure I can face that anymore,' I nod at the custard slice. You want it, Calum?'

'Aye, cheers,' he leans across the table.

Shirley smacks his hand away.

'Wait a minute. Hannah, you sure? You could do with some sugar in you.'

'I'm fine with the roll, you have it, Calum.'

Calum reaches for the cake again. He puts it upside down in front of him, peels the bottom layer of pastry off.

'I eat it from the bottom up, like leaving the icing till last,' he says, noticing my stare, 'it's the best bit.'

'Disgusting, he doesn't get that from me,' Shirley says.

I smile, keep my lips firmly closed. Calum's cake habits are doing nothing to help my churning tummy.

'Who was it anyway?' Calum asks, mouth full of custard.

I look down at the table, pick a slice of tomato out of my filled roll. I don't think I'll manage the bread, let alone something squashy and wet inside it.

Something red.

'Who was who?' Shirley replies, taking a bite of her roll and wiping her floured hands onto her trousers.

How can she stay so calm after what just happened?

I play with a bit of grated cheese, squash it between my fingers.

'The wifie who collapsed.'

'Hells bells, Calum,' Shirley hits him on the back of the head again, 'have a bit of respect. I didn't know her, did you, Hannah?'

I shake my head, pick up the roll; grated cheese falls out onto the table. I take a bite. It fills my whole mouth, takes an age to chew. The greasy butter, the wet cucumber, the soggy bread.

I keep seeing her face, the expression on it right before she fell. One minute you're buying Revels, the next...

Snap of the fingers. That's it.

(the difference between winning and losing a race)

'Had you better not get back to school?' Shirley looks at her watch.

'Nah, I've got a free period.'

'A free period?'

'Yes, Mum, remember I'm in sixth year now.'

'Well, should you not be using that so-called free period to do some studying or something?'

Calum rolls his eyes.

'Either that or you can help me and Hannah tidy up.'

'I'll see you guys later then, thanks for the cake, Hannah.'

'No problem.'

'You sure you guys are okay?'

'Yes, we'll survive.'

Calum waves as he leaves the shop, shirt un-tucked, hanging over his trousers.

'He's a bloody mess, that boy,' Shirley says, 'right, shall we get this place sorted out?'

'Yeah.'

Maybe I'll feel better if I'm doing something. Besides, I want to get the shop back to normal. Get rid of that body-shaped hole.

'Hells bells, I didn't notice that,' Shirley runs a finger along the break in the glass counter. I hear the crack in my head again, her chin splitting, teeth falling out.

'That's why she was bleeding.'

'She gave herself a right clout, didn't she?'

'Her teeth…' I look around.

'It's okay, I found them and put them in her handbag. The paramedics took it. Just in case.'

'Do you think she'll be okay?'

Shirley's still looking at the break in the counter.

'I don't know. Maybe I'll give the hospital a phone later.'

'Yeah.'

I'm not sure if I really want to know either way. I just want to get this day off me.

I could do with pounding the pool. But it's always so busy in the evening. Swimming lessons and aqua aerobics classes.

(swim club training sessions)

I kneel, pick up packets of chewing gum, slot them back into the cardboard container they've fallen from. Congealed blood puddles on the vinyl floor. I should get a cloth, wipe it up before it dries and crusts, but I can't face it. I've just washed my hands.

Shirley clears everything from the top of the counter, piles it up on the floor.

'I'll need to phone someone about this glass.'

The woman's purse sits on top of the stuff Shirley's cleared.

The lottery ticket and the bag of Revels are there too.

I lift the bag of Revels. Tears sting at my eyes.

She should be at home now, eating her sweeties; grimacing over the coffee one, dislodging her false teeth with the toffee one, biting the chocolate off the orange one, melting the minstrel one in her mouth with a gulp of tea.

Her change, she dropped all her change.

I crawl around on the floor looking for coins, get the brush, sweep out underneath the counter, drag out old penny sweets and dust, a few coins which have probably been there for a while. I drop them in her purse anyway, walk the length of the shop to make sure I find every rogue coin. It's the least I can do, fill her purse back up after what's happened to her.

I slide out a bank card, run a finger over the embossed lettering.

MS MARIÈLE DOWNIE

MS MARIÈLE DOWNIE

MS MARIÈLE DOWNIE

The old woman who collapsed becomes Marièle.

Ms Marièle Downie.

She has a name. She's real. And what a weird name, how do you even say that?

I flick through the other cards in her purse: Nectar card, library card, driving licence.

There's a photo of her. Younger, she has colour in her face, life.

Her address is there too.

I pass by her house every day on my way home. She's been so close to me this whole time, but I've never seen her before today. In a small town like this, how is that possible?

(wrapped up in my own concerns, my own wee world)

I slip the cards back into her purse, fold the lottery ticket in half, slide it in behind. I can take the purse with me when I leave, put that and the Revels through her letterbox.

Just in case.

4

YOU DREADED THE telegram boy stopping at your house. If you saw one cycling up your street, you'd pray for them to cycle right on past, to stop at another door. Even if that made you feel guilty later on, guilty that you'd passed the pain onto someone else, another mother, wife, sister.

'*Les anges de la mort*', Mama called the telegram boys.

Marièle dreaded them even more since they'd sat round the wireless and heard Churchill order the evacuation. The fear in her stomach never left her, it was there all the time.

George was out in France. One of the boys trying to get home. If only he would get in touch, let them know he was okay.

One of the lucky ones.

Marièle and Cath came out of the Palais to find everything white.

'That chap told us the truth,' Marièle said, 'it really is snowing.'

'Oh Marie, and you were so rude to him.'

'I thought he was just being fresh. How are we supposed to get home now?'

'We're not exactly dressed for the weather, are we?'

Marièle and Cath stood huddled in the doorway alongside the other dancers, nobody had come dressed for the elements.

'Maybe we should just start walking - it's too cold to stand here,' Marièle said, pulling her Camel coat tighter, belting it at the waist.

'Yes, you're right.'

They locked arms, began to walk in the direction of home.

'This is going to take forever, these shoes are useless,' Cath said, tightening her grip on Marièle's arm as she slid on the snow.

'Cath, Marie!'

As the days passed, the dread collected in her stomach, cloying and insistent until...

A knock at the door in the middle of the afternoon.

Somehow she knew without looking that the telegram boy would be standing there.

She felt almost sorry for him. He was so young, so smartly turned out in his Post Office uniform. It wasn't his fault he was so unwelcome. He was just the messenger.

The bearer of bad news.

But she didn't know for sure that it was bad news. It might be a telegram from George, telling them he'd made it home. Not to worry, he was fine. Or maybe he'd been hurt, but not seriously, and the telegram was just to let them know he would be in hospital for a few days.

Nothing serious.

'Telegram for Downie,' the boy said, and held out the slip of paper.

Someone chased after them through the snow.

A soldier, he was in uniform.

The snow was so thick, it was only when he came closer that Marièle recognised who it was.

'George, what are you doing here?' She asked.

'I sensed a damsel or two in distress and rushed home right away,' George replied. 'Your carriage, m'ladies.' He turned and she saw he dragged a wooden sledge behind him.

Marièle reached for the telegram, realised her hands were shaking as she slid the blue envelope open with a fingernail.

'Can I help you with that ?' The boy asked.

She shook her head, the lump in her throat made it hard to speak. She focused on his black tie, tried to bring herself back under control.

She unfolded the telegram, had to read it three times before the words filtered through, made sense.

POST OFFICE

TELEGRAM

Date : 08/06/1940

PRIORITY — DOWNIE, 24 BLACKNESS ROAD, ABERDEEN

DEEPLY REGRET TO REPORT YOUR SON CORPORAL GEORGE

DOWNIE S/10326973 HAS BEEN REPORTED MISSING IN ACTION

PRESUMED KILLED ON WAR SERVICE LETTER FOLLOWS

'No reply,' Marièle said to the boy.

'I'm very sorry,' he bowed his head, pushed his bike along the garden path. Marièle sat down on the front step, the wheel of the boy's bike squeaked as he cycled away. She looked up, saw thick blackout curtains twitching from the houses on the opposite side of the street.

'You're crazy! Do you think you're going to pull us both home on that thing?'

'Oh, ye of little faith, Marie. You'll never get home in those shoes.'

Marièle's teeth chattered, her toes had gone numb.

'Okay, front or back, Cath?'

'I don't mind, what would you prefer?'

'Come on, you two, get a move on. We could be halfway home by now.'

'Alright, alright,' Marièle climbed onto the back of the sledge.

'Here, take this,' George slipped off his overcoat, wrapped it round Cath's shoulders.

He took Cath's hand, helped her onto the front of the sledge. Marièle lent forward, put her arms around Cath's middle and pulled her backwards until she sat between Marièle's legs.

'Onwards, driver.'

George pulled on the rope attached to the front of the sledge. It jerked forward slightly, knocked Marièle and Cath off balance.

'You girls weigh more than you look,' George said.

He took the loop of rope, stepped inside it and lent forward, used all his weight to shift the sledge, and began to drag Marièle and Cath through the snow.

CORPORAL GEORGE DOWNIE

For a moment the formality of the telegram made her question who that was.

CORPORAL GEORGE DOWNIE
CORPORAL
CORPORAL

George. Big brother George.

MISSING IN ACTION
MISSING
PRESUMED KILLED
PRESUMED

What did that mean? Was he dead or wasn't he?

He might, even now, be trying to get a boat home. Had they just given up on him? George had better odds than most. They'd holidayed in France, Mama had taught them both to speak French. He'd be able to look after himself over there.

What sort of organisation just guessed what had happened to one of their employees? Just assumed the worst?

She listened to the news reports every day on the wireless. There must be boys scattered all over the place. All unaccounted for. Did they send a telegram to all of their families?

MISSING IN ACTION PRESUMED KILLED

'Who was it, Marie?' Mama shouted from inside the house.

'No grips on these blasted boots,' George said as he tried to get a footing.

Marièle looked behind, saw the tracks they left behind breaking up the clear snow. George's footprints, smudged and sliding, the parallel lines left by the runners of the sledge.

The snow was bright, lit their way in the blackout. It hurt her eyes to look at it for too long. She turned to the front again, felt Cath warm and heavy against her chest. Cath pressed her hands over Marièle's feet, rubbed her numb toes.

'How long are you home for?' Cath asked George.

'Just a few days, I'm afraid,' he replied.

'Oh, that's a shame.'

Marièle felt an ache clutch at her belly. It was a strange feeling, joy and melancholy combined. At the love she felt for George and Cath, at the beauty of the situation they were in, at the loss that this moment was fleeting. That she was losing George to the war, losing both of them to each other.

She inhaled, Cath's lavender perfume mixed in with the smoky chalk of winter, then breathed out. She could see her breath visible in front of her. Heard the crumble of snow as George pressed down with his boots, struggling under the weight of her and Cath on the sledge.

She didn't want this to end. Even though it was cold, even though it was late and she was tired, even though she could hear George's heavy breathing, knew he was exhausted.

It was just the three of them, the only three people alive in the whole world. While they trekked through the snow, there was no war, no rationing, no threat of imminent death. It was just the three of them.

'Marie, what are you doing out here?' Marièle stood as Mama opened the front door.

She watched Mama's gaze as it fell upon the blue envelope.

'Is it from George?'

Marièle handed Mama the telegram, watched as she fumbled with the piece of paper.

'What does this mean? *Je ne comprends pas,*' Mama asked, looking up at Marièle.

Marièle shook her head, ushered Mama back into the house.

'*Mon fils, mon petit garçon,* oh Marièle, our George!' Mama said, squeezing the telegram in her hand. 'Should we get Father from work?'

'I can't face going out there,' Marièle replied.

If someone stopped her, spoke to her, she would break down.

Oh God, Cath.

What would she say to Cath?

They sat down where they were, on the floor, facing each other across the hallway.

Mama reached towards Marièle and she took her mother's hands, the telegram lay on the floor between them.

'I believe this is you, mademoiselle,' *George said as he stopped pulling the sledge, let the rope fall towards the snow covered pavement.*

'Why thank you sir, that was quick,' Cath replied.

'Are you teasing me?'

'No, of course not, I didn't mean it like that.'

Marièle felt the heat from Cath's cheeks, warm enough to melt the snow.

'Don't worry, Cath, I'm just having you on,' George replied, holding out a hand to help her up from the sledge.

'See you later, dear,' Cath bent over and kissed Marièle on the cheek. Her lips were wet from the snow, which had started to fall again, and Marièle felt it burn against her cold skin.

'I'll see you to the door,' George said. Cath took his arm and they shuffled up the garden path until they were out of view behind the hedge.

Marièle stretched out her legs, lay back on the sledge. She could hear the murmur of voices as they said goodnight on the doorstep.

Snowflakes fell fast towards her. Every so often a flake would catch her off guard and she'd recoil, close her eyes. It was like the stars were tumbling down to earth. They melted against her cheeks, her eyelashes, her nose, her tongue.

Marièle jumped as someone knocked on the front door. She still held Mama's hand, felt it flinch in her own.

'Maybe it's the telegram boy come back, he made a mistake.'

Mama stood to open the door.

PRIORITY
CORPORAL GEORGE DOWNIE
MISSING IN ACTION PRESUMED KILLED

It wasn't a mistake.

'Claudine, I couldn't help noticing the telegram boy. Is everything okay?'

Mrs Walker from across the street. God, she didn't waste any time, did she?

'He's just missing,' Mama replied, 'they've lost him.' She started to laugh.

Marièle stood in behind the door so Mrs Walker wouldn't see her. Nosy old bisum.

'Well, there's hope then. I'll pray he comes back, he's a brave boy. Is there anything I can do?'

'No, thank you, he's only missing. *Mon fils, mon fils.*'

'Pardon?'

Marièle knew what the old bat was thinking.

Poor delusional French woman, she doesn't understand.

Marièle was used to the way people treated Mama, as if she was slow, stupid, just because she spoke with an accent, lapsed into French.

Mrs Walker had accused Mama of being a spy and a coward just because of her accent, and now she had the cheek to pretend to be concerned.

Don't listen to those girls, Marie, they're jealous of you. They've never been further than Stonehaven.

'Thank you for your concern,' Marièle stepped in front of Mama, shut the door on Mrs Walker.

George handed her his coat, and Marièle wrapped it around her shoulders. She dug her hands into its deep pockets, felt the scrunch of brown paper.

'What's this?'

'Oh, it's a birthday present from Cath. She gave me it just now.'

Cath hadn't told her she'd got George a present, kept that a secret.

Marièle squeezed the parcel, soft and spongy. She could see Cath now, sitting in her front room, ball of wool on her lap. She wasn't a great knitter, must have been at it for the last few months. Marièle let the surge of affection sweep aside the jealousy.

George lifted the rope, stepped inside it again and began to pull the sledge forward.

Marièle wrapped his big coat around her, pulled the collar up over her chin and breathed in the scent of lavender and lippy.

'Marièle?'

Marièle had just left work, turned at the sound of her name being called. A man in uniform hurried towards her. The sun shone behind him, in her eyes, obscured the man's features.

Was it?

Was it him?

George?

He came closer, stepped out of the sun's glare. She tried not to let the disappointment show on her face as she recognised him.

Arthur, Arthur Evans. One of the boys who worked in the shop with her and Cath.

Used to work there, until he was called up.

A lot of boys used to work in the shop.

'Artie, it's so good to see you,' she said, 'when did you get back?'

'About two hours ago.'

'Two hours and you come here, what will your mother say?'

'Ach, she'll not mind. I wanted to see you actually.'

Marièle stepped back. What did he want?

They'd been at the dancing a few times, but always in a group, and she'd let him hold her hand that time at the pictures.

He didn't think that meant anything, did he? Some of the boys got a bit carried away, especially when they were away from home for so long. Arthur was nice, but she wasn't interested in him romantically. She wasn't really interested in anyone romantically.

Her lips were wet from the snow, and Marièle felt the kiss burn against her cold skin.

'Can I walk you home?' He asked.

'Okay,' she nodded.

God, he looked different. Thinner, older. He'd grown up. She couldn't imagine him playing jokes on old Mr Jackson in the shop the way he had before.

'You were there? At Dunkirk, I mean?' She asked, trying to break the awkward silence between them.

'Aye.'

'Was it very awful?'

He nodded.

'I'm sorry, you're just home and here I am jumping in and asking questions.'

'You wouldn't believe some of the things I saw. I'll never forget them, as long as I live.'

He started to laugh.

God, he'd gone mad.

'What's so funny?'

'I'm sorry, you must think I'm such a fool. I was just thinking... me and a group of lads found a row boat. We didn't even question why it was lying there, why nobody else had used it. We all just piled in, started paddling with our hands. At first we went round in circles but then we got the hang of it. Got about, from here to that fence, then we noticed the water coming in, there was a big hole in the bottom of it.'

'Oh no! What happened?'

'What else? It sank! We had to swim back to shore, it was freezing.'

Marièle laughed with him. It wasn't even all that funny. It was more the absurdity of it. Amidst all that death and destruction, a slapstick comedy routine being played out.

'How did you make it home?'

'A fishing boat picked us up. Worst trip I've ever been on in my life. I was seasick all the way home. I think swimming back might have been better.'

She thought of George. Couldn't help it. Deep down, if she had the choice, she'd rather have George home than Arthur and that was an awful thing to think when he stood there beside her. After all he'd gone through. God, she wished she'd never thought that. Take it back, take it back.

'I saw George over there.'

'We got a telegram.'

'I'm sorry. I stopped to help him, but he was too... he was badly hurt. I sat with him until...'

She felt her legs wobble, stumbled. Arthur caught her.

'Marièle, I'm so sorry, I shouldn't have told you.' He held her upright, fumbled in his pockets and handed her a handkerchief.

'No. I'm glad, when the telegram said missing in action...' she took the handkerchief from him. She hadn't realised she was crying.

'Christ, excuse my language, but I thought you knew, I wouldn't have been so blunt otherwise.'

'No, don't feel bad,' she squeezed his arm, 'I'm glad you told me. I already knew, deep down.'

'I'm not very good at this. I'm ruining it. I kept thinking over how I'd tell you, and it wasn't like this.'

'Don't be silly,' she wiped her eyes and nose.

'He gave me something for you.'

Arthur rummaged in the inside pocket of his tunic, pulled out a silver cross on a chain.

'He said a French lady had given it to him – he'd sheltered in her barn.'

Arthur stood behind Marièle, fastened it round her neck. She was glad he couldn't see her face. She slipped the cross under her blouse, felt it nestle between her breasts.

Was it meant for her? She couldn't help thinking George had said her name when he meant to say Cath's.

'*Merci.*'

'What?'

'Sorry, I was in France there. Thank you. For bringing it back, for staying with him.'

'Well, here we are,' George stopped outside their garden gate.

'Thank you, kind sir,' Marièle held out a hand and George pulled her up from the sledge.

'Did you notice we were being spied on?' She asked.

'No, who?'

'Mrs Walker, who else?'

'Old busybody, I'll give her something to spy on,' George said and, without warning, grabbed Marièle and slung her over his shoulder.

'George, stop it, put me down.' Marièle kicked her legs but he held them firm against his chest.

'Can't have you getting your feet wet at this late stage in the journey,' he replied and carried Marièle towards the house.

She hung upside down, hair falling in her face, as she looked back along the garden path towards where the sledge lay discarded on the pavement.

July 2004

Life Bright For Wright

Success for Swimming Star at European Junior Championships

Hannah Wright's successful year continues apace. Hannah (15) has won gold in the 100m Butterfly at the European Junior Championships in Lisbon. Hannah, who qualified in second place for the final following the heats, powered to gold, taking half a second off her PB in the process.

'It was a really gutsy performance,' said coach Greg Candy. 'She wanted that gold medal and she took the race out from the start. It's the first time she's had to deal with heats and semi-finals and she has risen to the occasion brilliantly.'

5

I CYCLE FASTER, faster, faster, trying to get the day off me, leave it behind. I feel like some of that old woman got sucked into me when I gave her CPR. Some of the death and decay, stale and drying me up from the inside. I'm sorry for her, Ms Marièle Downie, but I don't want her on me any longer.

I'm young, still young.

(over the hill at twenty-one)

I stand tall on the pedals, let the cold air blast my face. My eyes water and my nose runs. It helps, reminds me I'm still alive.

I kick the garden gate open without slowing, don't hit the brakes until the last possible moment, until I'm almost in the shed. I shove my bike in, next to the rusty lawn mower, then let myself into the house.

'Dad?' I dump my bag on top of the glass cabinet in the hall. Swimming medals and engraved cups rattle inside, dusty and in need of a polish.

No answer.

A small part of me thought he'd be here. That he'd hear about what happened, come home to see if I was okay.

I push open the living room door. Dad's ashtray overflows on the coffee table. It stinks in here. Stale fags and no fresh air. He hasn't even opened the curtains. I pull them wide, open the window.

I pick up my bag and head upstairs. I need to change, shower. There's blood on my jeans and I can feel her clinging to me.

I peer in Dad's room as I head past on my way to the bathroom. It stinks worse than downstairs, dirty clothes, slept in sheets, another ashtray, glass of water on the bedside table with a rim of scum around the top of the glass. I open the window in here too. Waft the duvet up and down, make the bed.

I strip off in the bathroom, turn the shower on, hot, hotter. Let the steam fill the room, scrub myself clean, don't get out until my skin's bright pink. Condensation drips down the tiles, off the porcelain of the sink and toilet, down the mirror.

Back in my bedroom with a towel wrapped round me, I unzip my bag. It stinks of chlorine, I lean my face closer to the smell of it. Clean and comforting.

Something falls out of my bag as I pull at the towel and costume inside. It's heavy, thumps to the floor.

Purse.

The old woman's purse.

Shit, I totally forgot to drop it off like I'd planned.

I pick it up, can feel it contaminate me as soon as I touch it. This piece of her, bringing back what happened. I have to get rid of it. No reminders.

Another thought pushes through, irrational, like a superstition.

(my lucky costume)

It takes hold of me and I know I have to go back out, put the purse through her letterbox tonight. Her life depends on it. We're connected now. Me and that old woman.

She won't last the night unless I take her purse back.

I'll run. By the time I get my bike out again, I could be halfway there. I chuck on some clothes, grab my keys and leave the house. As I run, I pass her purse from hand to hand, feel the weight of it. My wet hair cold against my head.

I slow to a walk when I get to her street. Out of breath as I scan the house numbers.

There it is.

Her house.

Where she lives.

(lived?)

Do her neighbours know what happened? Have they noticed that she went out and never came back? Maybe family members have turned up?

As I walk up the path, I expect someone to shout on me, ask if I know anything, what I'm doing here.

I open her purse to double check I've got the right address. As I'm sliding out her driving licence, a scrap of paper flutters to the ground.

It's her lottery numbers, scribbled in black ink.

5   16   21   26   32   44

I slip the piece of paper in my pocket, read the address on the driving licence.

I'm in the right place.

I put the driving licence back in her purse, am about to push it through the letterbox when I stop myself.

Maybe someone's in there?

Husband, son, daughter, granddaughter. Does she live alone?

The house is in darkness.

I slide the driving licence out again.

MS MARIÈLE DOWNIE

16 SEPTEMBER 1922

MS.

That doesn't really give much away.

1922.

I count up on my fingers.

32, 42, 52, 62, 72, 82, 92, 2002, 2010.

Eighty-seven.

Shit, no way. She didn't look eighty-seven.

Certainly not before she keeled over anyway.

Eighty-seven.

To be honest, I don't know how old she looked. She was just old. She looked like an old woman.

Enough messing about. Just put the purse through the letter box and leave. Go home. End this fucking horrible day.

I jump at a noise from inside the house, grip the purse tighter to stop my hand from shaking.

Maybe someone is in there after all?

I ring the doorbell, hear it, tinny and echoing from inside.

Nothing. No footsteps. No light turned on.

What if it's her? Ms Marièle Downie.

(back from the dead)

My finger hovers above the doorbell. I'm too scared to press it again. There's something about the shrillness of it, disturbing the silence like that, it gives me the shivers.

I don't even know what I'm so afraid of. I'm just suddenly aware that I'm on my own.

Nobody else is about. One of those quiet wee cul-de-sacs. Dead end street, no traffic passing through, everyone else safe inside their homes.

I'm on my own out here. All on my own.

(the shadows on the wall as someone comes towards me along the hallway)

Stop it, stop it, Hannah. Stop freaking yourself out.

(closer, closer, the slow thud, thud, thud of approaching footsteps)

You're doing it on purpose. Why are you trying to spook yourself?

(a pair of feet on the other side of the door)

I mean it, Hannah, stop it.

(eye at the peephole, watching me, hand moving towards the door handle, rattling it up and down up and downupanddownupanddown)

I shove the purse through the letterbox, expecting a bony hand to shoot out and grab my wrist. The purse gets caught on the black bristles

46

lining the opening.

No, no, please, go in, go in.

I push with both hands, force it through.

It finally gives and I hear the thump as it hits the floor on the other side. Then I'm running again. Running, running, running, running, running. In the opposite direction, home, safety.

I slam the front door behind me when I get in, lock it. My chest hurts and I've got a stitch. I slide down the door, until I'm squatting with my back up against it. Something creaks in the house and I jump.

I move quickly, turning on lights and checking rooms. Don't care about the stale smell anymore, I slam windows and pull curtains shut.

What's wrong with me? I'm usually in the house on my own at night. I've never got myself so spooked before. I double-check all the doors, all the windows, even open cupboards, and look under the beds, behind the couch. I can't shake off the feeling that I'm not on my own, that someone's watching me.

Come on, Hannah. Stop being stupid. Breathe, just breathe. You're fine. There's nobody in the house. Relax, relax.

In my bedroom, I pull the curtains shut. Don't allow myself to look outside. In case.

(someone's out there, looking up at my window)

I need something to do, something to take my mind off everything that's happened. My wet swimming stuff's still lying on the floor. I hang my towel and costume on the radiator. The damp, chlorine smell helps.

Breathe it in, breathe it in.

Stroke, stroke, stroke, breathe, stroke, stroke, stroke, breathe.

I sprinkle my swim cap with talc to keep it from sticking, talc dusts my hands, the floor, and I rub the excess into the carpet with my feet.

Something's lying on the floor next to my goggles.

Revels.

A weight shifts in my stomach.

The old woman's Revels.

Shit.

I forgot about them. Took the purse back but not the sweets.

Superstition or not, there's no fucking way I'm going back there tonight. No chance. I'm not leaving this house, this bedroom. That's how people in horror movies end up dead. Not me. I'm smart.

(Higher English C
 Higher Mathematics D
 Higher Biology C
 Higher History C)

Just the thought of going back there makes me feel sick. I sit on the edge of my bed, the bag of Revels in my lap.

Sweat prickles up and down my back, across my forehead. I need another shower.

There's dots in front of my eyes. The room starts to blur, go out of focus. I think I'm going to faint.

I lie back on the bed, close my eyes. Everything's fuzzy, scribbled crayon flashes on the inside of my eyelids.

My fingers rest on the bag of Revels, the rippled edge of the bag. I can taste the chocolate in my mouth, on my tongue, anticipate the rush of sugar as it hits my bloodstream.

I have to eat them.

It's her turn to save me.

My hands are wobbly as I peel open the bag. With my eyes still shut, I reach inside it.

Orange.

Coffee.

Peanut.

Orange.

Malteser   Coffee   Peanut   Orange   Orange   Minstrel Minstrel Malteser PeanutToffeeToffeeToffeeToffee

I open my eyes, sit up, lick melted chocolate from my fingers. The red nail polish blazes.

It's too much, too bright, too red.

I blot cotton wool with nail polish remover, wipe my fingernails and toenails clean. Replace the red with a pale blue colour.

(one that doesn't look like blood)

Lie back on the bed, wait for it to dry.

My eyes open, awake, the light in my room seems to go out before I hear the click of the switch.

'Sorry, didn't mean to wake you,' Dad's standing in the doorway. 'All the lights in the house are on though, it's like bloody Blackpool tower. You okay?'

'Yeah, fine.'

'I ran into Shirley in the Sal.'

Shirley? Shirley? Still half-asleep, I fumble about for why that's relevant.

The old woman's hands, grasping for the top button of her blouse.

'Was she okay?'

'Aye, aye, nothing a couple of gin and tonics couldn't fix. It's you I'm worried about though.'

'I'm alright.'

'Sure?'

'Yeah.'

He hovers in the doorway.

'Okay, I'll let you get back to sleep.'

'Night, Dad.'

'Night.'

He shuts the door, the light from the hallway fades. I pull the duvet over me, can hear Dad pissing, the flush of the toilet, the creak of the hall floorboards, the TV switching on in his bedroom.

I can't sleep now, lie awake in the darkness. I slide my fingers underneath my jeans, inside my pants, rub myself. Impatient, aggressive. I rub harder and faster, harder and faster, harder and faster, until it hurts.

Keep going, keep going, keep going,keepgoingkeepgoingkeepgoingkeep fasterfasterfasterfasterfasterfasterfasterfaster

I come, out of breath, let the sleep take me.

6

'MISS DOWNIE?' A man in a suit and tie answered the door.

'Yes.'

'Come in, come in.' He held the door open and she stepped inside the room.

'Sit down.' He gestured to a chair. The room was almost bare of furniture. Two chairs faced each other with a small table in between. A pile of scattered paperwork lay on the table alongside a jug of water and two glasses.

She sat down facing the man. He didn't say anything, but filled the two glasses with water and handed her one.

'Thank you,' she said, taking a sip. Her lips were dry and she swirled the water around in her mouth before swallowing.

'*Je suis Monsieur Thompson. Parlez-vous Français?*'

'*Oui. Ma mère m'a appris.*'

Do You Speak French?

Have you ever been on holiday to France?
Do you have photographs of France?

You can help!

Blackout 10.59pm to 4:59am

Moon Set 5:36pm Rises 4:23am

du Maurier Cigarettes –
The filter tip will keep you fit!
It is now more important than ever that you empty your packet at time of purchase and leave it with your tobacconist.

'*Look at this in the newspaper, Mama, we have photographs we can send,*' Marièle said.

'Ne sois pas bête. *Why would they want our old holiday snaps?*'

'*They wouldn't ask unless they needed them.*'

Marièle looked out the shoe box of photographs that Mama kept under the bed. She pulled out a handful of them.

Her and George as children.

Mama and Father.

Mama with Mémé and Grand-père. They called him Grand-purr because of his two cats.

George had his arm around Marièle in one of the photos, was dressed in shorts and t-shirt, socks and sandals on his feet. One of his socks had fallen down, hung around his ankle. He wasn't looking at the camera, had been distracted by something off to the side. What was it?

She ached looking at these photos of him. That wee boy who lived to be barely a man. It wasn't fair. The missing him sucked all the air out of her.

Miss Marièle Downie
24 Blackness Road
Aberdeen

TO WHOMEVER IT MAY CONCERN

As per your recent newspaper advertisement, please find enclosed a selection of photographs taken while on holiday in France.
My mother is French and therefore we have spent a great deal of time in France over the years.

I hope they will be of some use to you. Please return them to us when you are finished with them, as they hold a great deal of sentimental value.

Yours faithfully,
Miss Marièle Downie

War Office
London SW1

Dear Miss Downie,
Thank you for your recent letter and photographs which were gratefully received. We request that you attend for interview on Friday 23 at 3pm to the enclosed address.

Yours Sincerely,
Mr Thompson

'An interview for what?' Mama asked.
'I don't know,' Marièle replied.
'Je n'aime pas ça. You can't go off to London alone. She can't go off to London on her own.'

'She's a big girl, Claudine,' said Father. 'She'll be fine.'

'But we don't even know what it's for.'

'It's from the War Office, Claudine, they don't have to explain. You know how dangerous gossip can be.'

Marièle re-read the letter. Was it real? What if she got there and discovered it was a hoax?

It didn't matter really. Whatever happened, she planned to join up as soon as she returned home. She wasn't going to spend the rest of the war counting ration coupons, totting up accounts, writing up receipts. Hang Mr Jackson and his excuses.

But I need you.

You are helping the war effort.

People need food, don't they?

I've pulled a lot of strings to keep you here.

It may not be glamorous but it's still an important job.

Someday they would ask her what she'd done during the war and she didn't want to be ashamed to answer.

She'd only ever had one job, one interview. And Mr Jackson's questioning had hardly been conventional.

MR JACKSON: So, Susan, you're here about the job?

MARIÈLE: My name's not Susan, it's Marièle.

MR JACKSON: What sort of a name is that? I'm going to call you Susan. Congratulations, Susan, you've got the job. Let's get you started.

MARIÈLE: Now? But, I'm supposed to go to school. Mama will wonder where I am.

MR JACKSON: No more school for you, Susan. You're a working woman now.

He led her to the shop counter, gave her an apron and left her to it. The apron was too long, trailed under her feet. She felt like such a fool, the new girl in the oversized apron. If it hadn't been for Arthur, she probably would have left then and there. But he stood her on a stool, pinned up her apron, told her if anyone gave her any trouble she was to let him know.

She'd only been fifteen. How the time had flown.

'D'accord, Miss Downie, I expect you're wondering why we asked you here.'

'Oui,' she nodded and took another drink of water. It was warm, must have been sitting out for a while. Had he been here all day? Seeing other girls before her?

'*Merci pour les photos*. They were very useful. You will of course get these back once we're finished with them.'

He picked up a few sheets of paper from the table. She tried to see what was written on them but the typeface was too small.

'The letter you sent us. You spent a lot of your childhood in France?'

'*Oui. Ma mère est Française*. We visited my grandparents every summer until they passed away.'

'I see. Are you fluent yourself?'

'*Oui*, my mother brought us up bilingual.'

'Us?'

'*Mon frère et moi*.'

'Ah, yes, George.'

She nodded. It was still hard to speak out loud about him. It felt strange hearing his name, they avoided using it at home. She hadn't mentioned him in the letter – how did this man know?

The letter looked official. It was stamped and signed. Besides, Father wouldn't let her travel all that way on her own if he thought it was anything untoward. He walked her to the station for the overnight train, kissed her on the cheek and wished her good luck. She watched him from the train window as he walked away along the platform, leaning on his stick, limping on his bad leg. The whistle blew and he was obscured in a cloud of smoke as the train pulled out of the station.

She read the letter again.

An interview for what?

You didn't question things anymore, just went along with them. The war had changed everything.

She folded the letter up, slipped it in its envelope and put it in her pocket. Ate the sandwich Mama made for her, washed it down with the Thermos of tea.

Mr Thompson took out a handkerchief and blew his nose.

'You have fond memories of France?'

'Yes, very much so.'

'And what do you think of the current situation?'

'It makes me very sad. Mama's glad *Mémé* and *Grand-père* didn't live to see this.'

'So you are sympathetic towards France in their current situation?'

'*Oui, bien sûr*, isn't everyone?'

'I should like to think so, but you'd be surprised.'

She glanced around the room.

No clock.

How long had she been here? The blinds were closed, the only light came from a lamp in the corner.

She looked out the train window, at her reflection in the dark glass. She'd never travelled so far on her own before. It was liberating. She was actually doing something.

She opened the letter again.

Friday 23 at 3pm

But an interview for what?

She didn't even know how long the interview would last. An hour? Ten minutes?

'You've travelled down from Scotland?'

'*Oui*, Aberdeen.'

'We appreciate you coming all this way. *Votre Français est très bon.* No trace of a British accent. That's what gives people away.'

'Gives people away?'

'*Oui.*'

Mr Thompson scribbled on a sheet of paper. Was she saying the right things? She was tired, had barely dozed on the train. This was as strange an interview as the one with Mr Jackson. At least then she had known what the job was.

'Would you describe yourself as patriotic, Miss Downie?'

'*Oui.*'

'To France or to Britain?'

'I feel strongly about both countries. They are both home to me.'

'How have you spent the war so far?'

'I've just been working in a grocer's shop.'

'Just?'

She shrugged. She felt as if she was dodging out of real work, hiding.

'Don't be embarrassed, Miss Downie – people still need to eat. Grocers are very important, what with rationing and food shortages.'

Exactly what Mr Jackson would say. She took a drink of water to cool the flush that spread across her cheeks. She could hear her tongue clicking against her palate when she spoke.

She smoothed out her skirt. Careful not to catch the stockings with her finger nails. She'd borrowed them from Cath, promised not to snag them. Marièle's only pair had a ladder in the heel.

Mr Thompson. She was to ask for Mr Thompson. She imagined a middle aged man, but couldn't conjure up a face, a hairstyle. It was an uninspiring name.

'Enough small talk. The reason you're here, Miss Downie.'

She nodded, smoothed out her skirt. Darn it, she'd snagged Cath's stockings. She hoped they wouldn't ladder. They were so hard to replace.

'We need people with language skills to help the war effort in France.'

'When you say in France?'

'*Oui*, to help out our French allies.'

'Doing what?'

'We have various uses for people like yourself, couriers, sabotage, wireless operators, that sort of thing. How do you feel about this, Miss Downie?'

'*Je suis désolée*. I'm not sure what you mean.'

'Sabotage, secret messages, that sort of thing. Underhand, some people call it – don't think it's very British.'

George had said something to that effect the last time he'd been home on leave. Something about fighting dirty when faced with dirty opposition. He'd argued with Father.

We shouldn't stoop to their level, George.

We need to if we want to win. You don't know what it's like.

Of course I do.

It's completely different from the trenches.

Yes, luckily for you too.

Father slammed his stick down on the table.

At the time, Marièle didn't know who to agree with, whose side to take. She just wanted the war to end.

For people to stop dreading the telegram boy.

'To be honest, Mr Thompson, I don't know much about it, but it seems to me that the Germans aren't exactly playing by the rules themselves, therefore I don't see why we shouldn't do the same.'

He nodded, didn't say anything.

'It's our freedom at stake, isn't it?' she continued. 'We have to fight for that.'

'Quite.'

She thought she saw a flicker of a smile, a dimpling in his cheeks, but then he bowed his head, scribbled something down. He scratched his moustache with the end of the pencil before he looked up again, as if the smile was nothing more than an itch in his whiskers.

Marièle had memorised the letter but that didn't stop her from reading it over and over. It contained just the basic information, all that she needed and nothing more. They hadn't even given her enough time to reply to it. There was faith being shared on both sides. Faith that she would turn up. Faith that they would be there and be legitimate.

But an interview for what?

She fingered the cross around her neck. Faith. Times like this you needed it more than ever.

She looked up as the compartment door slid over.

'Tickets please,' said the conductor.

She handed her ticket over.

'London, eh?'

'Yes, I'm visiting a friend.'

The lie came naturally, without thinking. Why? She could have said interview, appointment, meeting.

Interview for what?

'To quote the Prime Minister, our objective is to set Europe ablaze.'

'Before the Nazis burn it first?'

'Indeed. Now, Miss Downie, just because you speak the language doesn't necessarily mean that you're suitable. There are various skills we are looking for which we hope you will display during training.'

'What sort of training?'

'Oh, nothing to worry about now. Just basic stuff at first, a bit of PT, map reading, that sort of thing. The Germans have a very backwards attitude towards the fairer sex – don't think you girls are up to the task.'

She felt the fire in her belly. How dare they?

Oh, he was good, he was very good. Manipulating her. Making her angry so she would agree to help him and ignore the fact he was being so evasive. She was still none the wiser as to what the interview was for, but she was determined to sign up anyway.

London was cold and grey when she stepped off the train. Gosh, and people thought that Aberdeen was bleak. Aberdeen sparkled like glitter.

The fog was damp and clung to her and she pulled her coat tight. Where was the sky? She couldn't see it. She'd never been so far South before, the sky had disappeared somewhere on the way down.

She needed to find somewhere to freshen up, get something to eat before the interview.

Motorcars, army vehicles, buses and trams drove past, while the pavements were just as busy with people. London looked familiar but strange to her. She'd heard about it on the wireless, seen film of it in newsreels and at the pictures. She recognised bits of it without ever having been there before.

Sophisticated looking girls hung on the arms of men in uniform. Smart looking girls, also in uniform, hurried past, full of purpose, busy. Doing something. She looked down at herself. Her knee length skirt and silk blouse, the best clothes she owned. She felt so young and pathetic next to these girls. No, not girls: ladies, women. Maybe she'd join them, be one of them soon?

'*Les Allemands*, we want you to get under their skin, annoy them, hinder them, do you think you can do that?'

'*Bien sûr*. I want to help, only I'm still unsure what you're asking me to do. Do you want me to go to France?'

'Miss Downie, you're getting ahead of yourself. One step at a time, *s'il vous plaît.*'

God, he infuriated her. She wanted to shake him – stop being so evasive and answer me. It was okay for him to pry personal information out of her, but God forbid she asked him a question. Like a politician, Father would say.

'You want to help liberate France, don't you? Help end the war, bring our boys home?'

'*Oui, bien sûr.*'

'*Formidable*, that's all we want to know for now.'

Was that it, interview over? And who was 'we'? She had agreed to do something but she wasn't very sure what it was. She had signed on without realising.

She looked up as she went, a lot of the street names had been taken down, blanked out in case of invasion. She had the map from Father to help if she got lost.

Interview.

She looked for 143, walked on until she spotted a door number.

71.

She was on the right side of the road at least. She continued, counting the doors as she went.

73. 75. 77. 79. 81.

For what?

She stopped outside 143. Was this the right place?

It didn't look like much. What had she been expecting? Maybe a sign on the door, a plaque, a clue? Something to explain why she'd been asked to travel all the way down here.

Nothing though. As uninformative as the letter. She took a compact out of her bag and checked herself, ran a comb through her hair and applied a bit of lippy. It was an odd shade, two old stubs of lipstick melted together. Better than nothing though.

It was real, all of a sudden, and she felt the nerves flutter in her tummy. Back at home, telling her parents and Cath, it had been a game. Marièle playing at being a grown up. Yes, I have an interview. In London. You know? It's all very hush-hush, important War Office stuff.

For what?

She didn't feel so grown up now. A long way from home and out of her depth.

She snapped the compact shut.

Out of your depth you either sunk or swam, and she didn't plan on sinking.

'We'll need you to see our psychiatrist before we sign you on officially for the training.'

'Do you think I'm mad, Monsieur?'

'Non, non, please don't worry, just a formality you know. Now…' he rifled through his papers, 'we may be able to fit you in this week. Can you stay in London?'

'Oui, pas de problème.'

What would Mama and Father say? What would she tell them? She didn't know herself what was going on.

Secret work, helping France in some way.

'Bon. If you speak to the young lady at the reception desk, she'll sort you out with a place to stay and pass on any messages to your family.'

He put the paperwork down and stood.

Oh, she hadn't realised that was it. Interview over.

She breathed in, pressed one hand flat against her chest where the cross lay underneath her blouse. Pressed until she felt the shape of it on her palm. Then she pushed open the door.

A girl sat at a reception desk inside. Marièle looked around. She wasn't expecting this. What was this place? A block of flats? An office? A hotel?

'Can I help?' The girl at the desk looked up.

'Yes,' Marièle held up the letter, 'I have an appointment with Mr Thompson.'

'May I see the letter?'

58

Marièle handed it over. The girl read it, looked up at Marièle, looked at the letter again.

Marièle flushed, could feel the heat running through her. The girl was at least two or three years younger than her, but she looked so secure, so in charge. What would she make of the letter? When she'd spoken aloud there it sounded like a sleazy rendezvous. God, what if it was?

An interview.

But.

'It's been a pleasure, Miss Downie, *merci d'être venue.*'

He shook her hand as she stood up and they walked to the door.

'When do I…'

'*Ne vous inquiétez pas*, we'll be in touch with you.'

That 'we' again. She left with more questions than she'd come in with. It felt like a dream. Yes, that's what it was. A surreal, dream-like experience. Had it gone well? He seemed happy enough, but again, was that a smile or an itch? He'd asked her to stay around, that had to count for something.

She felt sweat prickle up her back and she exhaled deeply as he shut the door behind her. Phew, she hadn't realised how nervous she'd been, how much she'd been holding her breath in there.

The girl on reception probably knew the score. Maybe she sat there while an endless supply of girls arrived for an 'interview' with Mr Thompson.

Mr Thompson.

That probably wasn't even his real name. God, why hadn't she thought of that before? It was so generic, it had to be fake.

For what?

She could still leave. Turn around and walk out the door.

No. She had to see this through.

Interview.

'Mr Thompson is in room 26 on the second floor. Stairs are through there,' the girl pointed, 'then turn right.'

'Thank you,' Marièle nodded.

Had the girl smirked there? Marièle couldn't tell if it was a friendly smile or not. Oh hang it, if Mr Thompson or whoever he was tried anything fresh, she'd sock him.

'Between the legs,' George had told her when she'd started to get attention from members of the opposite sex. 'If anyone tries something you're not happy with, hit him between the legs.'

Mr Thompson better watch out. Marièle made her hand into a fist, punched the air a few times. Between the legs.

Out of sight of the receptionist, she checked herself in her compact again, put her hand under her hair, tried to bounce some life into the waves. The long journey had taken the curl out of them.

She turned right, followed the corridor. It was like a rabbit warren, door after door, while the corridor twisted and turned. She wasn't sure where she was anymore, disorientated – was she still facing the street?

She found herself counting door numbers again.

22, 23.

She stopped outside room 24. Darn it. That girl still had her letter. Should she go back and get it?

No, keep going. She could get it on the way out. Not that she needed it. She had memorised the little information it contained.

25, 26.

This was it. Door 26.

Behind this door she would finally get some answers. She knocked twice, hard. Didn't hesitate, didn't want to give herself time to chicken out. She knocked once more, harder, scraped the skin on her knuckles. A final practise in case she had to put George's advice into action.

She heard footsteps on the other side of the door, then the lock turned. A man in a suit and tie stood facing her.

Mr Thompson.

An interview for what?

60

July 2005

Going in the Wright Direction
GB call up for Scottish swimmer

Hannah Wright (16) has been named in the Great Britain team for the World Swimming Championships in Montreal. Hannah is one of the youngest competitors to be selected and is relishing the opportunity to make her mark on the world stage.

'I'm so excited to be included in the squad,' said Hannah. 'My swimming's been going really well and this is the reward for all the hard work I've been putting in.'

Hannah knows that she'll be less experienced than others in the team, however she insists she's not just going to make up the numbers.

'My aim is to get a new PB for the 100m Butterfly and if I do that then I've got a good chance of making the final.'

7

I COUNT AS I swim, add the metres in my head.

(the only way I know how to count)

25m

50m

100m

I swear I would have done better in Higher Maths if they'd asked me questions about swimming.

Pete's coach tells him to do 1,000m warm-up then 8 x 200 IM followed by 200m swim down. How many lengths will Pete swim?

Susan swims 100m freestyle in 1.02.33. What time should she be doing for 400m freestyle?

I'm tired, can't get a speed up. My arms are heavy and my legs slip through the water instead of propelling me forward.

150m

200m

Yesterday's taken it right out of me. What a strange fucking day.

I keep going for 800m then stop, lean against the tiled wall, out of breath. I give my steamed up goggles a wipe and rest them on my forehead. The days are gone when I could swim 70, 80,000 metres a week. Sprint 100m in less than a minute. How far have I swum in my lifetime? I've gone round the world a few times.

Where does your fitness go when it leaves you?

I glance at the clock. I should really be getting out if I want to make work on time. I can't face it though. Can't face work, can't face going back there after what happened yesterday. I pull my goggles down over my eyes, push off from the wall. Just a few more lengths, then I'll get out.

I cycle round the block twice before I finally stop outside the shop. I didn't realise it would be so hard coming back here.

'Hey, Hannah,' Calum nods at me from behind the counter.

He's reading a magazine, moves it to one side as I join him.

The crack's still there.

'Mum says it'll take a couple of days before someone can come to replace it,' Calum says, tracking my gaze. 'She's raging about how much it's going to cost.'

The glass is the only giveaway that something's happened here.

Something bad.

Everything else is back to normal.

It's kind of scary how back to normal the shop is.

Life carries on.

That old woman could be dead or alive for all I know, but the universe doesn't care, sweeps up the false teeth and keeps going.

'Where's Shirley anyway?' I ask.

'That's nice – aren't you pleased to see me?'

'Sorry, I didn't mean it like that.'

'I'm only joking. She wasn't feeling great this morning, didn't get in till late. She was pretty upset about what happened. Don't think it really hit her till after, eh?'

I'm about to say that Dad saw her in the pub last night but I stop myself.

I'm not sure how Calum feels about Dad. I'm not sure Dad treated Shirley all that well in their on/off/on/off/on/off.

It's weird to think Calum and I could have been brother and sister.

'Your mum was amazing yesterday,' I say.

'She's always been pretty good in a crisis – been on her own so long.'

Opposite of Dad. Getting up, going to work. Every night in the pub, living off beans and toast.

'So what's the plan?' I ask.

'I was thinking as little as possible. Then enjoy the rest of the weekend in freedom.'

'After yesterday, a quiet day sounds perfect.'

Calum turns the radio on behind the counter.

'Fuck sake, you two listen to some pish.'

'That's your mum's choice, not mine.'

Forth One blares out some chart nonsense. Calum messes about with it, flicks through stations until he finally finds something that seems to please him.

'How can you listen to that every day?' he asks.

Every day. Every day. Every day. Every day.

'I just tune it out, Shirley never has it on too loud.'

(white noise of the pool)

50m. 100m. 200m. 400m. 800m. 1000m.

Stocking shelves. Serving customers. Stocking shelves. Serving customers.

Every day. Every day. Every day. Every day.

It's still a routine, just not the one I wanted for myself.

'Frightened Rabbit are great, eh? They're at T in the Park this year,' he nods at the radio, drums his fingers on the counter. 'You going?'

I watch the glass either side of the crack bounce up and down, up and down, up and down.

'I doubt it.'

'Aww, you should, it'll be awesome.'

'Yeah, T's always kind of passed me by, what with training and that.'

'You're not training now though.'

(never again)

'Yeah, I guess.'

It's funny. Now that I have the opportunity to do all the stuff I missed when I was swimming, I don't care all that much.

I miss my routine

(800m, 1000m, 2000m)

Calum sings along with the radio. Looks a lot older than his age, but gives himself away with the goofy grin, the air guitar. The seventeen-year-old boy peeking out from that stubbled chin, pierced eyebrow, scruffy hairdo.

I run my finger along the crack on the counter.

Fuck, it's sharp.

I flinch, pull my finger away as the glass nicks me. I suck at the blood, the tang of it on my tongue.

'You alright?' Calum asks.

'Yeah, it's my own fault. That was a stupid thing to do.'

The blood keeps coming, the end of my finger throbs.

'Hang on,' Calum disappears into the back room, comes back with a plaster.

She gasps for breath, fumbles with the buttons on the collar of her blouse, blood pours down onto her hands but I don't think she's noticed she's bleeding.

The blood smears across my painted fingernail.

Blue. Bloodless. Dead.

I feel a bit queasy so I sit on the floor behind the counter.

'Sure you're alright?' Calum asks, kneeling in front of me. I can smell his body spray, strong and musky.

'Yeah, the sight of blood, you know?'

'I'll do it,' he says as I reach for the plaster. I hold my finger out for him. He undoes the plaster, slips it round the cut and sticks it down for me.

Calloused fingers.

Gentle.

A chill runs up the back of my neck, tingles the roots of my hair.

'Not too tight, is it?' He asks.

'Nah, that's great. Like mother, like son. Good in a crisis.'

'Anyone here?'

We both jump as a guy appears on the other side of the counter. Nervous laughter catches in my throat and I blush. I thought we were alone. It feels like we've been caught doing something wrong.

'Yeah, can I help?' Calum asks, standing.

I look up at Calum's back. His t-shirt has risen, I can see the top of his checked boxers, a line of downy hair at the base of his spine. It looks soft, I have to stop myself from reaching out and stroking it.

'These are out of date, by the way,' the guy says, putting a packet of Hob Nobs on the counter as he pays for his paper and a can of Irn-Bru.

'Are they? Shit, I mean sorry, sorry for swearing too.'

'No bother,' the man laughs, 'I'll take these instead.' He picks up a Mars Bar and a packet of Quavers.

Calum taps his foot as he serves the guy. He steps back to let the till drawer open and his t-shirt falls back into place. I want to lift it up again, place my hand against the fuzzy warmth there.

What's wrong with me? I stand, brush myself down. I'm light-headed, must be the blood loss.

Calum's a schoolboy. Thinking about him like that is just wrong. I'm no Mrs Robinson.

The guy leaves the shop and Calum holds up the Hob Nobs.

I take the packet, read the date.

(like me, best-before)

'It's only by a couple of weeks.'

Calum opens them, takes a bite of one.

'Taste alright,' he says, his mouth full.

There you go, nothing like a view of chewed-up biscuit to dampen your desires.

'You okay? You still look a bit pale,' he says.

'Yeah, give me a biscuit, that'll help.'

'Be my guest,' he holds out the packet.

'A bit soft, but they're fine aren't they?' The syrupy oats break apart, stick to my gums and the roof of my mouth.

'I'll check the others,' Calum says.

He hoists his jeans up as he walks to the opposite side of the shop.

Another reality check. How could I fancy someone with such stupid trousers?

Something catches my eye out on the street. Three girls looking in. They push open the door, banging into each other and laughing as they enter the shop.

They hide behind the greetings cards, pretend to be interested in them, but they're fooling nobody. They're here to perve on Calum.

'Blonde-Pigtails' picks up a card and points at it, 'Hot-Pants-and-Tights' grabs it off her and puts it back while 'Pierced-Nose' laughs.

I lean forward on my elbows. The glass pops as I put weight on it. The girls turn at the noise, look away, still laughing.

What's so funny?

They don't even register my existence.

(don't you recognise me?)

Too old, uninteresting. The way the school kids treat Shirley when they come in at break times.

Am I just some old wifie to them?

I'm not that much older.

I look down at myself. Ripped jeans, charity shop top, scabby Converse. The girls are glammed to the max, sparkling, even their hair glimmers. My hair hangs like straw, too much chlorine in it to ever shine like that. They wear lip gloss and creamy eye shadow. I wear waterproof mascara and smear Vaseline on my lips when they get too dry.

Way to make you feel like a zero.

They strut around the shop, pick things up, pretend to look at them, laugh, put things down again, giggle, giggle, giggle.

I get a weird satisfaction from Calum's lack of interest. Oblivious as they try to get his attention.

Engrossed in his out of date biscuits.

They're persistent, I have to give them that much. From their little play I work out that 'Hot-Pants-and-Tights' has the hots for Calum while 'Blonde-Pigtails' and 'Pierced-Nose' seem to be here for moral support and guidance.

Although I'm sure neither would say no given the chance.

(would I?)

The three of them edge closer, closer. Lionesses closing in on an un-suspecting wildebeest.

I get that rush of competitiveness, that bloody-minded streak that used to work so well in the pool.

'Can I help?' I ask.

They turn as one.

'No, just looking,' 'Blonde-Pigtails' replies.

My trick backfires. Calum turns, spots the girls, nods hello. They wave and smile. When he turns back to his biscuits, 'Hot-Pants-and-Tights' grabs 'Pierced-Nose' and 'Blonde-Pigtails' and they all hug each other.

Laughing. Laughing. Laughing. Laughing.

Jesus, am I so removed from my teenage years? There's not a hint of recognition, of empathy.

'Hot-Pants and-Tights' looks a bit sick now as the other two push her towards Calum. She pretends to struggle but lets them propel her forward.

Why don't I feel sorry for her?

Poor girl, trying to build up the courage to speak to the cute boy she likes. Why are they igniting my inner bitch?

You're fiery, Hannah – it's that red hair. Use it in the pool, no friends once you dive in.

I move out from behind the counter, feel them watching me as I walk towards Calum.

(beat you, I win)

'Hey,' I tap him on the shoulder, 'can I give you a hand?'

'Yeah, knock yourself out,' Calum points to a pile of out of date biscuits.

'Building yourself a wee tower there?'

'Thought we could play biscuit Jenga once we're finished.'

I laugh and hit him on the shoulder. Shit, I'm even ashamed of myself. What's wrong with me? Fucking over a schoolgirl to make myself feel better. Flirting with a kid to bump up my self-esteem.

I glance over to where the girls are standing. 'Blonde-Pigtails' flashes me the evils.

'Here, take these.' Calum loads me up with a pile of biscuits.

'Excuse me.'

'Blonde-Pigtails' and 'Pierced-Nose' are standing at the counter. 'Blonde-Pigtails' waves a bag of crisps at me.

'A little service, please.'

Now this is funny. I almost burst out laughing. These girls can give as good as they get. Maybe I'm out of my depth, taking on a group of hormonal teenage girls. What was I like at that age?

(wet and stinking of chlorine)

I dump the biscuits behind the counter, run the crisps through the till. Sure enough, as I look up to take the money, 'Hot-Pants-and-Tights' swoops in.

I hand 'Blonde-Pigtails' her change and she smiles, gives me an 'as if' look. She's right.

Calum's laughing, rubs his neck as he speaks to 'Hot-Pants-and-Tights.' All I've done is make an arse of myself and spur her on to a brave act of seduction.

It's quite touching really, this display of sisterhood. I don't remember ever having friends like that. I missed too much school, was always training, competing instead of partying. I had friends at swimming, but there was a hidden rivalry. A subtle gamesmanship that bubbled under the surface.

All my fault, too. I've always been so competitive, uptight. I'm hard to get close to.

I watch them flirt with each other. It deflates me.

I don't know why.

It's not like I fancy him or anything.

I don't.

I really don't.

Do I?

No. I don't. I'm being stupid. Really, really, really stupid.

It's been a hard couple of years, I've been lonely, feeling sorry for myself. That's all.

I peel open a packet of biscuits, snack on them as the flirting continues. 'Blonde-Pigtails' and 'Pierced-Nose' leave them to it, spy on 'Hot-Pants' through the shop window. Eventually she makes her goodbyes, gives me a massive fake smile as she leaves the shop.

Bitch.

The other two grab her out on the pavement and they all hug again, laughing. Am I really a girl? That age once?

(you've got shoulders like a man)

Calum goes back to his biscuits. I eat another Hob-Nob. Watch him bend over. The way his t-shirt rides up. The dark hair on the back of his neck. His bare arms.

Stop it. Stop it now.

It's just the flirting, the fancying someone, I haven't felt the thrill of that in ages.

I'm being stupid. It's not lust I can feel in my tummy, it's the out of date biscuits.

I don't fancy him.

I don't fancy him.

You do.

I don't.

Yes, you do. Just admit it.

No, shut up.

I turn away, flick through the *Daily Record*, try to distract myself.

68

Boris The Bonking Boar

Boris the boar has been having a squealy good time of it recently. The randy porker is now the proud father of over 121 piglets, after having his wicked way with fifteen

pigs. Boris's owner, farmer John Norman, noticed that Boris had a wicked glint in his eye and…

Jesus, who reads this pish?
I flick to the back pages instead. Past pages of football until…
No way.
No fucking way.
I think I preferred the story about Boris.

Jason Hungry For Gold in Budapest

Ughh. I'm an idiot. I've been trying so hard to avoid all mention of the European champs. Why did I open a paper?

Jason Livingston is going for gold at the European Swimming Championships in Hungary. Jason, British record holder for the 100m and 200m backstroke, is hoping to make his mark in the championships, which

take place this week.
'I've been working really hard and I feel a lot stronger and faster than I did this time last year. It'll be tough, but I'm in with a good chance.'

There's a picture of him in his GB tracksuit, hair wet and tousled. Not long out of the pool.
He looks good.
I hate that he looks good.
I miss him, miss that part of my life. That was my life.
I miss my life.
'Do you know him?' I jump as Calum speaks. He's looking over my shoulder at the paper.
'Yeah.'
'Think he'll win?'
I shrug.
'Probably.'
I shut the paper on Jason.

Shirley arrives as we're closing up.
'Sorry you two, did you get on okay? I meant to come in earlier, but

I just felt terrible.'

'That's okay,' I reply.

'I phoned the hospital, Hannah, the woman's very poorly but she's still hanging in there.'

'Really, that's great.'

Wow, something good to come out of today's madness.

'What's this?' Shirley says, as she discovers the pile of biscuits we've cleared.

'Some of the biscuits were out of date, Mum.'

'Were they? That's my fault, I've been meaning to do a proper stock check, just ran out of ink in the printer to run off the report. Hannah, I'll maybe get you to do that on Monday.'

'Yeah, no problem.'

Every day. Every day. Every day. Every day.

'Almost glad I'll be at school,' says Calum. 'Alright if I take off?'

'Hot-Pants-and-Tights' is back, standing outside the shop.

'Oh aye?' Says Shirley, 'who's that?'

'Blake, just a girl from my year.'

'What sort of a name is Blake?'

'Very good, Mum. I'll see you later, okay?'

'Okay, not too late though.'

'Yeah, yeah, see you Hannah,' he grabs his jacket and heads outside. I watch him and Blake walk off together.

You fancy him.

I don't.

Yes, you do. You bloody do.

'Seems like he's got over his wee crush,' Shirley says, wiping biscuit crumbs off the counter into the bin.

'What?'

'That wee thing he had for you.'

Me?

Calum fancied me?

Sometimes we'd all have dinner together, watch a film. He was about twelve though. I didn't pay much attention to him, wasn't always about.

(stroke, stroke, stroke, stroke, stroke, stroke, stroke, stroke, stroke)

'No,' I shake my head, blush.

'He used to talk about you all the time – Hannah, the famous swimmer. Oh aye, he had a real wee thing for you.'

I guess I was more attractive back then, when I was the local celeb.

(nobody wants you when you're a nobody)

Dad's not in again when I get home. Everyone's got something to do except me.

Pub.

Blake.

Europeans.

I make myself a cup of tea, slump down on the sofa with a packet of out of date biscuits. Don't have to be so strict about my diet these days.

I switch the TV on, channel hop for a bit, avoid the sports channels.

It's all rubbish. I press mute, put the biscuits to one side before I eat the whole packet.

(you'll put on weight now you're not training, those muscles are already going to flab)

The Lottery's on.

I pick up the remote, about to change the channel when I remember.

The Lottery.

The old woman's lottery numbers.

Shirley said she's still alive. I should check them for her.

The lottery balls flick up and out of the machine. The camera zooms in on them as they line up in a row. I jot the numbers down on Dad's old *Sun* which is lying on the coffee table.

32, 16, 21, 48, 5, 26, bonus 44

They put the lottery balls in order, flash up the winning numbers along the bottom of the screen.

| 5 | 16 | 21 | 26 | 32 | 48 | Bonus Ball | 44 |

Has she won anything?

I run upstairs, my jeans are lying on the floor. I dig in the pockets, find the piece of paper.

| *5* | *16* | *21* | *26* | *32* | *44* |

Back in the living room, I compare her numbers with the ones I've jotted down.

32, 16, 21, 48, 5, 26, bonus 44

She's done not too badly, got a couple, no, wait, three, she's won a tenner. Not too shabby.

| *5* | *16* | *21* | *26* | *32* | *44* |

32, 16, 21, 48, 5, 26, bonus 44

Hang on a minute.

| 5 | 16 | 21 | 26 | 32 | 44 |

32, 16, 21, 48, 5, 26, bonus 44

She's got five numbers.

Five numbers.

And the bonus ball.

She's won.
But what has she won?
It must be a lot.
I unmute the TV, maybe they'll say how much?
I'm too late though, the Lottery's over, they've moved on.

5   16   21   26   32   44

32, 16, 21, 48, 5, 26, bonus 44
I bring up the internet on my phone, Google.

```
Five numbers on the lottery
```

Scroll through the results.

```
3 numbers = £10
4 numbers = 22% of prize (£62 approx)
5 numbers = 10% of prize (£1,500 approx)
6 numbers = 52% of prize (£2,000,000 approx)
5 numbers + bonus = 16% of prize (£100,000 approx)
```

£100,000 approx
£100,000 approx
£100,000
£100,000
£100,000
£100,000 £100,000 £100,000 £100,000 £100,000

8

'*TU PARLERAS. Tu parleras.*'

Sabine looked away from the Gestapo agent, her eyes resting on a portrait of Hitler. It hung central on the wall, above the fireplace. A fire blazed in the grate, it was warm, so warm. Sweat trickled down her forehead.

'Sabine. *Je m'appelle Sabine Valois.* I've not been well, I'm staying...'

'Enough! You are lying.'

Sabine pitched back in the chair as the man slapped her across the face. Her gaze lurched from the portrait of Hitler down towards the plush, red rug that covered the office floor.

'Tell us the truth.'

He slapped her on the opposite cheek. The portrait of Hitler flashed past again in the opposite direction as her head rolled. She felt the man's fingers, burnt onto her skin, pulsing.

- .... . / -.- .. .. / -.... ..- .-. -. - / .- --. .- .. -. ... - / .... . .-. / -.-. --- .-.. -.. / ... -.- .. -.

She stayed silent, head lolled to one side, her eyes flickering. Hitler's image flashed on the inside of her eyelids. Her hair had come loose, tickled her nose. She wanted to scratch but her hands were tied behind her. Looped with rope around the back of the chair.

She looked down at the man's shiny shoes, could see her distorted reflection in the toe caps.

The same room as before, but this time a different man opened the door. He stood there for a few moments, just staring at her, before he eventually invited her in, asked her to sit down.

The intensity of his eye contact made her nervous, awkward. He sat opposite, his pencil tap, tap, tapping on the side of a notebook. He hadn't spoken, she was sure he hadn't. But he looked at her like he was waiting for her to answer a question.

Had she gone deaf?

No, she could hear the tap, tap, tap of the pencil. And his mouth, his mouth hadn't moved, his lips still, underneath his moustache.

Her eyes wandered the room. She couldn't maintain the eye contact.

It annoyed her, angry at him for making her feel like this. She let her eyes travel back to his, smiled. She could play this game too. She could stay quiet as long as he could.

The man cleared his throat.

'Miss Downie, thank you for coming back.'

'My pleasure.'

Pleasure, what a joke. She could think of a hundred different places she'd rather be right now.

'Now, I want you to know that everything you say in this room, everything we discuss, it's all strictly confidential. Just between you and me.'

Marièle nodded. Was this an attempt at reassurance? Was he trying to put her at ease? She had never felt less comfortable in her life. Even that first day at the shop was a more joyous experience. What was he going to ask her? What did he expect her to tell him?

Sabine shut her eyes. The room began to see-saw. Something dribbled down the side of her mouth. Saliva? Blood? She ran her tongue around her lips.

Blood.

'Your supposed friends have already told us all about you, we know who you are. Why not make it easier for us all. Tell us what you know.'

She kept her eyes closed. Didn't answer. Was he bluffing or had someone betrayed her?

If they already knew so much, what did they need her for?

She visualised the hand moving towards her face, waited for it to make contact again. When it didn't, she opened one eye. Two men stood in front of her now, she noticed a look pass between them, a nod.

Something about that nod.

She swallowed down the bile in her throat.

One of the men left the room, while the other one, the one who'd hit her, dragged over a chair. He took off his belt, slung it over his knee, sat down opposite her, hands folded in his lap.

'I'm glad we are alone. I don't enjoy this part of the job. Please, why don't you speak to me? I can help you.'

He smiled, ran a hand through his Brylcreemed hair.

'I've told you the truth. Je dis la vérité. I don't understand these other things you say, these accusations.'

'Come now. Please don't insult my intelligence. I don't want to see a pretty, young thing like you hurt. Cooperate. I hate this bloodshed as much as you do. I want to help you.'

He leant forward and she pulled back as far as she could go. The fire still blazed and she could see the reflection of the flames flicker in the revolver hanging from his belt.

'Come now,' he wiped away the blood that seeped from her lip,

74

licked his finger.

'I think you have mistaken me for someone else.'

He brushed her hair out of her face. She shivered. What was he doing? What was he going to do to her?

God, she couldn't bear to think of some of the things they'd warned her about in training.

'I've taken a shine to you, let me help you.' He stroked her cheek with his thumb.

This was worse than being hit. She wanted to spit in his face but her mouth was dry. No saliva. God, if he tried to do anything to her. The fire crackled. She was so warm, sweat stuck her thighs together, ran down her back.

'I am Sabine Valois.'

'Right, Miss Downie, to start with I'd like to talk about your home life, your family.'

He stopped, looked at her as if she was meant to continue. She expected a question.

'Well, that's rather a large subject area. Can you try to be more specific?'

He tapped his pencil, tap, tap, tap, tap, tap.

'What exactly do you wish to know?' She spoke again.

'Just start at the beginning,' he replied.

God, he was awful. Worse than the last man. This one didn't even attempt to deflect her questions, just ignored them. What was she supposed to say to that?

'Well, I was born in Aberdeen, spent a lot of my childhood in France, one mother, one father, one brother.'

Or at least she did have one brother. She hoped he didn't want her to speak about George.

'Brother,' he flicked through his sheets of paper, 'George, yes?'

She nodded. It was as if he'd read her mind.

How dare he say George's name, make it sound so normal, when just the thought of saying it made her throat thicken. She wanted to reclaim it from this God-awful man.

'I'm sorry to hear about your loss. How does it make you feel?'

How did he think it made her feel?

Awful, so awful, she was underwater, drowning, drowning without him.

'My family are devastated,' she replied.

'How does it make you feel about the war?'

'I wish it was over, so nobody else has to go through what we have.'

The man stood up and walked towards the desk. He unlocked a drawer, took something out. Chocolate. It was a bar of chocolate. She heard the crack as he snapped a chunk off, popped it in his mouth, chewed. Then another piece. She looked away. He was trying to provoke her, just doing this to tease, get a reaction. Did he think she was stupid? Some stupid little girl he could manipulate.

He laid the bar of chocolate on the desk where she could see it. In full view. She hadn't eaten properly in three days. Just try and give her a piece, she'd probably throw it right back up again.

He stoked the fire with a poker. God, it was already so hot in here. She couldn't think properly. How could he stand it in that suit? The chocolate would melt lying out on the desk. What a waste of precious chocolate.

It all happened so quickly. One minute he stoked the fire, the next he had crossed the room in two strides, lifted her skirt and pressed the hot poker against her thigh.

He leant forward, his face pressed to hers.

'If you don't talk, it will be worse for you. I abhor violence. I am nothing compared to my colleague.'

Sabine shut her eyes, his warm breath on the side of her face, the sweet tang of chocolate.

'What was your relationship with your brother like?'

'Your carriage, m'ladies.' He turned and she saw he dragged a wooden sledge behind him.

'The same as most brothers and sisters, I imagine.'

'What do you mean by that?'

'We were very close.'

He looked at her, chewed the end of the pencil.

'And your relationship with your parents?'

'The same.'

They sat down where they were, on the floor, facing each other across the hallway. Mama reached towards Marièle and she took her mother's hands, the telegram lay on the floor between them.

'Tell me about your holidays in France.'

'We would visit my grandparents, they lived there until very recently.'

'Do you miss your grandparents?'

'Of course I do.'

'Do you indulge in fantasies?'

'Fantasies?'

'Yes,' he nodded, waited for her to go on.

'I don't know what you mean.'

'Fantasies, pretence, dreams of a husband, a different life, sexual fantasies.' He looked down at his notes, as if it was a shopping list he read to her.

Her lips were wet from the snow which had started to fall again, and Marièle felt the kiss burn against her cold skin.

'No, no I don't.'

Where had the men gone? Were they coming back? God, how much more could she take of this?

Her wrists and shoulders ached. She longed to swing them free, let her arms hang loose at her sides. The sweat stung at her wounds. She needed a drink, water, she needed water. She'd drink some, then pour the rest of it down her leg, cool the burning.

God, they were pigs, pigs to do that to her. How could they act like that?

She made herself look at the portrait of Hitler. It was all because of him.

Down to him that George was dead, that she was here, that those pigs treated her like this. All down to that one man. Use the anger, use the hate. Use it to survive.

She hated him, hated them, all of them.

'Do you ever feel resentful towards your parents?'

'What? No, of course not.'

Your mother has a funny voice. Why do you call her mama? I was born here, I'm Scottish. Froggy Marie, Froggy Marie.

'Do your father and mother have a happy marriage?'

'Yes.'

'Can you elaborate?'

'What more is there to say?'

He smiled that annoying smile he had. He didn't answer questions, he asked them.

'They have their ups and downs like anyone else, but, yes, they're happy.'

'Would leaving your family for a period of time be difficult for you?'

'I'm here now, aren't I?'

It would be harder for them than it would for her.

'Ah, but if you had to go away for longer than a few days? Further than London.'

'They'd understand if it meant helping the war effort.'
'What if there was danger involved?'
Danger? What was he asking her to do?
An interview for what?
'We're all in danger while the war continues.'
'Could you put your parents through that? After George.'
Mama reached towards Marièle and she took her mother's hands, the
telegram lay on the floor between them.
'Am I at risk?'
He ignored her question, scribbled something down in pencil.
'How do you feel about keeping secrets from your family?'
Marièle felt the kiss burn against her cold skin.
'If it helps us win the war, I see no problem with it.'
'Us, what do you mean by us?'
'The allies of course.'
God, she hoped this would be over soon.

She heard footsteps outside, approaching the office. Were they coming
back? What were they going to do to her now?

That other woman, the one who'd been in the cell with her that first
day. She told Sabine they'd given her electric shocks. Clipped wires to
her bare breasts and shocked her. She urged Sabine to talk, tell them
what they wanted to hear. They're sadists, you're so young, so pretty,
don't let them hurt you. Just tell them, you can't imagine what they'll do
to you otherwise. The girl had shown her scars, sobbed as she pleaded
with Sabine.

Sabine ignored her. Listened but hadn't spoken back. She didn't
know whether the girl was for real or a plant put there to trick her. A
stool pigeon. They did that sometimes. She was sorry for the girl, but
she couldn't trust anyone, not now she'd been caught. The war had
hardened her.

Besides, she didn't plan on talking. She wouldn't give anyone away,
spill her secrets. She would keep quiet.

No matter what they did.

The footsteps stopped outside the door. She heard the key click in the
lock, saw the handle turn, then the door swung open. Why had they
locked her in? She was going nowhere. Even if she could get her weary
brain to come up with some sort of escape plan, she was too weak to
break free of these ropes. God, how had the Germans lasted so long?
They were stupid.

The two men were back. One of them carried a silver tray but she couldn't see what was on it. Something jangled as he placed it on the desk.

'This is your last chance to talk.'

'I have nothing to say.'

'I told you about my colleague, I warned you. Are you sure you won't tell us the truth?'

The man rummaged in a paper folder, pulled out a pile of cards, held together with string. He untied them, shuffled the cards, laid them on his lap.

'Now, Miss Downie, I'm going to hold up these cards and I want you to tell me what the image reminds you of.'

Marièle nodded. At last, a break from the intimate questioning.

He held up a card. It had some sort of inky splodge on it. Like when they made butterfly paintings at school. You painted one half of a sheet of paper, then folded it over so the pattern spread. Symmetrical.

'Spider.'

He held up another card.

'House.'

Her voice echoed around the room, lonely, a conversation with herself.

'Flower.'

'Butterfly.'

'Beach.'

'Sun.'

'Moon.'

'Horse.'

'Dog.'

'Cat.'

'Ball.'

God, she wasn't even sure if the cards make her think of these things. Any hesitation made her awkward, ill at ease. She had to keep speaking, quickly, quickly, quickly. Word after word after word after word. Just to keep herself from standing up and shaking him. She wanted to grab the cards out of his hands, throw them up in the air, see how he reacted to that.

He untied her arms. They floated free at her side, she'd lost all feeling in them.

He moved round, sat in the chair facing her. Shook his head, held out his hands, as if to say, I gave you a chance, there's nothing I can do now.

Then he grabbed her wrist, clamped her hand flat against his thigh.

The other man picked up the silver tray, it rattled as he walked towards her. He lifted a pair of pliers. They glinted in the firelight. Her stomach contracted.

Hitler surveyed the room.

Oh God, what were they going to do?

Her breath was quick and heavy, quick and heavy,quickandheavyquick andheavyquickandheavyquickandheavyquickandheavy.

She didn't want to give them the satisfaction of seeing her cry, but she couldn't stop the tears.

He slid her thumbnail between the teeth of the pliers, squeezed until she felt them grip, then pulled.

The man tidied the cards into a neat pile, tied the string around them again.

Was that right? Had she answered properly?

'Okay, Miss Downie, now a word association game.'

Game? Was this a game?

'I'm going to say a word and I want you to reply with the first thing that comes into your head. Okay?'

'Yes,' she nodded.

He laid his papers on his lap, folded his hands and stared at her.

'Rose.'	*'Red.'*
'Cat.'	*'Mat.'*
'Dog.'	*'Cat.'*
'Tree.'	*'Leaf.'*
'Horse.'	*'Door.'*
'Sea.'	*'Boat.'*
'Shell.'	*'Sand.'*
'Shoe.'	*'Stocking.'*
'Apple.'	*'Pie.'*
'Tram.'	*'Ticket.'*

She tried not to think. Snapped responses back at him.

He stopped firing words. Looked down at his bit of paper, nodded to himself. She wanted to scream. Speak, don't sit there contemplating.

'Okay, I think that will be all, Miss Downie.'

'Oh?'

Did she pass? Was she hired?

Was she mad?

He stood up.

'What happens now?' Marièle asked, standing but not moving

towards the door.

'Oh, I'll hand in my evaluation and then you'll be contacted. I'd stick around for another day or so if you can. I expect they'll want to see you again.'

Was that good news or bad? Did she want to be chosen by these strange men, for whatever job they wanted her to do?

Yes, of course she did. If it meant helping.

She sat in the chair, head slumped to one side, hands heavy and sticky.

The men were gone. They'd untied her, but she still couldn't move. Couldn't stand, couldn't walk, couldn't turn the door handle.

Not without her fingernails.

They'd taken them all.

Ten fingernails.

She could still hear the ting, ting, ting as the nails dropped into the steel tray.

Ting.

Ting.

Ting.

Ting.

Ting.

Ting.

Ting.

Ting.

Ting.

Ting.

March 2006

Hannah Re-Wrights The Record Books
Swimmer Breaks Scottish Record

Hannah Wright is celebrating Commonwealth success with a new Scottish record in the 100m Butterfly.

Hannah swam a personal best time of 59.76 and finished fifth in a thrilling final, missing out on a medal by less than half a second.

'Obviously it would have been nice to get a medal, but to get a PB and a new Scottish record, well you can't ask for more than that really,' Hannah said following her race.

'I've had such a great experience out here, and it really bodes well for the European Championships in July. I just want to catch those Aussie girls, they're so fast!'

In other results in the pool, fellow Scot Jason Livingstone finished sixth in the 200m backstroke final. Claire Richards narrowly missed out on the final of the 100m Butterfly but swam a personal best in the heats.

9

I WAKE EARLY, can't get back to sleep.

I keep thinking about that lottery ticket.

Has she really won?

£100,000

(it could be you)

I turn the bedside lamp on, my eyes shrink against the light, puffy and swollen. I reach over to the dresser, grab the nail polish remover and a bottle of pink polish. Might as well do something useful if I can't get back to sleep. Take my mind off everything. The old woman. The Europeans. Calum.

(the money)

I hate just lying in bed, can't do it.

(I've spent enough time lying still recently)

I paint my fingernails, then slide my legs up from under the duvet and do my toes.

When they're dry, I get out of bed, chuck my swimming stuff in my bag, throw on jeans and a top.

I'm brushing my teeth when I hear the paper being delivered.

The paper.

I can check the lottery numbers again.

I spit, rinse my mouth out, tie my hair back in a ponytail as I head down the stairs. The paper's lying at the front door and I pick it up, head into the living room.

Dad's asleep on the couch. Fully dressed, shoes, jacket, the works. His eyes flicker open as I pass him. He stretches, sits up.

'What time is it?' He asks. His mouth's sticky and he licks his lips. I can smell the booze off him.

'Just before seven.'

'What are you doing up? You don't normally work a Sunday?'

'I can't sleep.'

'You're not going swimming are you?'

'Yeah, I thought I might as well, seeing as I'm up.'

'That's nearly every day this week,' Dad says.

You keeping tabs on me? I want to ask, but I just shrug.

'They told you to take it easy.' Dad continues, 'You can't train the way you used to.'

'I'm not. Believe me. I'd die if I tried to do a proper session.'

I open the paper. Conversation over, flick through it, where do they print the lottery numbers?

I can feel Dad's eyes on me, don't look up.

Eventually I find the numbers.

5   16   21   26   32   48   Bonus Ball   44

£100,000.

'What's so interesting?' Dad asks.

'Nothing, just checking something.'

I don't know why I lie. What does it matter if I'm checking the lottery numbers?

(because it's a secret. My secret. Because I'm... the old woman is rich)

I have to see her ticket again. Check the numbers properly.

'Give us the paper over and make us a coffee, eh? There's a honey,' he says, lighting a cigarette.

I hand Dad the paper, head into the kitchen. Strong, black with three sugars. He's reading the sports pages when I take the coffee back through to him. He looks up at me as I hand him the mug, his eyes are bloodshot, flecked with red veins. I open the window, stand out of the way of his fag smoke.

He flicks through the paper, back to front.

Jason Swims New PB To Make Final

Dad clocks the headline, turns the page, glances up at me.

'It's okay, you don't have to hide it,' I say.

'Ach, I know, but... it's just not fair. You always wanted it more than him. He'd have given up years ago if it wasn't for you.'

I shrug.

'I never liked him anyway, truth be told. He'd fall in a bag of shite and come up smelling of roses.'

I kiss Dad on the cheek. Warm, flushed skin, more veins, purple and broken.

'Right, I'm off.'

'I mean it love, take it easy, for your old Dad.'

'Don't worry, I'm okay,' I lie to him for the second time that morning.

I do as I'm told. Take it easy in the pool. Plod up and down, up and down, up and down. Not even out of breath by the time I finish, might as well have stayed in bed for all the effort I put in.

Try to work out a plan in my head as I plod, plod, plod, plod.

The lottery ticket.

£100,000.

How can I check it?

There's no point getting all excited when I'm still only 98% sure that she's won. I guess I could go round there and knock on the door. It's unlikely she'll be in but someone else might be?

Son, daughter, grandchild?

(rival for the ticket)

As I'm getting changed I make up my mind, I'll cycle past her house on the way home. If someone's in, I'll explain what's happened. It's good news after all. Might perk her back to life.

Or pay for the funeral.

I feel like such an idiot as I walk my bike up her garden path. Why was I so scared the other night? It's just a house.

I must have been suffering from shock or something. In the daylight, it's harder to freak yourself out.

I ring the doorbell and wait.

Ring again.

And again.

Nobody's home.

The free paper sticks out of the letterbox, so I push it through, kneel and peer in.

I can't see anything, the hall's in darkness.

I push my hand through the letterbox, see if I can reach the purse, but it's no use. I only get as far as my wrist before I'm stuck.

(big old swimmer's arms)

As I pull my hand back out, I realise how dodgy I must look.

Local (Failed) Swimmer Caught Trying To Rob Sick (Possibly Dead) Old Woman

I'm not trying to rob her. I just want to confirm what I think is true.

She might never know, otherwise. She could be in hospital for months, recuperating, in a coma. She might even forget that she bought a lottery ticket what with all the drama of almost dying.

I'm the only link between her and the win.
(I could take it and nobody would ever know)
No.
I would never do that.
Steal from an old woman.
(if she died though...)
One of her neighbours must have a key.
I try the house next door.

Nothing.
The house on the other side.

Nothing.
Nobody at home.
Everybody needs good neighbours, but where the fuck are they?
I suppose that's it? Not much more I can do now.

I wheel my bike along the gravel path that leads down the side of her house, push open the gate into the back garden. It's nice and secluded. I dump my bike on the lawn, sit down on her back steps.

Her garden's pretty. She must have someone in to do it for her. She's too old to keep it this nice.

What do I know? Sitting here, making assumptions about her life. My only contact with her was when she lay on the shop floor and here I am making judgements.

Maybe before that she'd been super fit.
(like I used to be)

Her garden reminds me of Gran's. She had a veggie patch too, lettuces, potatoes, carrots. And a plum tree, made amazing jam. We've still got a couple of jars of it in the kitchen. It tastes fine once you scrape the white mould off the top.

Gran used to leave a key hidden under a gnome outside her front door. Dad always gave her such a row for it.

That's a bloody obvious place to leave a key. You could be robbed and killed before you even made it to the phone.

I've had a key outside my house my whole life, I'm not going to stop now.

Aye, but it's different now. Times have changed. It isn't the bloody Blitz spirit anymore, Mum.

They used to bicker, those two. But Dad misses her more than he lets on, and at least visiting her kept him out of The Sal some nights.

The old woman doesn't have a gnome at her back door.

She does have two large flowerpots though.

Worth a try, I suppose.

Without getting up from the step, I tip one of the pots. Dry, dead leaves fall from the plant, but there's nothing underneath except a circle of dirt on the paving slab.

It's a long shot, I know. Nobody leaves a key out anymore.

I might as well try both flowerpots. I reach towards the other one with my foot, tip the pot to one side. I push too hard though and the whole thing topples over. It cracks as it hits the crazy paving around the edge of the lawn. The plant slides out of the pot, roots clinging to a dried-out block of earth.

Fuck sake.

What was I doing, using my foot like that? That was stupid.

I lift the pot, about to put the plant back in when I hear something rattle.

I slip my hand inside.

No way.

It's a key.

A very dirty and rusty key, but a key nonetheless.

Wow, she's something else. Not content to leave a key under the pot, she actually hid it inside. I slide the plant back in, stand the pot upright again, wipe the key on my jeans.

It looks like it's been in there for a while.

Did she expect someone? A visitor who never showed?

Something tugs inside me at the sadness of it.

I scrape at the rust with my fingernail. I bet it doesn't even work anymore.

I might as well give it a try though.

I push the key into the back door lock. It takes some effort, but it seems to fit. I try to turn it but it's too stiff. I need pliers or something, something to get a bit of power behind it. It hurts my hand too much otherwise.

Come on, Hannah. Put those swimmers shoulders into it.

The key digs into my palms.

No movement.

I try again, squeeze my hands around it until my knuckles are white, jump down so I'm on the bottom step, stand with my legs slightly apart, lean all my body weight into the key.

I feel it move slightly.

I push harder, clench my face, my arms, my legs, everything. The key grinds against my fingers, rust flaking off.

It's moving, it's moving.

Gently at first then more and more and more until finally it clicks in the lock.

I push down on the handle and the door swings open.

Her house.

Her kitchen.

What am I doing?

Failed Swimmer Breaks Into Old Woman's House While She Lies Dying In Hospital

I could be arrested for this. Even though she's left a key out, practically inviting me in, it's still breaking and entering.

Well, entering anyway. I haven't broken anything.

Okay, I have cracked the flowerpot, but it's not broken and I'm not doing any of this with criminal intent.

I'll be quick.

The front door has to be directly opposite me at the other end of the house. I'll go straight there, check the numbers, then leave. Nobody ever has to know I've been here.

Her kitchen smells of mince and tatties. It makes me feel sick and hungry all at the same time. The lights are off and everything's dull, in shadow. I don't want to turn anything on though, draw attention to myself. Someone might notice.

I open the kitchen door onto a hallway. I'm right. The front door's at the opposite end, light shines in through frosted panes of glass. There are closed doors on either side of the hallway, must be her living room, her bedroom, her bathroom.

It smells of mince and tatties out here too.

What do people smell when they come to our house?

(who ever visits us?)

Stale beer, unwashed clothes, chlorine, slept on sofa?

I step into the hallway and the kitchen door swings shut behind me. I'm in darkness now, the only light faint in front of me. I'm unable to move. My knees shake.

I was wrong to laugh at myself earlier. It's still possible to freak yourself out during the day.

Anyone could be on the opposite side of one of these doors.

I hold my breath. My heart's thumping so hard, it's all I can hear, all

I can feel.

Thump, thump, thump, thump, thump, thump.

I inhale, exhale through my nose, try to slow my breathing down.

(pre-race routine)

Use the nerves to my own advantage.

(channel them into strength, speed)

A clock ticks somewhere. I tune into it, time my breathing with it.

Tick Tock	In In
Tick Tock	Out Out
Tick Tock	In In
Tick Tock	Out Out

Calm down, Hannah, calm down.

This is an empty house, an empty house, an empty house.

There's nobody here.

My eyes grow accustomed to the dark. I can make out a table at the other end of the hall, her purse on the floor.

All I have to do is walk forward.

Twenty-five baby steps.

Eight giant steps.

Mother may I?

(that's a joke, asking my mother for permission)

I don't move, can't move.

Not ready yet.

To dive in.

I reach behind me, touch the kitchen door.

I'm safe where I am. As soon as I step into the hall, that's it. I'll have to let go.

Dive in.

Jelly legs.

Tick Tock	In In	Tick Tock	Out Out
Tick Tock	In In	Tick Tock	Out Out
Jelly legs.	Jelly legs.		

I used to get jelly legs before I raced, but I used them. Like I used the butterflies in the stomach, the palpitations. Turned them into speed, strength.

Have I lost the ability to do that? I'm out of practise, but please don't tell me I've lost that. It's one of the few skills I have.

(sets apart the great swimmers from the good swimmers)

Jelly legs

Jelly legs

Tick Tock	In In	Tick Tock	Out Out

Maybe I never had it to begin with? I just imagined it. Created a false memory for myself. Made myself believe I was a great swimmer when I was just good.

Only good.

Not great.

(the real reason I failed)

I move one leg forward.

Left leg

Jellylegsjellylegsjellylegsjellylegs   Right Leg

jellylegsjellylegs

Tick Tock   In In   Tick Tock   Out Out

My arm's at full stretch now, I need to let go of the kitchen door.

Tick Tock   In In   Tick Tock   Out Out

I can feel it. A little bit of the old me returning. I felt it in the shop yesterday too. The competitive streak. The determination. The bloody-mindedness.

I've missed her.

(where have you been? where have you been hiding? don't you know I need you?)

I let go of the door.

Left leg

Right Leg

Left leg

Right

Left

Right   Left   Right   Left   Right   Left

I walk forward, towards the light of the front door.

Stop trying to spook yourself, Hannah. It's just an empty house. There's nobody here. No old woman. No relatives. No ghosts.

Just me.

I reach the front door, pick up the purse, along with some mail, the free newspaper.

I did it. I made it.

There's a phone on the table. I put the mail down next to it, carry the purse back along the hall to the kitchen. I'm out of breath. Tired.

(post-race cool down)

'There's someone here after all,' I say, spotting a fish bowl on the kitchen counter.

'What's your name? Are you hungry?' I say to the goldfish. My voice sounds hollow, hangs in the strangeness of the empty house. I open the tub of fish food, sprinkle a few flakes onto the surface of the yellow water. A scum line has formed around the top of the bowl. He could do with a clean.

The fish darts away from the shadow of my hand, but swims to the surface as I move away. The flakes float for a moment, before sinking to the bottom of the bowl.

'Your owner's not well. She might be dead actually. Sorry to break it to you like that. I don't want to upset you little fish.'

The fish sucks at the surface of the water, inhales soggy flakes of food. I run my finger along the side of the glass bowl.

'Poor fish.'

Does he care that his owner went out and never came back? Did he even notice? Maybe he'll only start to worry when his water gets too brown to see through or when he misses his food?

I sit at the kitchen table. I could do with a cup of tea, something to eat, but that would be a step too far. It's one thing breaking in but another helping myself to breakfast.

I play with the clasp of her purse.

Click it open, shut, open, shut, open, shut, open, shut.

Win or lose?

Win or lose?

Win or lose?

'What would you do?' The fish nibbles at the layer of coloured chips lining the bottom of the bowl.

'As many flakes as you can eat? A castle?' He swims in a circle, long tail rippling behind him.

I open the purse, slide out the lottery ticket.

5   16   21   26   32   44

I was right, five numbers and the bonus ball.

£100,000. £100,000.

I hold up the ticket for the fish. Read the small print on the back.

Is there any way I can do this without phoning, without turning up in person?

(without giving myself away)

HOW TO CLAIM
PRIZES CAN BE CLAIMED BY POST OR IN PERSON.
PRIZES OF UP TO £75 CAN BE CLAIMED FROM YOUR
LOCAL RETAILER.
PRIZES OVER £50,000 MUST BE CLAIMED IN PERSON.
PROOF OF IDENTITY WILL BE REQUIRED.

I should probably check she's still with us, before I go spending her money.

I head back into the hallway. I feel better somehow, knowing the fish is here, switch the light on now.

The phone book lies on a shelf underneath the phone.

I flick through it, find the number for the PRI. It rings a few times before a woman answers.

'Good morning, Perth Royal Infirmary.'

'Hi… I'm phoning to find out about a patient. She was brought in on Friday.'

'What's the name?' Fuck sake, what's her name again? My mind's gone totally blank. I lift a piece of mail.

TO THE HOUSEHOLDER

Shit, another one.

MS MARIÈLE DOWNIE

'It's Downie, Marièle Downie.'

'Hold on.'

I hear the clacking of computer keys as she types.

'Can you spell that for me?' She asks.

'Yeah, it's M.A.R.I.E.L.E. D.O.W.N.I.E.'

'I'll need to transfer you to Intensive Care.'

The phone beeps as I'm put on hold, then it rings again.

Intensive Care.

That sounds bad, but at least she's still alive.

'Hello, can I help?'

'Hi, yeah, it's about Marièle Downie.'

'Are you a relative?'

'Yeah, she's my aunt… my great aunt.' The lie slips out before I stop to think about what I'm doing.

'She's very poorly but she's hanging in there. She's still unconscious, but we're hoping she'll wake up soon. Are you able to come in and see her?'

'Yeah, I guess so. When's visiting?'

What am I doing?

'We make exceptions for Intensive Care. We can usually let you in at any time provided that the Doctor's not on rounds. Only for a short while though – fifteen, twenty minutes at most.'

'Okay,' I reply.

I can handle fifteen minutes.

'I'm really pleased to hear from you. We've been having a real job trying to trace next of kin. Was it the police who contacted you?'

'Right, yeah.'

The police. I'm lying about the police.

'Okay, my name's Jackie. I'll be here till about six if you want to ask for me.'

'Right, will do, thanks Jackie, bye.'

I hang up.

Shit, Hannah, what are you doing?

You can't go and visit her, pretend to be some long-lost niece. Especially now she's won the lottery. It's totally dodgy.

'She's alive,' I say to the fish, back in the kitchen.

Alive but unconscious.

Alive but alone.

Alive but with no traceable relatives.

No traceable relatives.

I can't leave her on her own.

That poor old woman. Marièle. Marièle Downie.

She has a name. She's a person with a name and she has nobody to visit her.

(no traceable relatives, no traceable relatives, no traceable relatives)

The lottery ticket.

It could be you.

It could be you.

It could be you.

Stop.

Stop it.

I feel sorry for her. That's all. Nothing more. She's dying and nobody cares enough to visit her.

Nobody cares enough to even notice she's missing.

(except me)

I'll go and visit. Return her purse. She'll need it if she wakes up. Maybe get some Lucozade, grapes, a card. Let her know someone cares.

'I owe her some Revels anyway,' I tell the fish.

I'm about to slip the lottery ticket back inside her purse when I stop myself.

'I'll just leave this here for now,' I say, 'in a safe place.'

I put the ticket in behind the bowl, hide it under the tub of fish food.

'Guard this with your fishy life, okay? This is our wee secret.'

The fish swims round in circles, mouth opening and closing, gills vibrating.

I let myself out of the house, lock the back door and pocket the key.

10

I understand the clauses of the Official Secrets Act
and am fully aware of the serious consequences which
may follow any breach or misdemeanour. I will not
divulge any information secured as a result of my
employment, entrusted to me in confidence by persons
under His Majesty. This applies not only during my
employment, but after my employment has terminated.
I have read and understood and hereby sign:

Signature..................... *Marièle Downie*

May 1943

My dearest Cath,

Well, I expect you're wondering what's become of me since
I left for the big smoke. It's all been a bit of a blur, I can tell
you. I have joined up with the FANY and am now doing a spot
of training for my duties. I'm afraid I can't give away much of
the nitty gritty, it's all very hush hush. What's new though? A
few of us girls are billeted together in a hostel in London. They
seem a nice bunch, although we've only known each other a
short while so are still on our best behaviour. I'm afraid I'm
not allowed to send you the address, they're very stuffy about
security. I'm sorry for the hurried goodbye, everything happened so quickly after I got the letter asking me to interview.
You understand why I had to get away, don't you? You more
than anyone.

Lights out soon and I must write a quick note to Mama and
Father before I'm plunged into the black. I'm sure they will
question you, but I'm telling all of you as much as I'm allowed
to.

Much love,
M

INITIAL REPORT
31st May 1943
NAME OF RECRUIT: Miss Marièle Downie

INITIAL INTERVIEW — PASS
Miss Downie speaks fluent French.
PSYCHIATRIC INTERVIEW — pass

NOTES — Brother K.I.A. (Dunkirk).
Concerns voiced regarding her age. Death of brother
had significant impact and should be taken into ac-
count. She has good language skills however, and
meets the required profile.
ACTION — Report for training, Scotland, assess again
following this.

'Ladies and gentlemen, welcome to the first stage of your training. Some of you may well have guessed from your interviews why you are here. For the rest of you, I'm sure it will soon become clear. This isn't a holiday camp. You are all being thrown in at the deep end and it's up to you whether you sink or swim. You've all been chosen as we think you should be able to swim, but we've been wrong before.

'So, before you get too comfy, up, up on your feet, that's right. You too, Miss. Everyone starts with the obstacle course. We time you now, and then again at the end of the training, give you a score, hopefully you'll have improved. No complaining, I told you this wasn't a holiday camp. Line up over there, yes, that's right. Now, I'll send you off in pairs. Right, you two first, then the rest carry on behind. Okay, you two, on the count of three. Three, two, one, off you go.'

He blew his whistle.

Marièle lined up beside her roommate, Eliza. They were next, dressed identically in the khaki blouse and loose-fitting trousers they'd been given to wear. Some of the other girls had fastened their leather belts tight around their waists, attempted to give some definition to the shapeless outfits. Marièle undid her already loose belt, slipped it back a few notches. There was no way she'd make it over that first obstacle if she couldn't breathe properly. Eliza's belt accentuated her curves, her bosom. She'd already attracted attention from the male recruits, despite her wedding ring.

'I'll never make it over,' Eliza said, her eyes on the girls in front of them. They both struggled to ascend the first obstacle, logs of wood piled high into a wall. Doris had managed to swing one leg over the top, but Celia's jumps had failed to even take her that far.

'It looks like Miss Lewis needs a leg up,' said the trainer.

'I'll go!' one of the men shouted.

'This is not an opportunity to get fresh with the other recruits, Captain Ramsey, you wait in line please.'

Marièle watched their trainer march towards the wall. Doris seemed to sense his approach, hauled herself over and disappeared. Celia clung to the top of the wall, tried to scrabble her feet up the wood.

'What do you call this, Miss Lewis?' The trainer glanced at his watch. 'Three minutes in and you're not even over the first obstacle.'

'It's too wet, my feet keep slipping,' Celia replied.

'This is Scotland. What did you expect? Now up you get.'

He bent down and pushed his shoulders under her bum, hoisting her up. Marièle watched her swing her legs over and she was gone.

'This is silly,' she whispered to Eliza. 'Are we not meant to be using our wits too? My wits are telling me to go around.'

'Is that right?'

Marièle jumped as she realised the trainer stood beside them.

She made a face at Eliza, who winked back.

'Right you two, ready to get going?'

He blew his whistle and Marièle set off running towards the wall. The trick was to get a bit of speed up. George was the school track and field champion and she remembered him explaining the high jump to Mama.

Speed, Mama, speed. The faster you go, the higher you jump.

Gosh, what would George think if he could see her now?

The wall loomed in front of her, closer and taller, closer and taller. She kicked off from the ground, gripped the top of it, felt a splinter stab into her hand, her plimsolls sliding and slipping as she tried to scramble up the damp wood. Her forearms burned as she heaved and tensed, pulled her body weight up. Eliza struggled next to her, panting and out of breath.

'Holy mother of goodness.'

Marièle giggled as Eliza swore.

No, no, no. Laughing made her muscles weak, she slipped back down the wall. Come on, come on, you're almost there.

'The mother of our lord is not going to help you here,' the trainer shouted.

Not him again.

Marièle couldn't face another of his wisecracks and heaved herself over the wall, leaving poor Eliza to face him on her own. The ground was soft where she landed, momentum took over and she sprawled forward. She picked herself up, trying to catch a breath as she ran on to the next obstacle. This was certainly being thrown in at the deep end.

June 1943

Dearest Cath,

Another letter from me. I know you'll be fretting at not being able to write back, but please don't worry. You'd think I was training to be a spy or something, the secrecy we have to abide by. I suppose it's just the times we find ourselves in. I do miss our chats and wonder how things are back home. We shall have a lot to catch up on when I next see you, make sure you remember all the shop gossip for me. I'm in a little bubble here. We were fitted for our uniforms this week, you'd laugh if you saw me. Gosh, I look a fright. Stiff and straight-laced, with sensible shoes, just like Miss Beryl at the shop! We even have to polish our buttons, they really do take it all very seriously. I suppose it is serious, it's a war after all. I don't see how shiny buttons help to be honest, though. If the Boche ever does invade, maybe the plan is to blind them with our buttons!

Have to dash, my roommate is pointing at the clock. Lights out in ten minutes and I must wash my face before bed. It's a strict life sticking to curfews!

Much love,
M

Marièle sat in the communal lounge, a cup and saucer balanced on her knee. She took a sip of tea and watched the others around her. A couple of the men played chess and smoked, Celia read a book while Doris chatted up one of the male officers. They'd spent the morning learning how to assemble and take apart a Bren gun. Then they'd had firearms practise out in the yard, peering round doorways and corners, shooting at targets which flew in and out of sight on ropes and pulleys. Marièle could still see the flash of the cut-out torso if she closed her eyes. It was strange to think they'd been shooting at pretend people earlier, yet here they all were now, civilised, tea and crumpets for supper in the lounge.

'Where do they get all this food from?' Eliza asked, spreading jam on another scone. 'I'm grateful for these morning runs, I'd never fit in my clothes otherwise.'

'I'm worried I'll have to take my overalls with me when we leave, it's all I'll fit into,' Celia replied, looking up from her book.

'Only the best for the British army,' Marièle laughed. 'I think it's all grown and made nearby. I'm surprised they've not had us out fishing, or pulling up tatties.'

'Tatties?'

'Potatoes,' Marièle put on a fake posh accent.

'Why do you think they're keeping us up late tonight?' Eliza asked, 'I'm so tired.'

'Another scheme, I suppose. Who knows? You can never get a straight answer round here.'

Marièle drank her tea and helped herself to a scone. Everyone looked tired. Different to that first day, turning up off the train in their skirts and stockings, hair done, even a bit of makeup. Doris still persevered with the lippy but the rest of them had given up. Would rather have an extra five minutes sleep. No point anyway, it all sweated off when they were sent on yet another cross-country run.

Marièle may have been eating more, but she'd lost weight rather than gained any. She lay awake at night, felt the poke of her hipbones, the tightness in her thighs, the shrinking of her bosom. She noticed it in her face too, her cheeks thinner; like the rest of them, she had purple shadows under her eyes, dirt under her fingernails, blisters on her feet. She admired Doris for still having the courage to chat up a fella, Marièle had never felt less attractive.

Just to have a morning when she wasn't woken up by someone blowing a whistle outside her bedroom door. That would be bliss. Or one night where she slept right through, undisturbed by Eliza's snoring, not lying awake thinking about George.

A room of her own, now that would be heaven. Her own room wasn't so far away right now. Just a train ride. It was odd to be so close but not to be able to visit. She couldn't even tell them she was so near. They all thought she was in London, living in the FANY hostel, learning to be a driver.

What were Mama and Father doing now?

Cath?

She glanced at a clock on the wall. Father would probably be reading or listening to the wireless. She wasn't sure about Mama, suddenly childless after all those years of doing nothing else but bringing up her children. Had Marièle made a terrible mistake leaving them? She had to do something though – didn't see herself following the life of Mama.

Marièle felt the homesickness tug at her. She bit down on the inside of her mouth. She wouldn't let herself cry. Not here in front of everyone, anyway. None of them did that. She knew Eliza cried herself to sleep some nights and she'd heard someone crying in the toilets the other day. At first she hovered outside, waiting for them to come out so she could check if they were okay, but then she changed her mind. Walked away quickly, so whoever it was would come out and think they'd got away with it. They all put on a front here, acting brave, trying to do well in the training, when they were all exhausted and missing things back in their normal lives.

Well, as normal as life could be these days.

'Right, you lot, on your feet. Yes, yes, I know, I'm tired too. I'd rather be in bed than having to organise you lot. Outside, please, outside.'

Marièle put down her tea, followed the rest of them, slipped her hands inside her pockets, away from the chill of the night air. The sky was clear, she could see the stars.

'Right. You each have an individual scheme to complete. Take a slip of paper, your task is written on it. Once you know what you have to do, off you go. No waiting around to discuss or confer, you're on your own tonight.'

Marièle took the slip of paper, stepped back so she could read it using the light of the house.

```
Find the dead letter box located 2km west and 3km
South of HQ — 56.910502, 5.84404. Memorise and de-
stroy the message waiting for you. Follow the in-
structions on the message, complete and return to
HQ by 02.30.


8 June 1943
NAME OF RECRUIT: Miss Marièle Downie
PROGRESS REPORT — Fitness improving, asks intelli-
gent questions, struggles slightly with map reading
and compass navigation — as a consequence did not
complete night mission in allotted time.
```

June 1943

Dearest Cath,

Well, how are you, darling? I'm being kept frightfully busy, which explains the rather erratic nature of my letters. Being in the FANY keeps me on my toes but it's rather dull work, I'm afraid to reveal. Reveal, that's a laugh, as if I reveal anything these days!

It seems I'm to remain a driver for now, so spend most of my days ferrying awfully important people around. Some of them are very pleasant and we have a joke but others are frightfully serious and downright rude to your friend – the lowly driver. Think Mrs Walker multiplied by about a hundred! Gosh, you should see me, driving around London . Me, who struggled on my old push-bike. I keep thinking of that afternoon we took the notion to cycle to Peterhead. What an awful idea, why did we do it? My posterior aches just thinking about it.

Well, I shall love you and leave you. Not much free time for me, I'm afraid. Much love to you and say hello to the gang at work. I do hope we haven't lost any more of our boys.

M

'Who do you keep writing to? Is it your sweetheart?' asked Eliza.

Marièle sat at the shared desk in their room, while Eliza sat on her bed, feet resting in a tub of hot water.

'No, I don't have a fella, it's my friend Cath back home.'

'Any of the fellas here caught your eye then?'

Her lips were wet from the snow which had started to fall again, and Marièle felt the kiss burn against her cold skin.

'I'll admit there are some handsome ones here, but nobody special.'

'I hadn't noticed, I'm a married woman after all.'

Eliza laughed, splashed water over the edge of the tub with her feet.

'You're not supposed to tell me that, no personal information remember?'

'Oh nonsense, they can't make me take off my wedding ring,' Eliza replied. 'Besides, you just told me about your friend Cath.'

'Gosh, I did. Oh dear, I'm never going to pass this training.'

'Do you see Mr Tracy up there?' Eliza pointed to a black and white cut-out picture of Spencer Tracy. 'My Bill looks like a young Spencer Tracy. That's why I've put that up there, they won't let me have a real photo of him.'

Eliza ran a finger across the picture.

'What do you think they'd do if someone struck up a romance here?' Eliza asked. 'Doris's already been caught sneaking over to the men's quarters.'

'I don't know. She's some girl, isn't she? I don't think any of the fellas are worth a week of six am runs though.'

'No, you're right, what a punishment! My poor feet,' Eliza rubbed at them, water dripped onto the carpet. 'I can't believe they made us go on a ten-mile hike today. Back home, I never go further than the shops or the pictures.'

'At least you didn't make a mess of your compass reading. I ended up adding an extra five miles on by mistake.'

'Oh yes, poor dear. Come and stick your feet in here.'

Marièle sat next to Eliza on the bed and pulled off her thick socks. She sunk her feet into the tub, her blisters stinging in the water.

'I hate these hideous socks,' Marièle balled them up and threw them against the wall. 'So itchy. This feels wonderful.'

The initial sting had dissipated and the water soothed her tired and aching feet.

'So, what do you tell your friend? Your letters would never get through if you told her the truth.'

'Oh, I've told her I'm enlisted with the FANY, not a lie, and that I'm a driver in London, a complete falsehood. I feel awful making up these stories, but I like writing to her. Maybe one day, I'll be able to tell her the truth.'

Eliza nodded and lay back on the bed. She laid her feet in Marièle's lap and Marièle rubbed at her damp toes and soles. Her feet were soft, the skin beginning to wrinkle.

'You are a dear. It's hard, isn't it? I've been meaning to write to my son, but he's so young, I just don't know what to say to him.'

'Gosh, Eliza, I didn't know you had a wee boy.'

'A minute ago you were telling me off for giving out personal information. To be honest, it's too upsetting to speak about him. Don't let on, but I've got a picture here under my pillow.' She reached underneath and handed Marièle a photo, its corners bent and creased.

'Oh, he's a wee sweetheart, what's his name?'

'Adam. He's only three, my little lamb. Abandoned by his mummy and daddy.'

Eliza slipped the photo back under the pillow, but left her hand there.

'How can you bear it?'

'It's hard, I won't lie. I turned them down a few times, but they were very persistent. I sometimes wish I hadn't answered that ad looking for French photographs.'

'That's how they got me too.'

'He's very resilient though. My mother-in-law and sister are looking after him. If Bill can go off gallivanting with the forces then I can do my bit too. It's his future after all. That's what I keep telling myself. Besides, it'll all be over soon, won't it?'

'If we're lucky it might even be over before this training is,' Marièle replied, squeezing Eliza's feet. 'Hopefully before the next obstacle course.'

```
11 June 1943
NAME OF RECRUIT: Miss Marièle Downie
PROGRESS REPORT — Miss Downie works hard and her map
reading has improved as a result. She possesses a
dry sense of humour and gets on well with the other
recruits. Concerns remain regarding her age, al-
though youth may work to her advantage in France.
```

Marièle stood in the empty hanger while the trainer fixed her into her safety helmet and harness. The doors of the hanger were open and the sun shone in as she was hoisted into the air and swung back and forward, back and forward, back and forward. It was hard to pretend you were in a parachute, the swinging motion was so relaxing.

'Ladies, this isn't meant to be fun, it's serious. You are learning how to parachute. How to fall from a great height and not get hurt.' The trainer shouted up at them.

Marièle tried to remember what he'd told her before she was strapped in, but the swinging motion was too hypnotic. She closed her eyes, let the harness take her weight. It was like a cradle, back and forward, back and forward, back and forward. Oh, to be a child again, not to worry about wars and George never coming home.

Back, forward, back forward, the seconds ticked away as she swung.

Tick, tock, tick tock, back, forward, tick, tock, tick, tock, tick, back, forward.

She kicked her legs out underneath her, as if she were on a swing, kick, kick, kick, faster, higher, faster, higher.

Tick, tock, tick, tock, tick, tock, tick, tock.

The silver cross hit against her chest as she swung faster and faster.

Tick, tock, tick, tock, tick, tock, tick, tock.

She wanted to go so fast that she rocked away the seconds, minutes, hours, days. She wanted to swing time away, rush on towards the future, the end of the war. They say time heals; could she swing so fast that the lump in her chest broke down and disappeared? Cheat the grieving process by speeding through it.

Or maybe she could go backwards in time if she swung the opposite way? Back to before the lump formed, stop George from leaving. Warn him not to go.

'You up there, Miss Downie?' She heard someone shout her name and opened her eyes. The trainer jumped, grabbed her by the ankle, slowed her down.

'This isn't a swing, it's a tool,' he shouted at her. 'Out you get, onto the landing apparatus.'

She joined another group of recruits. Took her turn at sliding down the wooden chute which hung over a crash mat, at jumping out of the old fuselage they had set up.

Her stomach lurched as she fell into space, then the ropes went taut, simulating the parachute descent. She hung in the air briefly before being launched into the drop and roll of her landing.

'Keep your legs together. You girls should be good at this, it's all about modesty,' the trainer shouted. 'You need to learn to fall the right way if you want to earn your paratrooper's wings.'

July 1943

Darling Cath,

It's me again. I know it's not long since my last letter, but I must confess writing to you is a comfort at the moment. Gosh, I'm homesick. My days keep me very busy but I have a bit of spare time before bed and that's when it hits me. I've got myself into the routine of writing a few paragraphs to you. It makes me feel better. It's like writing a diary, except that I can picture you reading and imagine your responses, it's almost like having a real chat with you.

I hope they'll give me some time off soon.

M

'I thought the wind would be louder up here,' said Eliza, 'but you can't hear anything over the engines.'

They lined up ready to jump, girls first, the men following on at the back. The trainer had taken them to one side earlier at the airfield, told them the reason for the order as they climbed into their bulky overalls.

'Don't let me down now, ladies. When you jump first it means the men won't chicken out. Can't see the girls getting the better of them, now can they?'

Marièle thought she'd be unable to go through with it when the time came. Thought she'd have to be forced out, had even told Eliza to go behind and give her a hard shove on the back if she hesitated. It was one thing jumping off the Fan strapped into a harness, but quite another jumping out of a plane and trusting yourself to a parachute.

When the time came though, she found it surprisingly easy. Much easier than the six am obstacle courses, the ten mile hikes, the cross-country runs.

The map-reading.

Something everyone should do at least once in their life.

She wished she could tell Cath about it, instead of inventing yet another story about driving officers around London.

'How can you stay so calm?' Eliza whispered. 'I thought you needed a push!'

'I don't know. It just feels okay now we're actually up here.'

'Speak for yourself, don't you worry it won't open?'

'*C'est la vie*,' Marièle shrugged.

The smell of the Lysander and the noise of the engines as they rose higher and higher soothed her. She sat on the edge of the drop hole, legs buffeted by the wind as they dangled under the plane, her static line attached to the fuselage.

She placed her hands flat on either side of her, felt the fuselage vibrating. She didn't need a shove on the back when the light flashed from red to green and the arm of the trainer swung down.

GO!

She was happy to go, happy to jump. Her head throbbed with the thrill of it, the blood pumping in her ears.

It was beautiful. The mosaic of fields and towns, growing and spreading out beneath you. Turning from coloured shapes into real things, from abstract to actual, as the wind rushed through. She preferred the abstract, felt a twinge of regret as things came into focus. It was almost a shame to hit land, to have to run and gather up your chute before the wind caught it and dragged you along the ground.

It was Doris who came up with the nickname, Marièle, Mariemerle, Merle.

Soon everyone called her it, 'Merle.'

'You deserve that badge, Merle,' Eliza said, as Marièle stitched the cloth wings onto her tunic.

29 June 1943
NAME OF RECRUIT: Miss Marièle Downie
PROGRESS REPORT

Marièle has performed well during training, no reason why she should not proceed apart from the obvious age issue. Her highest score on the obstacle course was 147, well above the 78 needed to pass. Has also performed well on other duties, although still lacks aptitude in map reading. Has a natural talent for parachuting and has outshone the other recruits — men included!

RECOMMEND HER FOR THE NEXT STAGE.

April 2007

Hannah Wrights Her Mark On The World Stage
Medal down under for Scottish swimmer

Hannah Wright was celebrating last night after winning a bronze medal at the World Swimming Championships and achieving a new British record in the 100m Butterfly. Hannah swam a personal best time of 57.89 and finished third in a thrilling final, missing out on second spot by three hundredths of a second.' A medal and a new British record, well you can't ask for more than that really,' Hannah said after her race. 'I knew I had it in me to get the British record, and I thought there was a chance of a medal if I swam that fast, so I'm just delighted with my performance.'

11

I'VE NO IDEA where to go when I get to the hospital, so I head in the first entrance I find. The signs aren't very helpful and I wander around for a bit, past the canteen, a shop selling newspapers and balloons.

IT'S A GIRL!

GET WELL SOON

I end up going round in a circle, find myself back where I started. I'm tempted to leave, just give up and head home.

Being here reminds me…

I stand at the entrance, swing my carrier bag back and forth, back and forth, back and forth, the Lucozade bottle hits against my shin.

Come on, Hannah, you can't leave. Not after you've come all this way.

I set off again, turn left instead of right this time when I reach the end of the first corridor. There's a woman sitting in a wheelchair, about halfway along. Maybe she knows where Intensive Care is?

I walk towards her, swinging the bag as I go.

'Help me.'

I stop, the bottle of Lucozade bashes against my leg again. I need to stop doing that, the grapes I've brought are going to end up mush.

'Help me,' she repeats.

'What is it?' I ask. I don't want to get too close in case a nurse comes running and thinks I'm the one she needs help from.

'I want to go home,' the woman says. 'I just want to go home.'

As I walk towards her, I realise she isn't looking at me, she's staring at the wall she's been parked in front of. I doubt she even knows I'm here. Poor old soul.

How do you end up like that? You get a bit older and people stop caring, stop treating you like a grown up. When Gran was sick, the nurses spoke to her like she was an idiot.

Dad lost it one day, had a real go at one of them.

'She's no a six-year-old, she's eighty-one and she's got more common sense than the lot of you put together, so show her some respect, eh?'

It was really embarrassing but I felt all proud of him, sticking up for her like that.

I keep going, can hear the woman still talking to herself as I turn the corner into the next corridor.

RADIOLOGY   →

OCCUPATIONAL HEALTH →

CHAPEL   →

Why do none of the signs mention Intensive Care?

There has to be someone around I can ask for directions. Where is everyone anyway?

A chill runs up my back and shoulders, someone walking over my grave.

When I was still at school, everyone used to go up to the abandoned TB hospital to get drunk.

(training again)

You're so dedicated, Hannah, I can't believe you don't drink.

I'd listen to them talking about it. Rusty bed frames, old gurneys, tables and chairs, just lying around the dusty corridors. All the windows smashed, the staircases rotting, ceilings and floors caved in. They said they heard things, things that couldn't be explained. Saw things move, shadows.

It's spooky enough wandering about an inhabited hospital.

I jump as a man turns the corner at the far end of the corridor. He's pushing an empty wheelchair.

'Can I help? You look lost,' he says.

'Intensive Care?'

'Oh, I'm sorry,' the man whispers. 'Follow me. I'll show you where it is. You're a bit out of the way.'

I follow him back the way I've just come. The wheelchair squeaks against the linoleum floor and the man's flat white shoes flap, flap, flap, flap as he walks.

I follow him along corridors, left, right, right, left.

He doesn't ask me anything else, who I am, who I'm visiting. Turns and smiles every so often. I guess he's seen people like me before. All hopeful with their carnations, their bunches of grapes. Before they end up eating the grapes themselves, put the wilted flowers in the bin, home to order more for the funeral.

He leads me into the lift, pushes a button, smiles at my reflection in the mirrored wall. The silence makes me uncomfortable in such an enclosed space, and I worry I'm going to burst out laughing. I clench my teeth together, focus on the red arrow counting us up the floors.

1 ↑
2 ↑
3 ↑

We leave the lift, the blue signs become more frequent now. I peer in open doors we pass, nurses drinking tea, patients propped up in beds, visitors in waiting rooms reading leaflets and old magazines.

'Not far now.'

He could be taking me anywhere. For all I know he could be some psycho leading me to my doom.

'Here we are then,' he says, and nods towards a set of double doors. 'Just in there.'

He's off, the wheelchair squeaking and his shoes flap, flap, flapping. Is he just paid to wander the corridors and pick up lost souls?

There was a man who worked here like that, but he died thirty years ago…

I shake my head, I'm an idiot, ghosts on the brain at the moment.

I push the double doors, there's a reception desk directly behind them.

'Can I help you?' A nurse looks up from the desk, face lit by the computer screen in front of her.

'I phoned earlier, about Marièle Downie.'

'She's just through here,' she says, coming out from behind the desk, 'in room three. We've kept her in one of the single rooms for now, but if there's any improvement we'll move her to the High Dependency ward.'

I nod.

'I'm glad you've come in, she's not had any visitors yet and it makes such a difference.'

I follow her to room three. She stops at the door, turns to face me.

'Now, I must warn you, it will look a bit scary. She's hooked up to a lot of wires and machines.'

'Is she okay? I mean, will she be okay?'

'Well, we can't really say for sure. She's unconscious, although she has stabilised. We're keeping her sedated and monitoring her…'

I tune out as the nurse keeps talking. Unconscious, sedated, monitoring, she's telling me all this personal stuff about a woman I don't even know.

'Are you okay?'

'Yeah, fine.'

'I know it can all be a bit overwhelming. Now you'll need to wash your hands when you go in and when you leave. If you use this hand wash here.'

I push the dispenser, rub the clear liquid into my hands. It smells of melon, leaves my hands feeling cold and shiny.

'Oh and what's in your bag. No flowers?'

I shake my head, open the bag for her to see.

'Okay, that's fine. If you turn your mobile phone off too, please.'

I do as I'm told.

'Take your time, I'll just be along here if you need me,' she says and leaves me to it.

I stand outside the door. This was a bad idea. I'm scared to go in. Of what I'll see, how I'll react. I want to leave, but the nurse can see me from where she's sitting, I feel her watching me. I have to go in or she'll come and check on me, speak to me in that whispered voice, put on that sympathetic face.

I push down on the door handle. Dive in. Room three.

She's lying there, head propped up on a hospital pillow, tucked under tight white sheets. A mask over her nose and mouth, a tube in her arm, another coming out from under the bed sheets at her midriff. Fluid-filled rubber bags hang from metal stands, another from the side of the bed, monitors all around her. The hum and suck of the machines.

A line of parallel stitches in her chin.

Neat.

I don't know what's worse, being unconscious and hooked up to all this, or being that old woman I passed in the wheelchair.

I shut the door behind me, lean against it, afraid to go any closer. I don't know what I expected. For her to sit up and wave me in, offer me the seat next to her bed?

She looks so small.

I take a step towards her, it smells funny in here. Clean, but not in a nice, fresh way. The blinds are closed, so I cross to the window, open them slightly. She needs a bit of light. Has nobody in here ever read *What Katy Did?* You don't get better hiding away in the dark.

I sit in the chair next to the bed, put the grapes, Revels and Lucozade on the bedside cabinet next to her.

I feel like an idiot for bringing all this with me.

Intensive Care.

She's in Intensive Care.

Grapes and Lucozade are hardly a miracle cure.

One hand lies free of the sheets, a drip plugged into the back of it. Skin bruised where the valve sticks out of her, wrinkled, purple and yellow.

Now that I'm close up, I can hear the in, out, in, out, in, out of her breathing. I don't think it's her doing it though. It's too rhythmic to be real.

(the breathing I aspired to when I swam, under control, in time with my stroke)

I clench my jaw, I'm going to cry.

Seeing her like this, and me, a total stranger, her first visitor. Not one card on her bedside cabinet.

(get well soon, Hannah, we miss you in the pool, can't wait to have you back at training, stay strong, you'll be back in the pool in no time…)

The back door key, rusting and unused inside the flower pot.

All my sneaking around her house, scared someone would see me, when nobody but me and Shirley even know she's in here. If she'd collapsed at home, she might be lying there now. One of those poor old souls, only found when the neighbours start to complain about a funny smell.

What does she have to wake up for?

There must be something.

Someone.

Is she in a coma?

Shit, I'm so dumb. What did the nurse say again? Sedated, unconscious. She didn't say the actual word.

Coma, coma, coma.

I walk to the end of the bed, pick up the clipboard hanging there. The writing's a scribble, hard to read, plus I feel like I'm spying on her. I put it back down. She's not well, that's all I need to know.

From this angle she looks long and shrunken, like she's been stretched out.

I sit down next to the bed again. Open the Lucozade, it hisses, fizzes to the top of the bottle, spills onto the bedside cabinet. Shit, this place is meant to be spotless and here I am making a mess. I wipe the Lucozade up with a tissue, pour myself a glass, my fingers sticky. Should I wash my hands again?

The Lucozade's sweet, bubbles against my tongue, takes me back to my childhood. Being off school, sick, lying on the sofa under a duvet. Dad would always bring me a bottle of Lucozade once I started to feel a bit better. Lucozade still tastes like recovery to me.

It's not like when I was five and I had the mumps

'Oh, I almost forgot,' I dig her purse out of my pocket, hold it up, even though she's totally out of it.

(Lottery ticket? No, I don't remember seeing that)

I open the drawer of the bedside cabinet. Her bag's lying there, her watch, her false teeth, a compact, a silver chain with a cross.

I slip the purse into her bag, pick up the necklace, let the weight of the cross sink into my hand, feel the slink of the chain as it follows, spilling into my palm like sugar. I do it over and over and over and over.

'Can you hear me? Are you in there somewhere?'

'Course you are, that's a stupid thing to say. I mean, are you on the surface, or are you lost somewhere, deep, deep down?'

'I like your fish, I gave him some food.'

'I'm sorry you collapsed in the shop. That was a crappy thing to happen.'

'I'm Hannah, by the way.'

'It was bad timing, collapsing like that.'

Should I tell her?
(is anyone listening in?)
What if she can hear me, and the lottery win jumps her back to life? Like Grandpa Joe and the golden ticket. She'll spring out of bed and we'll dance round the room together.
(then she shares the money with me)
£100,000.
Or maybe the shock will do her in? She's already weak, I might kill her.
(no need to share)
Or most likely, she can't hear me and I'm still the only one who knows she's won.
(it could be you)
It's pretty lousy, someone up there having a laugh. She must believe in God, she wears a silver cross. Is her God really that cruel? That unfair?
I lean in towards her, reach out to touch her hand, change my mind.
'Marièle, can you hear me?'
I'm whispering, why am I whispering?
'I've got something to tell you. You've won the Lottery. That ticket you bought before you collapsed, you had five numbers and the bonus ball. You've won.'
(we've won, I've won)
'So you need to wake up, because I don't know what to do with it if you don't wake up.'
(and I'm left with a winning Lottery ticket)
I watch her face for a flicker of a reaction.
Nothing.
Her eyes remain shut, no twitch in her eyelids, no murmur from her

mouth, whisper from her lips. Her hand stays still, the bruise shadowy and purple.

'Where you been?' Dad shouts from the living room when I get in.

'What are you doing home?'

'I live here, don't I? I got us a Chinese,' he says, getting up from the sofa. 'It's in the oven keeping warm.'

'You should have just had yours,' I reply.

'Can't I spend time with my own bloody daughter?'

'Yeah, sorry, I didn't mean it like that.'

I sit down, check off dates in my head.

Have I forgotten something?

Mum's birthday?

Gran's birthday?

My birthday?

It's not his wedding anniversary either, although he wouldn't be here for that anyway. He usually spends that day in the pub getting completely wrecked. As he does on the anniversary of Gran's death.

(and most Saturday nights)

As yet I'm the only girl in Dad's life not to leave him, so there's no fixed date for that.

'I got you a chow mein, that okay?' He says, bringing the plates through. 'It's pork.'

'Yeah, great,' I reply. 'That smells good. I'm starving.'

I take the plate off him, tip out the contents of the foil container, a sticky syrup of noodles and pork.

'Prawn crackers too,' he says, dumping them on the coffee table, greasy translucent stains on the brown, paper bag. He disappears again, comes back with two lager stubbies.

'You want?' he asks, holding one up.

'Yeah, why not,' I reply.

(make up for my teenage years)

I could do with a drink tonight, after seeing that old woman. I'm not really that keen on lager, never acquired a taste for it, but I can force it down.

Make Dad happy.

Watching you on the TV tonight, I was so proud of you

Dad prises the stubbies open, sets one down in front of me. I help myself to a prawn cracker, feel it stick and prickle on the end of my tongue.

'What's the occasion?'

'Bloody hell, does a man need a reason to buy dinner for his only daughter?'

'No. Course not.'

'I just thought we deserved it, overtime burning a hole in my pocket. Besides…'

I stop eating.

'Besides, what?'

'Ach, well, I saw the results of the Europeans, thought you might need a wee pick-me-up?'

'How did he get on?'

'Gold, another PB.'

I imagine the photo in tomorrow's paper. Jason. Up on the medal rostrum, or in the pool at the end of the race, fist pumping the air.

I twirl my fork round the noodles. Spear a bit of pork, a water chestnut, shove it all in my mouth. Crunch down on it, swallow the tears.

Tears at Dad's loyalty to me, tears of disappointment that it's not me in the sports pages anymore making him proud, something to brag about down The Sal. In another life, it's me out there, at the Europeans, breaking records, winning medals. Instead I'm sitting here with Dad, eating takeaway and drinking lager.

I take a swig, gulp down the lump, burp as it collides with the gassy fizz somewhere on the way down.

'Pardon me,' I laugh.

'Very ladylike,' Dad shakes his head. 'Where you been today anyway?'

I hesitate, about to make something up, lie about where I've been. The lager's gone to my head though, made me slightly tipsy, and the love I feel for Dad right now won't let me lie.

'I ended up going to visit that old woman.'

'What old woman?'

'The one who collapsed the other day, she's in the PRI.'

'Did you? Jesus, I'd forgotten about that.'

I slurp on a noodle, feel it slap against my chin, wipe the juice away with my hand.

'Are you alright?'

'I'm fine, don't worry.'

'I'm allowed to worry about my daughter.'

'I'm fine, honestly.' I take another prawn cracker, my stomach bloated, all this food buoyed up with fizzy lager.

'Was she okay?'

'I don't know, she's unconscious, hooked up to all sorts of machines.'

Dad picks at a bit of pork he's dropped in his lap, eats it, then wipes at the trail of juice dripping down his t-shirt. He crunches on a prawn cracker, white crumbs fleck his beard and moustache.

'I'm stuffed,' I say and push my plate away, lie back on the sofa. 'Thanks, Dad, that was great.'

He nods, gets up and clears the plates away. I hear the clatter as he dumps them in the sink, then he comes back through pulling open another two stubbies.

'Another?' He asks.

'Yeah, thanks,' I reply.

'Will you go and see her again?'

'Not sure. Maybe. They said I was the only visitor so far.'

'Really? Poor old soul.' He shakes his head.

The Lottery ticket is on the tip of my tongue. One more bottle of lager and it would be out there, I'd be telling him. I hold back though.

Dad picks up the remote control, starts channel hopping, puts the volume up.

'What's the use of all these bloody channels, eh?' He says. 'All a load of shite.'

'I think I might head up to bed,' I say, finishing my beer.

'You swimming in the morning?'

'Not sure.'

'Do you think you should?'

'Probably not.'

Hearing about Jason though, doing so well, it makes me want to pound the pool.

'Got a goodnight kiss for your old Dad?'

I bend down, his moustache and the crumbs of prawn cracker tickle my lips as I kiss him.

'Thanks again for dinner.'

Dad waves his hand in a 'don't be silly' way. I leave him flicking through the movie channels.

I'll find him on the sofa in the morning, empty bottles on the coffee table, TV on, wallet lying open at the picture of him and Mum.

I tramp up the stairs. Sometimes I think about destroying that photo. Pulling it out of Dad's wallet and ripping her up into pieces.

Poor old Shirley never stood a chance. Her face that day in the shop, when he opened his wallet to pay for lunch and she spotted the photo. Dad didn't even realise, just put his change away, carried on flirting in his own useless way. Shirley saw me watching, smiled as if nothing had happened, but we both knew.

Sometimes I feel like shaking Dad, she's not coming back, she left us. But he knew her better than I did, loved her more, misses her more. Sometimes I wish she'd died, at least then she'd be worthy of his grief.

It's still early but I'm worn out, full of food and gas. I sit on my bed, peel my socks off, pick at my feet. I get the cotton wool and the nail polish remover, rub it over my toenails and fingernails, wipe away the colour. Paint them purple, hide the stained and cracked nails underneath.

As it dries, I lie back on my bed, wake hours later, still fully clothed on top of the covers.

(like father, like daughter)

12

THE GUNSHOT WOKE her. She never really slept properly these days anyway, never let herself relax. Always on the periphery of sleep, she had odd fragmented dreams, often in Morse code.

- .... . / -.- .. .. / -... .. .-. -. -. - / .- --. .- .. -. ... - / .... . .-. / -.-. --- .-.. -.. / ... -.- .. -.

She was exhausted but her body kept going. It was her eyes that gave her away. Dry, itchy, always wanting to close but not able to. They reminded her how much she wanted to lay her head down, allow herself to drop, drop, drop all the way. To go past the dreams into a sleep where she knew nothing and woke refreshed.

- .... . / -.- .. .. / -... .. .-. -. -. - / .- --. .- .. -. ... - / .... . .-. / -.-. --- .-.. -.. / ... -.- .. -.

A second shot, closer this time, forced her out of bed. Was that a car engine she could hear?

She slid the pistol out from under her mattress, put on shoes, a skirt, jumper. Her fingers throbbed, swollen with chilblains from cold nights tapping skeds back home. Her paddle finger doubled as her trigger finger.

She edged towards the window, the wooden shutters were closed but she left the window open at night.

Make sure you have an escape route planned in case you need to make a quick getaway.

She listened for a signal. A warning. Their agreed whistle. The go-ahead to hide or flee.

Nothing came though. Just the sound of a dog barking.

```
17 January 1944
Circuit code name:      Sand Dune
Organiser:              Alex Sylvan
Agent:                  Marièle Downie
Field Name:             Sabine Valois
Code name:              Blackbird
Agent to join Sand Dune circuit (27-land) as re-
placement w/t operator/possible courier, following
the regrettable capture and disappearance of pre-
vious. To be transported by felucca on 20.02.1944.
Arrangements have been made and communicated to cir-
cuit organiser.
```

.. / .- -- / .... .- -... .. -. . / ....- .- -.. --- .. ...

She stood at the window, peered through the slats in the shutters. Who was out there? She was in danger, felt her skin prickle.

Trust your instincts. They will keep you alive.

'*Merde*,' she whispered – it was too dark to see anything. She crept across the bedroom, opened the door onto the kitchen. Her escape route was meant to be out the bedroom window, but she couldn't be sure that it was safe. It sounded like someone was out there.

She was grateful she had left her transmitter in the cachette. At least she didn't have to worry about them finding it here.

'Sabine, who's out there? *Qu'est-ce qui se passe?*' Madame Poirier peered out from her own bedroom. She held a candle, dressed in a full-length night gown, hair in a net. She'd never make it if they had to run.

'*Je ne sais pas*, stay there, ssshhh, *ne fais pas de bruit.*'

Madame Poirier nodded, stepped back into the darkness of her bedroom.

Congratulations to all of you on completing the training. You will be pleased to hear that most of you are now entitled to go on leave. You will be contacted individually concerning any future arrangements.

Please always remember that, even if you do everything we have taught you, we still cannot guarantee your safety. Never let your guard down or relax your defences.

Sabine padded across the stone floor towards the front door, lifted the latch. She hesitated, preparing herself to pull the door, slowly, slowly, slowly open when she saw a shadow.

Feet.

The door thrust open against her. It caught her on the side of the head and she fell backwards, dropping her pistol.

She put a hand to her head, felt the blood, wet and warm. It stuck in her hair, dripped down her forehead into her eyes. She felt around for her gun, saw the boot connect, heard the pistol spin away across the stone floor.

Oh God, this was bad, very bad. A torch shone down on her and she looked up to see the German soldier.

The trainer stood in front of the full-length poster, pointing at the various pictures of men, uniforms, insignias, while the class recited back at him.

Gefreiter
Leutnant
Oberleutnant
Hauptmann
SS Hauptsturmführer

SS Obersturmführer
'Sabine Valois?' He pointed his Luger at her.
'*Qu'est-ce que c'est que ça?* Assaulting me at home like this.'
'We have orders to take you in for questioning. We know Sabine Valois is an alias and that you are a British spy.'
'What? *C'est ridicule.*'
.. / .- -- / ... .- -... .. -. . / ...- .- .-.. --- .. ...
Je m'appelle Sabine Valois.
I am twenty-one years old.
I am living with my aunt while I recover from rheumatic fever.
My name is Sabine Valois.
J'ai vingt-et-un ans.
I have been ill. Rheumatic fever.
The doctor sent me to the country to recuperate.
I am staying with my aunt. My parents and younger sister live in Paris.
Je m'appelle Sabine Valois.
Je m'appelle Sabine Valois.
.. / .- -- / ... .- -... .. -. . / ...- .- .-.. --- .. ...
'Sabine, *ma nièce, ma nièce*, are you hurt?'
Madame Poirier rushed from her bedroom. The soldier looked up, lifted his pistol, shot her in the forehead. Sabine heard the moan of surprise and the thud as Madame slumped to the floor.
'Your aunt is a terrible actress. On your feet.' He fixed his pistol on Sabine. Dizzy, she put out a hand to steady herself as she stood, felt something wet at her feet. A puddle of blood. The smell of it was all around her, rich and musky.
What now? What now?
Parts of her training flashed in and out, like a Morse signal, what should she do?
- .... . / -.-. .. .. / -... .. -. .-. -. . - / .- --. .- .. -. . ... - / .... . .-. / -.-. --- .-.. -..
/ ... -.- .. -.
The blood soaked into her shoes, she felt it pool between her toes.
.. / .- -- / ... .- -... .. -. . / ...- .- .-.. --- .. ...
Je m'appelle Sabine Valois.
Je m'appelle Sabine Valois.
She'd memorised the story they gave her. Recited it over and over and over, until she felt like she'd erased her real memories. She had to make it believable, it had to roll off the tongue. There could be no holes, nothing they could stick a fingernail in and pick at. They had well-manicured hands, those Gestapo officers.

Je m'appelle Sabine Valois.
How dare you suggest that I'm lying?
I am speaking the truth.
Je dis la vérité.
I am Sabine Valois.

She took the Marièle part of her and shut it away. Bullied Marièle into submission, let Sabine take over.

Merle, the pianist, sending skeds back to Britain. Chilblains on her hand from the paddle.

Tap, tap, tap, tap, tap, tap, tap, tap.

- .- .--. / - .- .--. / - .- .--. / - .- .--. / - .- .--.

Oh God, oh God.

--- .... / --. --- -.. / --- .... / --. --- -..

Please let her wake up, let this be a nightmare. Maybe she had finally succumbed? Allowed her eyes to close, slipped down, down, down, down.

But no, this was all too vivid, too real.

She'd been caught and dear Madame Poirier…

Sabine had told her to go back to bed, left her there to die, instead of giving her a chance to run, to hide. Madame had trusted Sabine, tried to help her.

--- .... / --. --- -..

Sabine felt the nausea in her stomach, saliva coating her dry mouth. She swallowed back the sick, felt it burn her throat on the way down.

The soldier gestured for her to move towards the door. His Luger in her back as he pushed her outside. Her feet stuck to the floor as she walked, leaving footprints on the stone.

Should she try a persona?

The swooning invalid.

The simpleton.

The seductress.

Sabine.

She and Eliza had giggled through that part of the training, embarrassed and awkward to role play in front of the others. It had seemed funny back then.

18 January 1944
Agent Downie is to report to HQ on 22 January at 13:00.

'I know you've not been given much time for leave since completing the training, but I'm afraid it is vitally important that we get you out there sooner rather than later. The network is in a bit of a pickle and we think

you can help.'

She was being sent to France. For real. All that play acting, pretending the boys were Gestapo Officers as they interrogated her, learning how to strip and reassemble a Bren, memorising the Morse alphabet. There was always a voice at the back of her head, whispering, this isn't real, no danger here, it's all pretend.

It was unlikely she would die during training, no matter how bloody awful she felt during a six am ten-kilometre run.

Being sent to France meant putting herself in actual danger. It meant the possibility of her parents receiving another telegram.

If she was caught they wouldn't care that she was young, that she was female. She was a spy, and in the real world spies were tortured and executed. This had been drummed into her constantly over the last few months.

The average lifespan between arrival and capture for a w/т operator in France is six weeks.

'You're being sent out as pianist for the Sand Dune circuit but it's more than likely that you'll need to help with courier work too – they're a bit short-staffed. You will report to Alex Sylvan.'

Six weeks. Six weeks. Six weeks. Six weeks.

One, two, three, four, five, six.

Forty-two days.

One thousand and eight hours.

Funny to think this could be all the time she had left. Even funnier the way she kept nodding, as if this was completely fine with her.

In Britain, you listened and nodded.

In France, you tried to survive. Stay alive.

Six weeks was an average, she might not even last that long.

- .... / -.- .. .. / -... .. -.-. -. - / .- --. .- .. -. ... - / .... . .-. / -.-. --- .-.. -..
/ ... -.- .. -.

But she was different.

Clever, above average.

She would come home.

There was a car parked outside the farmhouse, a black Citroën. She had heard an engine. God, why hadn't she acted on it?

A man dressed in black and a driver sat in the car.

The soldier pushed her into the back seat, followed in behind. He pushed his pistol into her ribs, handcuffed her.

Sabine.

She was Sabine.

What had the training reports said about her? Was she up to this? Or had they sent her over here with the hope that they'd get a couple of weeks out of her?

She'd lost count. Had she made it to six?

At least she'd made it through the training, that was more than some.

Celia received a telegram about her husband, left and hadn't come back.

Doris, 'dismissed with regret' after being monitored talking English in her sleep. Too much of a risk, everything had to be done in French, even sleep-talking.

The others had been sad to see her go until Marièle pointed out it meant they were being monitored while they slept.

Maybe it was that sort of thinking that had got her this far? What did her brain tell her to do now?

'There's still time to say no.'

- .... . / -.- .. .. / -... ..- .-. -. - / .- --. .- .. -. ... - / .... . .-. / -.-. --- .-.. -.. / ... -.- .. -.

'I want to go.'

'We would never force someone into going, despite the value we place in your work. It's a huge risk, you do understand that?'

Marièle nodded, didn't ask what had happened to Sand Dune's previous pianist. Was it someone she'd trained with?

'You will travel by felucca on Sunday evening.'

'Felucca?'

'I'm sorry,' he shuffled some papers, 'I can see that you're a whizz at parachuting, but I'm afraid a parachute landing isn't possible at this time. I know you'll be disappointed, but really how you get there isn't important. More that you get there and help Sand Dune back up and running again.'

What had happened to Sand Dune?

If she asked, she might change her mind about going.

But I'm Merle, she wanted to say. She felt sick at the thought of going by felucca, it was a bad omen. This was her life they were playing with. They didn't care if she lived or died, she was just w/t replacement, just like the girl who came after her would be w/t replacement. They didn't care that if she didn't parachute in, the whole mission was doomed, jinxed from the start.

But of course she had to stay quiet. If they knew she had thoughts like that they would stamp her record.

Not in a fit mental state.

Flights of fancy equalled no France, and she still wanted to go. She had to go.

It was stupid of course, he was right, it didn't matter how she got there. She couldn't shake it off though, that nagging feeling of doom.

She looked down, tried to avoid eye contact with the men. Nobody spoke.
Should she protest?

Je m'appelle Sabine Valois, what is the meaning of this?

Madame Poirier. That moan she gave out. Worse was the sinking realisation that fear of being shot herself cancelled out some of her grief for Madame. She wasn't ready to die. She didn't want to die.

- .... . / -.- .. .. / -... ..- .-. -. - / .- --. .- .. -. ... - / .... . .-. / -.-. --- .-.. -.. / ... -.- .. -.

'Press here, and here.'

Sabine pressed her finger into the ink pad, then marked her new document with the printed loops and whorls.

Funny, how similar Sabine's fingerprints were to Marièle's. Or was it the other way around?

Froggy Marie, Froggy Marie. Her name embarrassed her when she was at school. She avoided saying it. Now she was sad to let it go. Even if it was only meant to be temporary.

Would she ever be Marièle again? Had she lost herself forever to Sabine? Marièle felt like a friend from back home. Someone she used to know. The only part of her they let her keep was the cross from George. It was French, looked authentic. And Marièle's grief, of course, that never left her.

Je m'appelle Sabine Valois. *I am twenty-one. I am blah, blah, blah.*

She was fed up repeating the story over and over and over.

As her departure date got closer, they played tricks on her, tried to trip her up.

'Marièle, *please can you empty out your coat pockets for us.*'

'Je suis Sabine.'

'Good girl, Sabine, très bon.'

She emptied her pockets. They'd given her a French coat to wear, complete with French labels, wanted to double check she hadn't pocketed anything that would give her away.

British bus tickets, British money, British cigarettes, British wrappers.

'Now, we'll swap your documents. You'll get them back when you return.'

If she returned.

-.... / .-- . . -.- ...

Sabine handed over her identity card, her clothing coupons, her ration book, replaced them with French ones.

'We get to dress you up like a French doll,' one woman laughed as she fixed Sabine's head scarf.

'It feels like I'm being dressed down, look at me,' Sabine replied.

Frumpy skirt, woollen pullover, flat shoes.

Lucky for Doris she talked in her sleep, you would have had a fight on your hands, Sabine thought, as they wiped off what little make up she had on.

One of the men said something in German and the others laughed. Sabine didn't know much German, but she understood enough to know it was a joke about her appearance. At least that meant they probably wouldn't rape her. That was the part of the training where nobody had laughed.

What was her limit? Could she take the pill if she had to?

'This is the bit that's always a bit sensitive.'

He held a lipstick in his hand, French branding of course. The attention to detail was astonishing. Sabine doubted that your average German soldier would recognise the name and style of a French lippy, but she didn't want to end up dead over something so trivial.

'Sensitive?'

'This isn't just a lipstick.'

'Ahh, I see, another one of your gadgets. What's this one, a flick knife, a compass, a machine gun?'

He didn't smile, looked at her with that same apologetic expression that people had worn after George. He clicked something with his fingernail, unhinged the bottom of the lipstick. A small, translucent pill fell out onto the palm of his hand.

Sabine looked at him, nodded, and he put the pill back inside, clicked the catch shut again, handed her the lipstick.

The woollen jumper they'd given her irritated her, she scratched at the crook of her arm until she broke the skin.

'Now, let's go through the contents of your handbag.'

'A girl's handbag is very personal to her.'

'Not in France,' he smiled.

'Torch, compass, six hundred francs, comb, hair ribbon, head scarf...'

Sabine only half-listened. She picked up the photograph of her fake Parisian family.

Fake mother.
Fake father.
Fake sister.
'I always wanted a sister,' she said, looking at the strange girl who smiled back at her. The photo was creased, worn around the edges. It had to look well-used.

- .... . / -.- .. .. / -.... .. .-. -. - / .- --. .- .. -. ... - / .... . .-. / -.-. --- .-.. -..
/ ... -.- .. -.

Mama and Father back home. So many, many miles away. The middle of the night there too. They would be in bed. Were they asleep? Mama always claimed to have a sixth sense. Was she lying awake right now while Father snored? She wished she was home with them, that last visit on leave had gone so quickly. They'd never recognise her now. Would walk past her in the street. Sabine couldn't bear to think of what Mama and Father would do if they received another telegram.

She handed the pile of letters over, she'd spent the last couple of days writing them. Part of the procedure for being sent to France.

Just a quick letter to say I'm doing fine. Sorry, I've been unable to write more. I've been so busy here, they certainly keep us on our toes.

Hello from London, not much has changed in the last week or so. Still driving the top brass around.

Met my first Yank today. Very nice despite what we used to say in the shop. He gave me some nylons and a bar (a whole bar!) of chocolate for driving him and his CO around London.

Went with a couple of the girls to the flicks to see the new Clark Gable picture.

Missing you both dreadfully and, of course, still think of George everyday. I hope to be able to get some leave soon, but we are terribly busy and the girls with husbands and families seem to take priority.

If you're reading this letter, then I'm afraid that something terrible has happened to me. I suppose I can tell you now that I have not been in London these past few weeks. I'm so sorry for deceiving you. I only did it to stop you from worrying, a white lie, Mama. I love you both very much. Please know that you were never far from my thoughts and thinking of you helped me through my darkest times.

The Last Will and Testament of Marièle Francesca Downie, being of sound mind.

'A parting gift for you, my dear, from Major Buckmaster.'

'Thank you,' Sabine opened the gold plated powder compact.
'No tricks with this one, it is what it is.'
'Did I look so disappointed?'
'He likes to give everyone one, as a parting token of his appreciation.'
She clicked the compact shut, slipped it in her handbag.
'Now I can see how dowdy you've made me look every time I powder my nose. I'm joking of course, merci, c'est trés joli.'
'If you wait here now, someone will come and get you when it's time to leave.'
He held out his hand and she shook it.
'We don't say good luck,' he said, 'so I'll just say au revoir, jusqu'à la prochaine fois.'

The driver started the engine and the car moved forward. What about the rest of the circuit? Had they all been caught, killed? Was she the only one left?

The Germans are fond of night-time raids.

Oh God, she needed to start thinking straight. Caught. No idea what had happened to the rest of them. No idea how much the Germans knew.

What did they tell her in training?

Don't speak. Try not to speak. Even under extreme torture…

Her hands shook, handcuffed behind her. She clasped them, picked at the swollen chilblains.

She didn't want the men to see how afraid she was.

The headlights of the car lit up Madame Poirier's farmhouse. Madame had been so good to her, sheltering her, feeding her, caring for her.

As the car turned and drove away, Sabine caught a glimpse of something.

A shape beneath her bedroom window.

What was that?

She turned her head to look, inhaled as the headlights illuminated what lay there.

The man beside her laughed.

Then the car drove away. Away from the farmhouse, away from Madame, away from Alex's body.

126

Hannah Struggles To Get It Wright
Shock as Scottish Swimmer Fails To Make European Final

Hannah Wright has had a disappointing European Championships, after failing to make the final of the 100m Butterfly. Hannah, world bronze medallist and British record holder for the event, came fifth in her semi-final, failing to qualify for the final which will take place tonight.

'I've been struggling with a shoulder injury for the last few weeks,' said Hannah following her semi-final swim, 'so my preparation has not been as I'd hoped, but I don't want to make excuses. That was a poor swim and I should have done better. I'm really disappointed.'

Hannah has pulled out of the relay squad and will fly home to seek medical treatment on her shoulder.

'The Olympic trials are at the end of the month and these are my priority now,' said Hannah.

13

I CAN'T WAIT to get in the pool this morning. Dad's right, I'm pushing myself too much, but I really need it today.

The discomfort woke me before my alarm clock. Head throbbing, queasy tummy, dry mouth. I had two beers last night, two lousy beers, but I still feel crappy this morning. My body just can't handle alcohol after so many years of being good.

You're so dedicated, Hannah, I can't believe you don't drink

Is this how Dad feels every morning? Or does drinking every night mean the hangover never catches up?

I stand on the poolside for a beat longer than normal. Enjoy the anticipation of hitting the water. Then I dive, stay under for the whole length. Strong butterfly kick propelling me forward.

Water and white noise. Water and white noise. Water and white noise.

I reach the wall and rise to the surface, gasp the air in, water dripping from my body.

How did I live without the pool all those months? No wonder I lost the plot. I can't imagine what I'd have done if they told me I could never swim again, not even for fun. I've got so much pent up energy, so much that needs swept out of me by thrashing up and down the pool.

I push off again, without thinking go into my butterfly stroke. My leg kick's strong, skims me along the surface of the pool like a flying fish.

Like a dolphin.

If I started deep enough, I could propel myself right out of the water.

I turn and go into a second length of butterfly. I'm not as fit as I used to be, my arms heavy. This is good though, I'm tiring myself out, getting rid of the aggression. I'll probably pay for this later, but I don't care. I hit the wall, turn and go into front crawl. Instead of slowing down, I pick up the pace. Eight-beat leg kick, head down, as fast as I've gone in a long time.

I need the pool to stay alive, I start to dry up on land after a while. Sometimes I wish it would rain so much the pavements and the roads filled up, turned into one long swimming pool. I'm so ungainly on dry land, it's easier in the water.

You're a wee selkie, Hannah

I'm wide awake, refreshed by the time I cycle to work.

'Hey,' Calum greets me when I get to the shop.

(twice in one week, what did I do to deserve this?)

I run a hand through my hair, wish I'd brushed it properly, put on some make-up.

'It's an in-service day at school, so you're stuck with me again,' he says.

I nod, grab onto the word school, repeat it over and over and over. School, school, school, school, school, school, school.

He's at school, a schoolboy.

You can't have a crush on a schoolboy. It's wrong. Wrong.

'Mum's got accounts to do so she asked if I could work. I'm glad to get away to be honest, she always gets dead crabbit when she's doing accounts. Starts ranting about Presto.'

'It's not been Presto for about fifteen years.'

'I know, but it'll always be bloody Presto to Mum.'

Poor Shirley. She's been struggling to stay afloat ever since that supermarket opened.

I dump my bag in the backroom, being here undoes all my good work from the pool. The positive energy sucked out of me. It's not that I'm ungrateful to Shirley for giving me a job, getting me out of the house, it's just that working in this shop is not where I thought I'd end up.

'Not much of a day off, having to come in here,' I say.

He shrugs.

'I'm going to a party on Friday night, need some beer money.'

(with Blake?)

I'm about to ask him if his mum knows he's underage drinking when I realise how ancient that makes me sound. I'm only a few years older than him, but my closest female friend is his mother. Shit, what's happened to me? Where has my life gone?

Is that how he thinks of me? That woman who works with his mum?

When I was in school, anyone over the age of twenty seemed old. It's weird how your concept of age changes the older you get.

Here's me, barely in my twenties and on the scrap-heap already.

I have to stop myself being so negative. I can't help it though. It's not just this shop or this town, it's this life I hadn't planned for myself.

'You been swimming?' Calum asks.

'Yeah, can you tell?' I reply, wet hair dripping down my back, leaving a damp patch on my top.

'Do you go every morning?'

'Just depends.'

'Don't you get bored? I mean it's not the most exciting thing in the world, is it?'

I shake my head. I never got a chance to get fed up of it, not properly. It got taken away from me before I was ready to let it go. Having the decision made for you changes everything.

'Can you still do it? I mean, I know you can swim, but can't you go back to it properly?'

'They said it's fine for me to swim every so often but I couldn't manage proper training anymore. I probably go too much to be honest, but I enjoy it.'

'Man, that's pretty crappy, isn't it?'

'Yeah,' I want to elaborate but I can't, just nod instead.

Pretty crappy doesn't cut it. I can't think of the words to describe just how shit it is. To have to give up the one thing you love, the one thing you're actually good at.

On my worst days, I look at the people around me and tell myself how much better I am than them.

I'm different.

I hate myself for doing it, but I look down on them, like they're beneath me. I should be doing more exciting things, more important things, instead of stuck in this small-town life. On my worst days, I just can't stop the part of my brain that tells me I deserve so much more.

Everyone feels that way though, right? That their life isn't going to be like everyone else's? Normal, uneventful. That the universe owes them more than just the mundane.

My shoulder aches.

It's my own fault, I pushed myself too hard in the pool this morning. Sometimes I get so angry, I want to make it hurt even more. I want to punish my shoulder for fucking everything up, even though it's part of me and I'm only hurting myself.

It's such a non-event of an injury too.

A sore shoulder.

I've got a sore shoulder.

Not a life threatening illness or a horrific accident. Just a sore shoulder.

I grab boxes of sweets from the back room, carry more than I should, let the weight tug and pull at my shoulder. If you want to hurt, I'll make you hurt. It's dumb of me and I know I'll regret it later, but for now I don't care.

'What are you doing that for?' Calum asks as I stock the shelves. 'Mum's not here, we don't need to work.'

He leans on the counter reading *NME* and drinking a can of Fanta.

I shrug, move older bags of Maltesers to the front, fill the back of the shelf with the new stock.

Maybe he doesn't think of me as being like Shirley after all? Maybe he sees me as being like him? Just working here to make some money, fill in the time until real life begins?

For him, university.

(for me?)

I move onto a box of Revels, dig a pen into the brown tape sealing the box and rip it open.

The old woman's favourite.

Marièle's favourite.

There I go, making up a life for her again. How do I know they're her favourite? Because she bought them once and never even got to eat them?

Dried banana chips always remind me of Gran. In the car going home after a swimming gala, me in the back, still in my tracksuit, wet hair, Dad driving, Gran in the passenger seat. She turned round and took a bag of banana chips out of her handbag, gave me a handful to eat. I didn't believe her when she told me they were banana.

That could have been a one-off, the only time she ever had them. She might have given them to me because she thought they were fucking rotten.

It's weird, I never saw her eat them again, but they always remind me of her.

Maybe it'll be the same with Revels and Marièle now?

'Leave that, you're making me tired watching you. Fancy a cup of tea?'

'Okay,' I stand and kick the box of Revels to one side, follow Calum into the back room.

I sit on the table as he puts the kettle on.

My shoulder is really killing me now. I squeeze it, try to massage the ache away.

'You alright?' Calum asks.

'It's my shoulder, I did too much in the pool.'

'Is it still injured?'

I want to scream at him for asking such a stupid question. Of course it's still injured, do you think I'd be here right now if it was okay?

But it's not Calum's fault.

A sore shoulder.

It's such a stupid fucking thing to have to give up a career for.

'I'll always be injured.' I reply. 'That's why I had to give up.'

'Sorry. Can I do anything? To help I mean?' He asks, coming towards me.

'No, I just have to rest it.'

He's standing right in front of me now.

It's weird, kind of awkward. The way he's not moving.

The way he's looking at me.

The kettle clicks off but he just stands there, not breaking eye contact. Can he feel it too? The friction, the way the air has gone all fuzzy around us.

(water and white noise)

I can sit here and let it go on or I can break it. Jump down off the table and move away, finish making the tea.

(dive in)

This is a decision I need to make very soon.

I know I should choose the tea, but I'm not moving. I'm still sitting here and he's still standing right in front of me. He moves his arm to my shoulder, starts to rub, circular movements, kneading the pain. His fingertips brush my neck and still I don't move.

This is bad, this is very bad, but I want him to kiss me. I haven't kissed a boy in so long.

I can feel the heat prickle up and down my spine and I can't stop myself.

I grab his hips, pull him forward. His hands move to my hair, my face, and we're kissing. Warm and damp. Months of making myself come, of no human contact, make me want him and I open my legs and wrap him towards me.

His breath's hot and sticky and I can feel his cock pushing against his jeans. The shop's open, anyone could come in, but somehow that only makes it more urgent, more desperate.

His hands are all over me, inside my clothes, tugging at buttons. It's been so long, he only has to rub me for a few minutes and I'm shuddering and gasping. He looks at me, his expression weird. Like he's never made a girl do that before. How experienced is he?

It feels good though, I'm tingling and ringing, toes curling. I see Jason, head between my legs, the smell of chlorine seeping from our naked, sweaty skin. Hear his voice telling me to relax. I push the image away, concentrate on the moment.

'Hang on,' Calum says.

He reaches into his wallet, slides a condom out from behind a bank card, pulls his jeans and boxers down, unravels the condom down his cock.

He may be a schoolboy but he's definitely done this before.

Why am I disappointed? Because I'm not the first? The experienced older woman turning the boy into a man.

(he's probably done this more than me)

He slides me toward him, slips his cock inside and then I'm leaning back on the table as he pushes into me. My shoulder's burning. With each thrust I think it's going to give way underneath me. The sex is quick though, quick and frantic. He comes, panting and heaving, kisses my forehead.

He pulls out of me and I stand, do up my jeans. My legs are wobbly and I lean against the table, sort my clothes out. He turns away from me, I hear the snap of rubber as he removes the condom, ties a knot in the end of it. He chucks it in the bin, fastens his jeans.

We don't speak. It's weird now it's all over. It felt right when it was happening, but now...

I finish making the tea, take mine out onto the shop floor. I think my hangover's back; I need some fresh air. I open the front door, stand out on the pavement with my tea.

I can feel him watching me from the counter and it's worse than standing next to him so I go back in. His hair's all ruffled, his cheeks flushed.

I feel sick.

I'm not the classy Mrs Robinson, I'm a dirty old woman. It's so sleazy, doing it at work. And I came so easily, he must realise how hard-up I am.

'I've wanted to do that with you for ages,' he says.

I take a swig of tea to avoid having to answer. We stand in silence behind the counter.

'How's your shoulder?' He asks and starts to rub it with his hand again.

He wants me to say the sex helped, made me forget the pain, but the truth is it's fucking agony. Worse than before. I move away from him, try not to make it obvious that I don't want him to touch me. But now it's over, I don't want any contact with him.

I just want out of here, away from him. I feel sticky and unclean, I need a shower, I need to be on my own.

I'm a total bitch, turned into such a cliché. The dirty old woman who seduces a schoolboy. What's wrong with me?

I'm relieved when it's time to close up.

'Do you fancy doing something?' Calum asks as we cash up the till.

'Sorry, I can't tonight,' I reply, avoiding eye contact.

(it's a school night, it's a school night, it's a school night)

'No worries, maybe another night?'

'Yeah,' I reply.

I'm such a chicken, I should be straight with him. That's not going to happen again, it shouldn't have happened today, but I'll say anything to get out of here without a confrontation. I'm so grateful for my bike, it gives me an excuse not to have to walk beside him. I cycle as fast as I can away from the shop. The cold air feels good against my hot and crawling skin.

Dad and Shirley. Dad and Shirley. Dad and Shirley.

Like father, like daughter. Like father, like daughter. Like father, like daughter.

Fuck, I can't bear it. It all feels so wrong, so smutty and sordid. I'm angry at myself for letting it happen but I'm angry at myself too for being so disgusted.

(I'm allowed to get my kicks)

My shoulder's so sore by the time I get home that I can barely get off my bike. I dump it in the garage and head into the house. I'm crying now, I can't help it. Crying with shame and pain.

The light's on in the living room. Great, the one night I could do with him being out.

'Hi sweetheart,' I hear Dad shout as I reach my bedroom.

I ignore him, I can't speak. The lump in my throat is so big that I can hardly breathe. I fall on my bed and sob into my pillow. How did I end up like this?

I hear Dad's footsteps on the stairs. I should make a run for the bathroom, hide from him, but I don't move.

'Hannah? Hannah, you okay?'

I look up. He's standing in the doorway, blurry through the tears. My nose is running and I wipe it on my sleeve.

'What's wrong?'

'My shoulder,' I manage to say between gulping sobs.

'Oh, sweetheart.'

He sits on the edge of my bed, pulls me into a bear hug, crushing me. It doesn't help my shoulder but I don't care.

I let him crush everything away.

When it first started, Dad would help me with all the exercises the physio gave me to do, doing his best to get me better. He'd laugh as I grimaced, tell me it was all for the best, that it would be worth it in the end. Neither of us realising how serious it was. Both of us sure that the exercises were working, that my shoulder was improving. That this was only a blip.

The Olympics just around the corner.

I get so down thinking of us then. How hopeful we were, how optimistic. It was just a sore shoulder that needed stretched.

I can't bear to fast forward us.

To the present, to this room, to me crying and him crushing me.

14

THEY'D TOLD HER to try and sleep on the voyage over. As if she could sleep here, on the felucca. The chug of the engine, the constant soaking from the waves, the punch of the sail. The

up and	up and	up and	up and
down	down	down	down

Captain Kalinowski and his crew had left her alone so far. One of them, Piotr, had handed her a wool blanket and a tarpaulin when she'd boarded the Seafox in Gibraltar. He smiled at her, said something in Polish she didn't understand. He was so young, not old enough to grow the stubble that the other crew members kept their faces warm with.

She wished she had a beard herself. The spray stung against her face, made her eyes water and her skin tight.

The men dressed in cord trousers and woollen jumpers, fingerless gloves, hats pulled down over their eyes. How many times had they made this crossing? She could tell by their weather-beaten faces, calloused fingers, that this was a regular trip for them. When had they last been home? Could they go home?

Marièle looked out of the train window. This would be the first time she'd been home in over ten months. A few days leave before being sent to France. She laughed to herself as she thought of the telephone call she'd made to Cath earlier in the week.

'I can't wait to see you dear, it's been so long. Mrs Walker keeps asking where you are. She said to me the other day, that Miss Downie's been away for about nine months now hasn't she? I tapped my nose and said, "careless talk, Mrs Walker." Let's push a pram past her house when you get back for a giggle!'

Mrs Walker could think what she liked. Those French girls, ooh la la. Froggy Marie. Froggy Marie.

..-. .-. --- --. --. --. -.-- / -- .- .-. ... .

The scenery was familiar now, getting closer to home. It was time to become Marièle again, put Sabine aside for a few days. It wasn't just Mrs Walker who could make up stories. Marièle had to remember that, for the duration of her leave, she was Ensign F43A, driver and orderly in the FANY.

She'd been on board almost three days now. At least she thought it was three days. She'd dozed for some of the time, was sure she'd counted three sunsets.

The seasickness was starting to pass. Her stomach more accustomed to the rocking motion of the felucca, the lurching from side to side.

up and	up and	up and	up and
down	down	down	down

They were so low in the water, she felt every wave, every fish pass underneath.

She hadn't eaten properly since that first night, when she'd thrown up over the side after a slice of ham and a boiled egg.

The picnic she had was sheltered underneath the tarpaulin, a Thermos and some sandwiches. She peeled open two slices of bread, wished she hadn't. The grey blobs of meat paste made her gag.

Captain Kalinowski sat on the opposite side from her, folding flags. She forced herself to take a bite of the sandwich, tried not to think of the filling as she chewed then swallowed. She had to prove that she was more than just a seasick female. She was sure the Captain and his crew talked about her behind her back: young girl, useless, why risk their lives for someone like her? Couldn't even stomach the boat trip to France, there was no way she'd last five minutes in the *réseau*.

'Would you like something to eat?' She offered the sandwiches to Kalinowski.

He shook his head, continued folding flags.

'Can I help with that?' She asked.

'*Nie, nie*, we choose a flag depending on who we run into.'

He held up a union jack and then a swastika, spat over the side of the boat.

She was nervous as the train whistled, slowed down and pulled into the station. Silly of her, this was home.

No matter how long she'd been away.

No matter what she'd done since leaving.

She wore her FANY *uniform, brass buttons and epaulettes on her khaki jacket, belted around the waist, blouse and tie, skirt rubbing against her calves.*

What would people think when they saw her in it? It made her self-conscious, going home dressed like this.

The train stopped and she put her beret on, might as well complete the look.

She stepped down from the train, looked along the smoky platform for Mama.

She was at the ticket office, under a poster.

IS YOUR JOURNEY REALLY NECESSARY?

Marièle's journey definitely was. It was the last time she would see her family, see Cath, before being sent to France.

Sabine unscrewed the lid of her Thermos. Maybe tea would help? Mama didn't understand the British and their tea.

They use it for everything. Too hot? Have some tea. Too cold? Try some tea. Feeling sick? Tea. Well? Tea. C'est un remède miracle, n'est-ce-pas?

Sabine needed a *remède miracle*. She clamped the plastic cup between her knees, tried to hold it steady as she poured from the flask.

up and	up and	up and	up and
down	down	down	down

She couldn't put the cup down on the deck; even if the felucca stayed still long enough for her to pour her tea, the deck was covered in about an inch of water so her cup would just float away. The Seafox in miniature. Maybe she should get a knife, scrape 'Seabrew' onto the side of the plastic cup.

I hereby name this vessel the Seabrew.

She spilt as she poured, but it wasn't hot enough to burn her legs.

Piotr and the navigator Aleksy stood nearby.

'Would you like some tea?' She asked.

Piotr smiled, took a step towards her but Aleksy shook his head.

'Nie, we have our own supplies.'

She lifted the cup, it wobbled in her hand as the felucca lurched and tea dribbled down her chin, salty and lukewarm.

'Mama, Mama, I'm here,' Marièle waved. Mama turned at the sound of her voice. Confusion flickered across her face before recognition turned it into a smile and she ran towards Marièle.

'Marie, my Marie, chérie, it's so good to see you.' She hugged Marièle and then held her out at arm's length. 'My, my, I didn't recognise you in that uniform – you look so official. And your hair? Your father won't approve of that, non, he will not.'

Marièle let Mama kiss her again and again. She'd forgotten they'd dyed her hair. Had gotten used to the dull brown shade, although it had taken her a few days and, she was ashamed to admit, a few tears. Still, to play the part of Sabine, she must have the right shade and hairstyle.

Au revoir to lovely blonde hair and salut to this hideous brown creation.

She felt horribly unclean. Funny, surrounded by all this water, but she hadn't had a proper wash since leaving the submarine.

Her hair stuck to her head and she could feel the stickiness under her armpits. Not even Chanel No5 could penetrate the stench. She longed for a bath. The men splashed their hairy armpits with seawater, didn't seem to mind the grime. Would she ever be able to get rid of the fishy smell that clung to her? Like the old harbour wives who brought the fish into the shop, you smelt them coming before you saw them.

She could taste salt, felt it coarse against her skin.

up and   up and   up and   up and
down   down   down   down

She'd taken to mopping the deck. Sometimes she would use an old tin can and bail some of the excess water overboard first. She couldn't sit still any longer, sheltered under the tarpaulin like an old woman. She wanted to help. Besides, the longer she sat, the more her joints seized up, the salt water rusting her stiff.

Kalinowski had argued with her.

'*Nie*, sit down, be careful, you'll go overboard.'

'Honestly, Captain, I'm not an idiot. I don't want to fall in there anymore than you want me too. I can't swim for one thing.'

Kalinowski laughed, said something in Polish to Aleksy.

'What's so damn funny?'

'Nothing, *nic*. I'm sorry for laughing. It is not good that you cannot swim. If you like, I can teach you?'

Sabine felt his laughter take hold, it pulled at her insides, made her stomach muscles ache. God, the absurdity of it. What on earth was she doing?

'It's a deal,' she replied. 'And I will teach you to parachute.'

He nodded, spat in his hand and held it out. She hesitated, then did the same, the saliva slippery between their palms as they shook hands.

Mama held her hand as they walked from the station towards home.

'And see, they got this too,' Mama said as they passed the debris of yet another German bombing raid.

'This was very close,' Mama shook her head. 'Madame King had her windows blown in from the blast.'

Marièle squeezed Mama's hand, grateful that the bomb had not been closer to home. She'd been so worried about Mama receiving a telegram, but what if it happened the other way around?

'The boys are always playing there, collecting shrapnel,' Mama said, 'I wish George had been a few years younger. He might have enjoyed the war.'

'What are you playing?' Sabine asked as Kalinowski dealt the cards to Piotr and Aleksy.

'Rummy. You play?' He replied.

'Yes, of course, deal me in.'

Piotr moved and Sabine joined them around the upturned crate. Kalinowski continued to deal, added her to the game. Aleksy moved as if to play.

'Now hang on a second,' Sabine stopped him. 'I believe I go first, left of the dealer, or do you have different rules in Poland?'

Aleksy laughed, held out a hand to indicate she should play, 'Captain has his own rules.'

They played a few hands before she realised Aleksy was right. She was sure Kalinowski was cheating. They played for cigarettes though, so she didn't mind if she lost.

Despite what you may think, very few village girls in France smoke, or can afford to smoke. Smoking in a public place will arouse suspicion and bring the Boche down on you quicker than you can exhale.

They'd given her French cigarettes for the men in the circuit and to use to barter with, but she'd already decided to leave them on board for Kalinowski and his crew.

'Come on, your turn,' Kalinowski nodded to Aleksy. Aleksy looked at his hand, then the cards discarded on the crate. She could see him working something out in his head. Piotr rolled his eyes at Sabine.

'Show me your cards,' Aleksy demanded.

'*Nie*, what's your problem?'

'Cheat.'

'How dare you accuse me of cheating.'

Both men got to their feet. Piotr shook his head as Aleksy kicked the crate over, sending cards and cigarettes all over the deck. Sabine began to pick them up as they floated around her feet.

Aleksy made a hand gesture at the captain, 'You are a crook.'

'*Dupek*.'

'What does that mean?' Sabine asked Piotr.

'I cannot say,' he replied.

| up and | up and | up and | up and |
| down | down | down | down |

Just at that moment the felucca hit a wave, knocking them all off their feet. The Seafox rode the wave, rose with the undulation before sinking so low that foamy spray rushed in over the sides. Sabine felt the cold seep through her clothes, her woollen jumper heavy, weighing her to the deck.

'Are you alright?' Piotr asked as he helped her to her feet.

'Yes, are you?' Her teeth chattered and she could barely speak.

'Bail,' said Kalinowski, handing her a tin can.

The salt water stung at her fingers, her cracked knuckles. As she emptied a can of water over the edge of the felucca, she watched a handful of playing cards and a few cigarettes drifting out to sea.

The table was set when they arrived home. Bread, jam, tea, scones, all lying on plates underneath a fly sheet.

'Mama, where did you get all this?'

'Oh now, ce n'est rien. If I can't give my only daughter a decent welcome home, then I am not fit to be a mother. Besides, look at you, you're not eating properly.'

'But, there's so much, and jam, how did you get jam?'

'I've been saving my coupons and Cath was very helpful when I went in to the shop.'

'Mama, I'm shocked. I go away for a short time and you and Cath are on the black market.'

'Oh, don't give me any of your nonsense. Assieds-toi and tuck in. Father said he would be home early but we'll just start. Make sure you leave him a scone though.'

As Mama poured their tea, Marièle heard the front door open.

'Father.'

He held out his arms and kissed her on the cheek before pulling her into a hug. As he let go, she saw his eyes fill with tears. He turned away, coughed into his handkerchief, then faced her again.

'What the devil have you done to your hair?'

Sabine sat opposite Kalinowski, an upturned box between them. Piotr lay asleep on the wooden bench, which ran the length of the deck, a tarpaulin draped over him. The wind had died down and it was the calmest sea they'd had since setting off.

'It's almost pleasant out here now,' Sabine said.

'The sea is beautiful on days like this, but you can never trust it,' Kalinowski replied, swigging from a hip flask.

'That's why we only have half a deck of cards left and we're stuck making conversation to amuse ourselves.'

'Exactly.'

Sabine sipped the cold dregs from the bottom of her Thermos. The tea was on the turn and she could taste the milky sourness. The remains of the meat paste sandwiches lay on the box between them. They were still edible, although the bread had gone stale; they'd picked off some mould around the edges. Sabine had finally found her sea stomach. She laughed to think how green she'd been just a few days ago.

'We're not far away now. The next part's the tricky bit,' Kalinowski said. 'We have to be careful as we navigate our way in. The coast is well monitored.'

As they'd got closer to France, Sabine had repeated her story again and again in her head.

My name is Sabine Valois.

J'ai vingt-et-un ans.

I have been ill. Rheumatic fever.

The doctor sent me to the country to recuperate.

I have been staying with my aunt. My parents and younger sister live in Paris.

Je m'appelle Sabine Valois.

Je m'appelle Sabine Valois.

'I saw a picture just a few months ago,' Cath said. *'It made me think of you. Millions Like Us, it was called, girls driving trucks and ambulances. It looked so glamorous.'*

'I'm sorry I've been so secretive in my letters to you.'

'That's alright,' Cath pointed to a poster on the inside of a shop window, *'careless talk and all that.'*

BE LIKE DAD – KEEP MUM!

'I know, but still,' she squeezed Cath's arm.

'You look so tricky in your uniform.'

'I feel like an old frump. Look what they did to my hair.'

'Why did they make you dye it? What does it matter?'

'Oh I don't know, another one of the many regulations I suppose. All part of being Ensign F43A sir!' Marièle saluted and Cath laughed, dimples showing in her cheeks. Marièle had always loved those dimples.

'Oh, stop it, what will I tell my grandchildren? That I worked in a Grocer's shop?'

'Don't be daft. People need to eat, don't they? Besides, Mama told me you helped her out with some jam.'

'Sshh, she was meant to keep that quiet,' Cath blushed.

'When has Mama ever been discreet? I think they wrote that poster back there just for her.'

Oh, those dimples, they made her ache.

- .... . / -.- .. .. / -... ..- .-. -. - / .- --. .- .. -. ... - / .... . .-. / -.-. --- .-.. -.. / ... -.- .. -.

Marièle used to imagine the children Cath and George would have, her nieces and nephews. Dimpled cheeks and deep brown eyes.

What was worse? Cath with George, or Cath with someone else?

'What is a young girl like you going to France for anyway?' asked Kalinowski.

'Well, Captain...'

'*Nie, nie*, enough with this Captain nonsense, my name is Marek.'

'Well, Marek, the same reason as all your previous passengers, I suppose.' Marek nodded, took a drink from his hipflask.

They'd taken the sail down and turned off the engine. Sabine missed the constant hum of it, the chug chug chug as it broke down yet again. The swearing and hammering as the crew forced it to splutter back to life.

She could just about make out land in the distance.

France.

It made her homesick, but she wasn't sure what for.

'You know I take you people over, but I'm never sent to bring you back,' said Marek.

The average lifespan between arrival and capture for a W/T operator in France is six weeks.

'Girls, girls, wait a moment.'

'It's only one of those street photographers, ignore him.' Marièle said.

'Let's see what he wants.' Cath tugged Marièle back towards him.

'I got a lovely photograph of you both. Something to remember your day out together.'

What if this was their last one? The way he said 'something to remember,' it was almost as if he knew Marièle would be gone soon. He'd done nothing wrong but she was suddenly angry at him. His words made her aware of how fast the time passed, how the day would soon be over. How precious her time at home was.

- .... . / -.- .. .. / -... ..- .-. -. - / .- --. .- .. -. ... - / .... . .-. / -.-. --- .-.. -.. / ... -.- .. -.

'How much?' Cath asked.

'For you, one shilling.'

'Okay, I'll take it,' Cath replied and handed over the money. The man took her name and address, gave her a receipt.

'*You'll never hear from him again,*' Marièle *said as they walked away.*

Sabine swallowed more cold tea, felt it thick in her mouth.

'My brother was killed during the evacuation of Dunkirk. Going to France is small compared to that.'

Marek looked at her, held eye contact as he took a bite of sandwich, swallowed it down with another mouthful from his hipflask.

'Why are you doing this, Marek? It can't be easy, making this crossing time and time again.'

'I cannot go home while the Germans are in Poland,' he replied, and spat.

Piotr stirred in his sleep, muttered something.

'I'm sorry,' she replied. 'We think it's bad back home, but we forget what happened to you.'

He waved a hand, lit a cigarette.

'Don't apologise, you did not march into my home.'

Sabine took a bite of sandwich, could taste salt. It got everywhere, like sand. George trying to get home. Sand in his hair, in his eyes, in his mouth. Or was he in so much pain that he didn't notice the irritation?

What colour did sand go when it mixed with blood? What colour were the beaches in France?

'*I've got it, ye of little faith,*' Cath *waved something at Marièle.*

'*What?*'

'*This,*' Cath *sat down, handed a small, square photo to Marièle. 'I was hoping to get it before you left.*'

Marièle *looked at the photograph of her and Cath. Neither of them aware of the photographer, no self-conscious smiles, no embarrassment. They both looked relaxed, natural.*

Happy?

Mid-walk, arm in arm, Cath smiling, dimples puckering her cheeks. Marièle turned slightly inward, leaning towards Cath. He'd captured her thinking of the nieces and nephews she'd never meet, she could tell by the way she looked at Cath.

- ..... . / -.- .. .. / -... ..- .-. -. - / .- --. .- .. -. ... - / .... . .-. / -.-. --- .-.. -.. /
... -.- .. -.

'*I take it all back, it's a lovely photo.*'

'*It's yours, I want you to have it.*'

Marièle wouldn't be able to take it to France, they'd never allow it.

'*I couldn't. You paid for it.*'

'*No, I insist.*'
'*Well, keep it for me, keep it safe till I get back.*'

Cath's father used to tell them stories about the trenches, about how he would scrape a fingernail up the pleat of his kilt and it would be crawling with lice. How the wet hem hung heavy against his bare legs, cutting and chafing his skin.

She'd be in danger in France, but was it any more than George, than Cath's father, than father himself had gone through?

There was a splash at the side of the boat. Piotr opened his eyes as Marek and Sabine stood. Sabine ssshhed him back to sleep. A seal's head stuck out of the water. It looked at them then dived back under, only to resurface again a few metres away.

'He looks like my dog,' said Marek. 'He has the same eyes.'

They stood and watched as the seal's head bobbed on the surface of the water.

'I came home from work one day and my dog was gone, the garden gate was open.' He reached inside his jumper, pulled out a photograph. 'Here,' he handed it to Sabine.

She took the photo expecting to see a dog. Instead she saw a young girl and a woman. The photo peeling at the corners, warm from Marek's body heat.

'Is this your family?' She asked.

'I was too late. We were planning to leave Poland, but I was too late. I came home from work and the gate was open. I don't know where they are.' His voice broke and he coughed, turned away and drank once more from his hipflask.

'That's awful. I'm so sorry.'

Sabine laid a hand on his arm. His jumper was damp, the wool cool and itchy. She looked out to sea again, the seal had gone.

'That is why I take people like you to France,' he said and shook her hand away.

Marièle's father had closed the blackout curtains and lit a candle. The wireless seemed to crackle in time with the flicker of the flame. She couldn't keep her eyes from the dripping wax.

THIS IS THE BBC HOME SERVICE.
HERE IS THE NEWS AND THIS IS
ALVAR LIDELL READING IT.

Marièle's father leant forward and turned the volume up.

The candle stood on top of the piano. Marièle watched the shadows it cast on the wall, the floating dust motes, her mind wandering from what was being broadcast on the wireless. One of the last times all four of them had been together, they'd sat like this, listening to the BBC broadcast. When it had finished, they'd turned off the wireless and George had played the piano while they sang along.

'Keep the Home Fires Burning' (Till the Boys Come Home)
Lili Marlene

Over three years now since they'd got the telegram about George. God, where had the time gone? Three years and the war still going on.

The Seafox drifted just off the coast of France. It was dark, but Sabine could hear the sea hitting land somewhere in the distance.

Aleksy held a torch, flashed a message.

.. / .- -- / .... .- -... .. -. . / ...- .- .-.. --- .. ...

They waited, scanning the darkness in front of them. And then Sabine saw it. A light flashing back at them.

.. / .- -- / .... .- -... .. -. . / ...- .- .-.. --- .. ...

Aleksy put the torch down.

'Not long now,' said Marek.

YOU'RE LISTENING TO THE BBC WORLD SERVICE
AND NOW THE PERSONAL MESSAGES BULLETIN.

Marièle's father turned down the volume.
'Leave it,' said Mama. 'I like to listen to these.'
'They don't mean anything to us.'
'Ça m'est égal, I don't care.'
Her father raised an eyebrow at Marièle, turned up the volume.

REBECCA IS TAKING THE TRAIN TO LONDON.
THE APPLE CRUMBLE IS PIPING HOT.
THE ELEPHANT NEEDS A DRINK

'I'm going to make supper,' Mama said, wiping her eyes with her sleeve.
'What's wrong? I thought you wanted to listen to this?'
'I'm going to make supper.'
Marièle stood to help, but Mama waved her back into her seat.
'Non, non, it's your last evening at home, you sit there.'
Marièle felt the heaviness of her last night with them, knew Mama

and Father felt it too.

JANET HAS MADE A FRUIT CAKE
THE CAT IS WEARING A BLUE RIBBON

'Some sort of code, I suppose,' Father said and puffed on his pipe.
'I don't know, it certainly sounds like that. Nonsense, isn't it?'
Father nodded. She listened to the phut, phut, phut as he sucked on his pipe.

THE DOG BURIED THE BONE IN THE PARK

'Probably for those top brass chaps you ferry around London,' Father said.
'I would imagine so, but they don't tell us anything.'

JOHN IS TAKING LOUISE TO THE PICTURES

Her father put down his pipe, reached across, put his hand on hers.
'George was right, Marie. I've changed my mind. I'll never forgive myself for fighting with him that night.'
'It didn't mean anything, it was just a silly argument.'
'Promise me you'll be careful, when you go back.' His breath was smoky, smelt of tobacco.
She nodded, saw the tears in his eyes and couldn't reply. Her throat was tight, squeezing her voice down, down, down. He opened his mouth, about to say something else, when Mama came back into the room carrying a pot of tea.

Marek raised a hand. Sabine listened. She could hear it, above the sound of the sea lapping against the felucca, the sound of another boat approaching. The oars as they slapped the top of the water.

Marek whistled and someone whistled back.

'Don't look so worried,' Piotr said. 'It's all going to plan.'

'*Bonjour*,' Aleksy called as the rowboat came into view.

There were three men aboard, one rowing, another sat in the stern while the third stood in the bow. It pulled up alongside the felucca.

'And I thought the Seafox was small,' Sabine said to Marek.

One of the men threw a rope to Aleksy, who caught it, wound it in a figure of eight, pulled the rowboat in until it bobbed against the side of the Seafox. Piotr and Aleksy lifted the cargo, passed it to the men on the rowboat, who handed over a few packages in return.

'I hope you have some food in there,' said Aleksy, as he traded boxes of supplies.

'Better food than you had coming over, I'm sure,' replied the man standing in the row boat.

'I take it you're Sabine,' he held out a hand. Sabine leant over the side of the felucca and shook it. It was softer than she'd expected. He was dressed in a brown leather jacket and had a scarf tied round his neck.

'*En fait, quel âge avez-vous?*' he asked.

'It's not polite to ask a woman her age. Monsieur Sylvan, I presume?'

'I'm Alex, that's Sebastian,' he pointed to the man who had been rowing the boat, 'and that's Roy, but no point getting to know him. You two are swapping.'

'What was that?' Roy said, standing. The boat wobbled underneath him and he grabbed onto Alex to steady himself.

'They will take you home,' said Alex.

'Smashing, thanks for everything.' Roy replied.

'*De rien.*'

Roy shook his head, looked at Sabine.

'Keep speaking in bloody French, I haven't got a clue what they're on about, this could be a boat to Timbuktu for all I know.'

'You're fine,' she replied.

'First thing I do when I get back, is learn some bloody French.'

Marek held out a hand, helped Roy climb up into the felucca.

'Some trade this is,' Marek said, 'I hand over this lovely *mademoiselle* and we get this in return.'

Sabine looked around the felucca. Just her left now.

'Thank you, Marek.'

Marek nodded. He took her hand, squeezed it between both his own. Rougher than Alex's had been.

'*Powodzenia*, stay safe,' he said. 'You take care of this one, Alex.'

Her hand felt cold and empty when he let go and she wished he was still holding her. 'Goodbye,' said Piotr and waved to her, '*powodzenia.*'

Aleksy untied the rope, threw it to Alex, and Sebastian began to row away from the felucca.

Marek held up a hand. Sabine kept her eyes on it until it disappeared into the darkness.

'*Bienvenue en France.*'

All Going Wrong For Wright
Swimmer forced to pull out of Olympic trials

Olympic hopeful Hannah Wright has been forced to pull out of the British Championships, which will take place in Sheffield later this month. Hannah, who currently holds the British record for both the 50m and the 100m Butterfly, has been suffering from a shoulder injury and is unable to compete at the trials.

'I'm really upset that I'm not able to defend my British titles,' said Hannah, 'but it's taking longer than I'd hoped to shake off this injury. I'm still hopeful that I'll make the team for the Beijing Olympics.'

R u free 2day? Do u want 2 meet up? x

I still cant believe what happened. It was amazin! xx

U r gorgeous, the sexiest girl Iv ever met X

Do u want 2 do something 2nite? xx

R u ignoring me? X

What have I done wrong? Why wont u reply? X

I scroll down the inbox in my mobile, delete messages as I go. Wish I could delete Calum as easily.

I'm such a bitch to think like that, but he just won't leave me alone. Texting, trying to call me. I've been ignoring my phone for the last couple of days in the hope that he'll take the hint.

It's a joy to get back in the pool. My shoulder's still niggling, but I can deal with it. The benefits of a swim outweigh any pain at the moment. Just half an hour to myself, away from Calum's constant texting, Dad's worried looks across the living room, Shirley's questions.

Are you okay?

You look a bit pale.

Has something happened?

You know you can talk to me if you're worried or upset.

You're due some annual leave, why don't you take a few days off this week?

Thank fuck for annual leave. I can take my time in the pool, no rushing, no clock watching.

I treat myself to a shivery bite when I'm out, a hot chocolate and a Twix from the vending machine. I'm on holiday after all. I sit at one of the plastic tables in the café, stir the frothy cream into my hot chocolate as I watch the old women going into the pool for the over-50s Aquafit class.

Did Marièle ever go? Have any of them noticed she's missing?

I dunk a finger of Twix in my drink, suck at the chocolate and caramel before biting through soggy biscuit.

The women in the pool have all linked arms and are walking round and round in circles. The instructor on the poolside shouts at them to change direction every so often. The water in the centre of them swirls and whirlpools.

I finish my Twix, gulp down the powdery dregs of my drink. As I stand to throw the empty wrapper in the bin, I spot him through the window.

Calum.

He's sitting on the pavement next to my locked-up bike.

Fuck sake, what does he want?

It's all schoolboy angst and drama. I don't want to hurt his feelings, but it was a shag, that's all. And one I wish hadn't happened.

The pool windows are tinted so I can watch him without him realising. He's sitting on the kerb, picking at the ground with a stick. His schoolbag lies next to him. I fluctuate between pity and anger. If I was sixteen again then yes, I would definitely be flattered by all the attention. But I'm not, and I've got a feeling he wouldn't be so interested in me if I was sixteen. I can't believe he's so besotted after one fumble in the back room.

I sit back down, try to work out an escape plan.

The over-50s are lying on their backs, arms at their sides, using their hands to scull, to try and keep them on the surface of the water. A couple of them manage to stay prone, but most of them sink in the middle.

I could leave my bike? Sneak round the back of the pool and walk home?

Or I could just hang around here, wait for him to give up and go away?

Come on, Hannah, stop being an idiot.

I'm the grown up, he's the schoolboy, isn't that what I keep telling myself?

I sling my bag over my shoulder, head outside.

Chris is at the door having a fag.

'You're late today, aren't you?' He asks.

'Yeah, got a few days off work, so I'm not rushing about.'

'Doing anything exciting?'

'Nah, not really.'

Calum clocks us, gets to his feet. I'm such a bitch, but I know he's watching us, so I put on a bit of an act. Pretend to be really engrossed in Chris's chat, laugh at his jokes, even though he's talking utter pish and I'm not really listening.

Calum looks properly hurt when I eventually walk towards him. I feel rotten, regret acting like that.

I had sex with him, I should be grown up enough to deal with the fallout.

'Hey,' I say. 'What are you doing here?'

'What choice do I have? You keep ignoring me.'

My pity dissolves again, replaced by the pissed-off part of me. I ignore him, unlock my bike, let my hair fall in front of my face to avoid eye contact. How can I have been so intimate with him a few days ago and now feel this awkward around him?

'Are you just going to keep on ignoring me then?' He asks.

I unwind the chain from the frame of my bike.

'You just sleep with me and that's it?'

The truth is I don't know what to say. My head is full of lame clichés.

'That was the best day of my life. Why won't you give it a go?'

'Calum, I'm really sorry. I didn't mean to hurt you. I don't want a boyfriend right now.'

'So you're just a slut then?'

'Okay, I'm going now.'

He stands in front of my bike. I manoeuvre it round him but he moves in front of it again. My heart's thumping and I grip the handlebars. I really feel like banging the front wheel into his shin, but I restrain myself.

Use the nerves, use the adrenaline, channel it into speed, strength.

'Calum, get out of the way.'

'Not until you give me a proper answer.'

'Answer to what? Yes, I'm a slut. Happy now?'

'I didn't mean that.'

I push my bike round him, run over his foot as I go. Shit, that didn't go well at all. I jump on my bike, start pedalling, scared to turn round in case he's coming after me.

I didn't think he could be like that. So full of rage. We've always got on so well, had a laugh together. I hate that I've ruined it.

I breathe in deep through my nose, blow out through my mouth.

In.

Out.

In.

Out.

I'm trembling and the bike wobbles underneath me.

In. Out. In. Out. In. Out. In. Out.

Force down the lump in my throat. I will not cry. I will not cry because of him.

I can't go home, not yet, not after that. I head towards Marièle's house instead. I need some peace. To be somewhere where nobody will find me.

The fish swims to the top of the bowl as I let myself in.

'Hey, fish, you must be hungry.'

I dump my bag at the kitchen table, lift the tub of flakes.

High in vitamins.

Nutritionally balanced.

A healthy diet for goldfish and fancy goldfish.

'Are you fancy, or just a normal goldfish?'

I sprinkle some food into the bowl. He bobs upside down like he's doing a headstand, sucks at flakes as they settle on the bottom.

I turn the kettle on, open cupboards as I wait for it to boil.

Tin of macaroni cheese, tin of ham, bag of rice, packet of spaghetti, loaf of bread.

The bread's mouldy so I throw it in the bin. The lid swings back and forward, back and forward, back and forward. Somehow her house doesn't seem so scary when I'm using it as a hideout.

I help myself to a mug, find a jar of coffee, shake the carton of milk that sits in the fridge, sniff at it.

'I think the milk's off,' I pour it down the sink. Curdled lumps drop out of the carton, sour and sickly. I turn the hot tap on, fast, gushing, try not to gag. Steam rises around the sink, melts everything down the plughole.

'Looks like it's going to have to be black.'

The fish sits on the bottom of the bowl, his tail rippling out behind him, like hair under water.

'You still keeping our secret?' I ask.

I reach in behind, lift out the lottery ticket.

5 16 21 26 32 44

I've sold these tickets every day for the last eight months or so but I've never really looked at one properly before.

The hand that's meant to resemble a face. Two fingers for eyes, two fingers crossed for luck, giving you the thumbs up. A smiling mouth gashed into the palm.

Play.

Play with me.

You might win.

It could be you.

Turn your back and he'll give you the finger.

Fingers crossed, fingers crossed, keep your fingers crossed.

What does that even mean anyway?

What good has crossing your fingers ever done?

It's what I kept saying when I first got my injury. What other people kept saying to me.

I'm keeping my fingers crossed.

We'll keep our fingers crossed for you.

It didn't do me any good.

£1.00

It depresses me to look at the price, that small amount. Marièle about to hand over her pound, the coins tumbling and spilling onto the shop floor. I turn the ticket over. The tiny pink writing makes me go cross-eyed.

SAFE CUSTODY OF THE TICKET IS THE OWNER'S RESPONSIBILITY.

PLEASE WRITE YOUR NAME AND ADDRESS ON THE TICKET FOR SAFEKEEPING.

WINNINGS HAVE TO BE CLAIMED WITHIN 180 DAYS.

One hundred and eighty days.

Twenty-four weeks.

Six months.

How long is she going to be unconscious for? I should write her name and address on the back of the ticket.

But.

She might never wake up.

(I could write my own name and address on it, nobody would ever know)

I slip the ticket back in behind the fish bowl, finish my coffee, rinse the mug out under the tap and leave it upside down on the draining board to dry.

What now?

I open the door to the hallway, there's a pile of mail lying on the mat at the front door. I flick through it, out of habit rather than nosiness. It's mostly junk.

Indian takeaway menu.

A leaflet from Sainsbury's

It'll always be bloody Presto to Mum.

Charity letter from Amnesty International.

Another from the Red Cross.

I dump the lot on the phone table.

Five doors leading off the hallway. Which one is the living room hiding behind?

I try the most obvious one.

Jackpot.

(it could be you)

I close the living room blinds, switch on a lamp. Don't want to advertise the fact I'm hiding out here.

I sit down in an armchair. A coaster stained with mug rings, lies on a side table within reach of the chair.

Stand.

I'm in her chair. It's wrong to be in her chair. I smooth down the lace antimacassars. Slightly discoloured from where her hands and head have rested all these years.

Like the ones Gran used to have.

This is where she sits.

Where she sat.

I go for the sofa instead, pick up the remote control, switch on the TV. Noise blasts out of the speakers and I point the remote at the TV. My finger press, press, pressing on the volume button.

DOWNDOWNDOWNDowndowndown

I channel hop, about to put my feet up on the coffee table when I stop myself. Remember where I am.

Her home.

Have some respect.

It's all shite on the TV.

LOOSE WOMEN.

THE WRIGHT STUFF.

SECRET MILLIONAIRE

(not quite a millionaire, but...)

THIS MORNING.

THE JEREMY KYLE SHOW. *My older lover acts like I don't exist. We had sex in a shop and now she's ignoring me. Schoolboy lover for washed-up swimmer.*

Fuck sake.

I keep flicking.

My finger stops, hovers over the channel button as the screen shows a swimming pool. I recognise that pool. I've swam in that pool.

NOW: LIVE SWIMMING FROM THE EUROPEAN CHAMPIONSHIPS

I put the remote control down on the coffee table. I know I should keep going, move away from this channel, turn the TV off altogether, but I can't.

Next up in the pool, we have the heats of the women's 100m butterfly.

100m butterfly.

My stroke.
My distance.
My event.
My British record.
Heat one.
The commentator names the eight girls as they stand behind the starting blocks. Swinging their arms, peeling off tracksuits. Costumes slick against skin. Caps and goggles being adjusted. The camera moves from left to right, each girl gets their five seconds of airtime. I recognise most of them. It's not that long since I competed against them. What do they care that I'm not there? One less person to have to beat. One less person to keep them out of the final.

They may have acted like they were upset, like they cared. But nobody cares when a rival drops.

Painted nails wave at the camera, a few smiles for the viewers back home. A couple of girls ignore it completely, just stare straight ahead. Focused. Already swimming the race in their head.

Take your marks.
The girls are still, poised on the blocks.
Beep.
They dive, streamline into the pool. The camera switches to its underwater view now. Froth and bubbles as eight strong pairs of legs breakout. Then they're up on the surface of the water, into their stroke.

The camera focuses on the girl in lane four, edging into the lead. Her shoulders, just under the surface of the water, rise with every stroke. Strong and supple shoulders, muscles relaxing and contracting, working.

I'm in the pool with them. I swim every stroke, every kick, every pull. I count my strokes, I'm racing them. I'm racing them and I'm winning.

Turn and push off the wall, leg kick under the water, propel myself to the surface and back into my stroke. Final length. Feel my muscles burn as I hit the last twenty five metres, my arms heavy, lactic build up.

Ten metres to go. My legs are slowing, my chest heaving. I have to maintain my stroke, not give in to the tired ache.

Five metres. The wall is in sight. Keep going, keep going.

Four metres, you're almost there now.

Count the strokes.

Three metres, dying but almost home.

Two metres, head down now.

One metre, bang, your hands hit the wall.

The winning time flashes up at the bottom of the TV.

1:01:78

Slower than my PB.

I won that heat.

I would have won that heat.

I'm out of breath. I reach forward to pick up the remote control, need to switch this off, put myself out of my misery. But I don't switch over. I leave it on.

I should be there. I should be competing. I'd make the final, a medal contender. My PB would have been faster by now if I'd been able to keep going. Fulfil my potential.

Heat 2.

Slower than my PB.

I was strong when my shoulder gave up. I had a whole season of training behind me. I had a faster time in me, I know I did. I just didn't get a chance to prove it.

I was flying before my shoulder gave up.

Heat 3, and of course we have Claire Richards going in this one.

Claire Richards. Claire. My teammate.

Ex-teammate.

She sticks her tongue out for the camera as she's introduced. She's had it pierced.

(Jase must love that)

Her nails are long, painted with Union Jacks. As the camera moves on to the next girl, Claire pulls her goggles down over her eyes. She may be acting the fool for the camera, but she's focussed. She knows what she has to do.

She's so slim, so fit. Her skin's brown, muscles toned and smooth. The Twix from earlier sits heavy in my stomach and I put a hand down my waistband, rest it on the loose flesh of my belly.

Take your marks.

Claire wins Heat 3.

Fastest time going into the final.

0.6 of a second off my PB.

(she'll get it in the final)

I used to hammer her in training. Leave her standing. Now she's fastest going into the final. Favourite for the gold.

The camera zooms in on her as she treads water. She leans her arms over the lane rope, pulls her cap and goggles off, shakes the hand of the girl in the lane next to her. Then a thumbs up for the camera and a big smile. The camera zooms back out again as she makes her way out of the pool, pulling herself over each lane rope like an eel.

I tune in to the commentator.

And what a swim from Claire, she's having a great season, isn't she?

Yeah, she sure is.

That second voice, I hadn't been paying attention before but it's a voice I recognise.

She's one of your teammates, isn't she?

Yeah, I know she'll be really pleased with that. We've all been working really hard.

And it's paying off. After your great swim at the start of the week and now this, you must be doing something right in Bath.

Yeah, we've got a great set-up there.

Jase.

It's fucking Jason.

He's doing so well for himself, they apparently now have him in the studio giving his expert opinion to the world.

Without being disrespectful to the rest of the girls, that European title is hers to lose. And she's not far off Hannah Wright's British record.

She's flying at the moment. She's worked really hard in training so she deserves it. I know she's had that record in her sights, and it's no easy record to beat. Hannah set a high standard.

My gut tightens as he says my name.

Indeed, I'm sure if Hannah's watching this she'll be pleased to see her old teammate...

Shit, I can't take this.

I hit the power button. The TV flashes off. I slam the remote control down on the coffee table; the back pings loose and the batteries spill out, rolling across the table and onto the floor.

I'm shaking, shaking, shaking all over and I pound the sofa cushion. Punch it, punch it, punch it. I don't know what's worse. Being completely forgotten about or being talked about like that.

As if they know what it's like.

They have no right to talk about me like they know how I feel. Like I had my shot, gave up on my own terms.

(as if I'm happy)

I had it in me to set a better record, a faster one. One that Claire Richards couldn't come close to. She's stolen my place in history.

I'm out of breath, panting, my chest heaving, in and out, in and out, in and out. My heart hammers and I can't stop the tears. I think I'm going to be sick.

I slide off the sofa, lie on the floor in front of it. Push my face into the carpet, feel it prickle against my face.

I feel so awful, so fucking awful. Why does it hurt so much? And I have nobody, nobody. I hurt too much to get in touch with my swimming friends, too ashamed to get back in touch with my school friends.

I'm all on my own.

So what happened? I read in the paper that you got injured.

It's my shoulder.

What happened to it?

What do you mean?

Did you fall or hit it or something?

No, it just happened.

Those Union Jack nails flicker in front of my eyes. My own nails are chipped and peeling. I push my hands away from me, under the sofa, into the dust and crumbs.

I need to paint my nails.

Marièle must have nail polish somewhere.

I get up off the floor, try the door directly opposite the living room.

A cupboard.

Coats and jackets hang from a rail, shoes and boots on the floor beneath. It smells of lavender, smoky and floral. I shut the cupboard, try the next door.

It swings open onto her bedroom. I stop in the hallway.

Should I go in?

I have to. I have to wipe off this chipped layer of polish and start again with a fresh coat. I step into her bedroom, the door shuts behind me. The lavender smell is stronger in here, sickly, cloying, like those parma violet sweets.

The bed's made, shoes lined up underneath, clothes folded on a chair in the corner, make up and bottles of perfume neat on the dressing table. Chanel No5.

I spray it onto my wrist, my neck. The scent hangs, misty, and I breathe it in. The bottle clinks against the varnished surface of the dressing table when I put it down. I rummage through tubs and tubes and aerosols, find a bottle of clear nail polish and a bottle of red. There's no remover though, so I sit on her bed, use my teeth to scrape off the dried polish stuck to my nails.

The red polish is sticky, can't have been used for a while, so I apply a layer of the clear stuff over the top. It slicks over the red. The brush of the clear liquid turns pink, contaminates the rest of the polish. I lay my hands out flat on my thighs, wait for it to dry. Flakes of polish lie across Marièle's cream duvet cover.

There's a pile of books at my feet.

Angela's Ashes
The Cinder Path
Women Agents of WW2
Great Expectations

A shelf above her bed. An ornament of a blackbird, the porcelain shining, another of a Chinese fisherman. He's holding a fishing rod, made from a toothpick and a piece of thread, a glass fish tied to the end of it. I push at the fish with my pinkie, it swings from side to side.

I blow on my nails, dab at them with a fingertip. They've not dried completely and my finger imprints the sticky polish.

Two photographs stand in frames next to the fisherman, a layer of dust static across the glass.

Old photos, no colour in them, yellow rather than black and white. One's of a man in uniform. The other is of two girls walking along the street.

Is one of them Marièle?

It's hard to compare the girls in the photo with that old woman lying in the hospital bed.

So young, but before you know it you're living alone with just a fish for company.

(I don't even have a fish)

B	L	A	C	K
I	R	D	E	F
G	H	J	M	N
O	P	S	T	U
V	W	X	Y	Z

SABINE HAD NEVER cycled so far in her life. The suitcase containing her Mark III radio was slung in a basket on the back of her bike, the brown leather creased and worn. She was glad she didn't have to carry it, the weight of it already made her bicycle unsteady.

The bicycle is the easiest way to get around once you are in France. It is a common way for women to travel and means that you can take back roads and avoid public transport, including any road blocks or document spot checks.

Sweat ran down her back and forehead, grit from the dusty road stuck to her damp skin. She was grateful for the breeze that blew up her skirt and cooled her legs.

No matter how much Madame Poirier tried to feed her up, she simply did not have enough food to combat the endless hours of cycling. Sabine could feel her clothes, specially measured for her back in London, loose around her waist and bust, her thighs firm.

It took Sabine a moment to remember where she was. Light shone in through the slits of the wooden shutters. Even though she was on dry land now, she could still feel the rocking motion of the felucca.

| *up and* | *up and* | *up and* | *up and* |
| *down* | *down* | *down* | *down* |

She could smell coffee and sausages cooking somewhere in the house. As her ears tuned in and she began to wake up properly, she realised that she could hear voices through the wall.

Sabine slipped her arms out from the sleeping bag Madame Poirier had made for her. The parachute material was soft and slippery against her skin. She ran a finger along the fine black stitching which held it together. It had been dark when she'd arrived last night. Madame Poirier sat up waiting for her, had sent Alex away, even though he wanted to brief Sabine on Sand Dune. Madame had fed Sabine, bread and cheese, before packing her off to bed. It all felt like a dream now, she'd sleepwalked through most of it.

All these drops we get, I tell the boys bring me the parachutes, I can use them. They groan and moan, we must bury them, Madame, we must. It's such a waste. They think they can fool me, but I'm not stupid, I know.

Sabine could hear Madame Poirier now. It sounded like Alex was with her.

'Look at the time, it's after nine. I need Sabine. She is not here to sleep, she is not here for un jour férié.'

'Sssshhh, I will not have you waking that poor girl. She's no use to you exhausted. Let her get some rest before you send her off on one of your missions. Laisse-la tranquille.'

'This is important.'

'Everything is important to you. What use is she if she drops dead of exhaustion halfway down the road? Have some coffee, sit down and speak to me.'

Sabine stopped next to a roadside shrine, set up inside an alcove in the wall. A statue of the Virgin Mary, blue paint peeling from her shroud, too long exposed to the elements. There were dead flowers in pots lying next to the statue, stubs of candles standing rigid in pools of wax.

She untied the silk scarf around her neck, careful not to tug on the silver chain underneath. The cross bounced against her chest as she cycled.

She wiped her face with the scarf then spread it out on the saddle of her bike. A map had been printed on the silk. She glanced at it quickly, before tying it back around her neck and setting off on her bike again.

Sabine closed her eyes, could feel the sleep dragging her down. She sat up. She had to get out of bed, if she let herself drift off she would sleep the whole morning away. Alex already thought she was lazy and weak, she had to prove to him she was an asset.

She knew the attitude of some of the men towards women agents.

She climbed out of the sleeping bag, her legs wobbly and unsteady. The pack containing her clothes lay on the floor next to the bed. Madame Poirier had stripped her of what she'd been wearing the night before.

I think we might be better off burning these rather than trying to wash them.

Sabine pulled a skirt and pullover from the pack and put them on,

washed her face using the hand basin in the corner of the room. As she
dried her face she looked up into the mirror on the wall.

God, she looked a fright.

She splashed more cold water onto her face, tried to shock some life,
some colour into her skin.

I have been ill. Rheumatic fever.

Oh well, she looked the part if nothing else.

Sabine propped her bicycle against a railing. She took one of the tables
outside the Café Rouge. There was a poster on the wall behind her.

POPULATIONS ABANDONNÉES,
FAITES CONFIANCE AU SOLDAT ALLEMAND!

It had a picture of a German soldier surrounded by children, the children
were smiling and eating bread.

Someone had scrawled '*Vive la France*' over the soldier's face.

A man went past on a donkey and cart, he nodded at Sabine and she
smiled back. A group of German soldiers were seated at a table on the
opposite side of the square. Sabine looked up at the clock on the church
tower.

Never wait more than five minutes for a rendezvous.

A bell jingled and Sabine turned to see the door of the café open and
the waitress step out. She carried a notepad, wore a blue spotted apron
tied around her waist.

Alex had said that she was nineteen, but she didn't look much older
than fifteen. She was very pretty, like a young Greer Garson, slim with
blonde hair.

PM FC DO OA PF MU BJ BD JU PM FD BT AR UA FG

The soldiers spotted her and one of them wolf-whistled. The girl
blushed, ignored the jeers coming from the other side of the square.

'*Oui,*' she said to Sabine.

'*Je voudrais un café et une pâtisserie, s'il vous plaît.*'

The girl began to write, then hesitated, looked up.

'How do you take your coffee?'

'*Noir et très chaud.*'

A flicker passed over the girl's face. She nodded and disappeared
back into the café.

Sabine's stomach churned, she needed the bathroom. The soldier's
voices carried across the square.

Je m'appelle Sabine Valois.

Je m'appelle Sabine Valois.

One of them said something and the others all laughed. Her dowdy disguise must work. They weren't interested in a sickly French girl. Not with Natalie around.

Natalie reappeared with a cup of coffee and a crescent shaped pastry. She leant forward to put the tray on the table. As she did so, she bent in close to Sabine. Sabine felt a shiver run up her spine as Natalie whispered in her ear.

PM FC DO OA PF MU BJ BD JU PM FD BT AR UA FG

She wiped under her armpits, her back, the first proper wash she'd had in days. Then she sprayed herself with perfume, ran a comb through her hair.

'D'accord, *Sabine Valois, you will have to do.'*

She stood in front of the bedroom door, breathed in then counted.

'Un, deux, trois.'

Once she opened the door, that was her. She needed a few seconds to compose herself before she was thrown in at the deep end.

'Quatre, cinq, six, sept.'

The voices whispered now, they must have heard her moving around, realised she was awake.

'Huit, neuf, dix.'

She pushed open the door.

'*Mademoiselle*, stop, *arrêtez-vous.'*

Sabine gripped the handlebars of her bicycle.

Stop or keep going?

The shout had come from behind her, she didn't recognise the voice.

Je m'appelle Sabine Valois.

DB JT CL FG IY CA VG XA

Please don't be German, please don't be German, please don't be German.

It was an older man. He stood in front of his house and waved her over. He was dressed in a waistcoat and trousers and smoked a pipe. Sabine caught the aroma of pipe tobacco as it wafted from where he stood. The smell was comforting, reminded her of father, of being home, safe. Her warning voice told her not to make such a rash assumption. She shouldn't risk her life on something so silly as a smell.

Keep your wits about you and learn to trust your gut. Usually the first hunch you have about a situation will be the right one. If something, no matter how trivial, feels wrong then it probably means that you're in danger.

Sabine wheeled her bike towards the old man, leant it against a tree.

'*Bonjour monsieur, comment allez-vous?*'

'*Je vais bien.*'

'*Pas mal.*'

The old man disappeared inside his house then reappeared with a bottle of wine and two glasses.

'I've seen you go past my house three times today, *mademoiselle*. You look thirsty, please have a drink with me.'

'*Merci*, but I really should be...'

'I won't take no for an answer. You won't find wine like this in all of France. If those Germans knew I had this... Come, sit down.'

Don't accept food or drink from strangers, especially if you haven't seen it being prepared.

Sabine looked at the man. He smiled at her, his face shook slightly. She shouldn't let her guard down, even for an old man trying to be kind. She hated having to be so suspicious of everyone. They'd trained her to always be on her guard, not to trust, to think the worst. It was a sad way to live, but the only way to stay safe.

She nodded, sat down next to the man. If Alex could see her now. Wasting valuable time, having a break, drinking wine.

God, it was strong. She felt it blossom through her, tighten round her head like a vice.

'*C'est très bon.*'

'I told you, didn't I? I used to have a vineyard nearby,' he gestured behind his house, 'but it was destroyed during the invasion.'

'I'm sorry.'

'Those allies were supposed to be helping us,' he shook his head. 'Instead they trampled my land then ran away back to England.'

Sabine opened her mouth to argue, felt the anger rise. George was one of those allies, he died over here. And they would be back, they weren't cowards. Maybe it was even George who had trampled through his vineyard, hungry and trying to get home.

But she was Sabine. Not Marièle. She did not have a brother called George.

DB JT CL FG IY CA VG XA

She'd seen a new poster in the village that day, it showed an RAF bombing raid.

AND THESE ARE YOUR ALLIES?

It angered her to think that people actually believed the propaganda. But she took a sip of wine, counted to ten.

Un, deux, trois, quatre, cinq, six, sept, huit, neuf, dix.

She shook her head, pitied the old man for his loss, drank the wine while he moaned.

'To be honest, sometimes I don't think the Germans are all bad. Don't look at me like that. Obviously I'd rather they weren't here, but we have food, don't we, a roof over our heads?'

'Not everyone does,' she answered. She found it harder and harder not to argue with him. Not to scream at him for being such a fool.

'We have suffered more than anyone, in this war and the last one.' Sabine nodded, swirled wine around her mouth rather than answer him. 'What's a girl like you doing cycling so much anyway?'

Je m'appelle Sabine Valois.

'I've not been well, rheumatic fever. The doctor prescribed fresh air and exercise. I've been staying with my aunt, helping her out.'

The man nodded, stroked his whiskered chin as he sucked on the pipe. Sabine inhaled the smell, held it inside her, could feel Father with her. She downed the remains of her wine, held the glass up to the old man.

'Well, I must be on my way, monsieur. *Merci pour le vin.*'

'Nonsense, nonsense. We are on Berlin time you know.'

He refilled her glass. The red wine chugged from the bottle. Her lips were dry and she licked them. She began to feel light-headed. If she drank anymore, she might start to argue. Give herself away.

Losing your inhibitions can result in you giving important information away or letting your guard down.

'Those Germans, if they knew about this wine...' the old man laughed and shook his head. 'You know they think they can ban me from drinking this. *Les jours sans*, they say. They can't make me do anything.'

Sabine nodded, slugged the rest of the wine from her glass. She had to get away from here, from the old man and his contradictions. She risked her life to save old fools like him.

She set down her glass, put a hand over the top of it.

'*Non, monsieur*, I must be going.'

She swayed back to her bike, giddy and off balance. Her bike swerved from side to side as she tried to manoeuvre it back onto the road.

'*Au revoir, mademoiselle*, come back again. My wine has made you feel better, *oui*?'

'*Oui, merci monsieur.*'

Sabine turned to wave at the man, lost control of her bike and crashed into a bush at the side of the road.

The kitchen and dining area lay just off Sabine's bedroom. Madame Poirier and Alex sat at an oak dining table which ran the length of the room.

'Good morning, Mademoiselle,' said Madame Poirier, standing up from the table.

'What's left of it,' said Alex.

'Je suis désolée, you should have woken me, I didn't mean...'

'Don't listen to him my dear, now, assieds-toi, sit, let me fix you some breakfast.'

Sabine sat opposite Alex. He rocked in his seat, smoked a cigarette. The top few buttons of his shirt were open and Sabine could see the wiry, dark hair from his chest. He stared at her, flicked the ash from his cigarette onto his greasy breakfast plate, pulled a fleck of tobacco from his tongue. Madame Poirier tutted, put an ashtray down in front of him.

Alex was better looking in the flesh than he was on the wanted posters, but he still didn't get her hot under the collar.

PM FC DO OA PF MU BJ BD JU PM FD BT AR UA FG

Madame Poirier thought they were crazy about each other, that all the fighting and arguing was really just a *façade* for the mad, passionate love affair.

The wanted posters had gone up that day in the village. Sabine hadn't stopped long to look, didn't want to draw attention to herself. It wasn't the greatest likeness but there was no denying it was Alex.

They had accentuated some of his features, made him look menacing and fierce, as if he'd come and kill your children in the night. Trying to scare the villagers into giving him up.

REWARD 1,000 FRANCS

Sabine didn't think he would do anything as evil as the poster suggested, but there was a side to him that scared her. A side that was unstable and dangerous.

It was worse now that he'd become an outlaw.

Madame Poirier said that being inside all day drove him crazy.

I wouldn't be surprised if he snapped and went on a rampage. You must go and see him, you are very calming, *mademoiselle*. Go and sort him out.

His current hideout was a woodsman's hut outside the village. Sabine cycled there before curfew. He'd left a cracked flowerpot lying outside to signify that it was safe to come in. At least he still followed safety procedures, that had to count for something.

Her hope was dashed when she entered the hut and found him opening a crate of guns and ammunition.

'Alex, what are you doing?'

'What do you mean, what am I doing? You heard about Monsieur Allard, didn't you?'

'*Non*, what happened? Tell me.'

Sabine knew exactly what had happened, but she hoped to buy some time. Calm Alex down.

'What sort of useless agent are you, Sabine? Why did they send you? You have no idea what's going on here.'

'I've been running around the French countryside doing errands and sending skeds for you all day. Excuse me if I don't keep up with the local news.'

He ignored her, emptied another Sten from the straw lined crate. Sabine put a hand on the gun.

'Tell me what's so important that you're happy to risk all our lives for it.'

He pulled the gun away from her, threw it down onto the mattress in the corner of the room.

'Those *salauds* murdered Monsieur Allard today. Burnt his house and hung him up from a tree.'

He slammed his hand against the wall of the hut and Sabine flinched. Was he going to take that temper out on her? Would hitting her help to calm him down?

She had seen the smoke rising from the outskirts of the village, smelt the fire. Heard the murmur among the villagers, then the eerie silence that followed. The stillness as their confusion turned to realisation.

That could happen to us.

People went home, hid themselves inside, locked their front doors.

'The railway line?' Sabine asked.

'Of course, the railway line, what else?'

It was their fault.

Sand Dune.

Alex, Sebastian and three other *résistants* had blown up part of the line three nights ago. Sabine and Madame Poirier sat up waiting for them to come home. Toasted their success.

Now an innocent man was dead.

A man who Sabine had drank wine with, a man who actually toasted the health of the German soldiers for leaving him alone.

'What are you planning to do?'

'Kill the *salauds* who did that to an old man.'

'And what good will that do? Get yourself killed, take a few with you maybe? They will seek more and more retribution. Sand Dune will collapse. All the good work we've done will be for nothing.'

'I don't care, I can't sit here hiding like a coward.'

'If you do this, you might as well have hung that man yourself. Stop being so selfish. You need to leave France. I can send a sked, get you to London.'

Alex spun on her, lifted a hand. Sabine closed her eyes, braced herself. Instead he grabbed her by the shoulders, shook her.

'How dare you speak to me like that? I'm not going to run away.'

'Don't be a fool. This is what being brave is, Alex. Making hard decisions.'

His grip weakened and there were tears in his eyes. Spittle clung to his bottom lip and his voice clicked as he spoke.

'Get out, get out,' he pushed her towards the door of the hut, slammed it behind her. She looked in the window, saw him sink onto the stained mattress.

The room was warm from the stove, drops of sweat ran down Sabine's forehead and she wiped them away with her sleeve.

Madame Poirier put a plate down in front of Sabine. A fried egg, a sausage and a slice of bread. Then she took the metal coffee pot from the stove, filled a bowl and put it down next to Sabine's plate of food.

'Merci, Madame.'

'You need a proper meal after being at sea.'

Sabine dipped the bread in the egg yolk, used it to soak up some of the fat from the sausage before putting it in her mouth. She felt oil seep from the pores on her face, the egg yolk smooth and creamy.

'Now, Sabine, it is very important that you start work today. I need you to visit Natalie Charron at the Café Rouge, she should have a message for me. You must say to her je voudrais un café et une patisserie, s'il vous plaît. *She will ask you how you take your coffee and you should reply* noir et très chaud. *Then you must check in with Sebastian, he says that he has found a safe house which you can use for your first few skeds back to London.'*

You must never transmit for more than twenty minutes and never for more than three days in the same house.

Sabine looked up, she had only tuned in to the last part of Alex's instructions. She had been dipping a slice of sausage into her egg, enjoyed the spurt of juice as she bit into it. She hadn't realised how hungry she was. How good a hot meal could taste after going so long without. She swallowed, took a gulp of coffee; thick and bitter, it coated her teeth and tongue.

Madame Poirier sat at the dining table knitting. The gramophone was on in the corner, crackled music, a man singing.

Ma Pomme

'What are you listening to?' Sabine asked.

'Maurice Chevalier, you've never heard of him?'

Sabine shook her head, 'I don't think so.'

'He's very handsome, like Alex.'

Madame looked up from her knitting, raised an eyebrow.

'When will you believe me when I say we are not having a love affair?'

Madame shrugged, went back to her knitting. The needles click, click, clicked.

Sabine helped herself to a glass of water from a jug in the centre of the table, closed her eyes and listened to the crackled voice.

There was a knock at the front door and Madame stood to open it.

Sabine knocked her glass of water. A German soldier stood in the doorway. She dabbed at the water which poured over the edge of the table and dripped onto the floor.

Gefreiter

Leutnant

Oberleutnant

Hauptmann

SS Hauptsturmführer

SS Obersturmführer

He'd caught her off guard, her gun was in the bedroom.

'*Bonjour,*' Madame Poirier said to the soldier, 'come in.'

The soldier took off his hat, wiped his boots on the mat before entering the house. He spotted Sabine and nodded at her, she nodded back, sank into her seat at the table.

He hovered in the doorway, shuffled from one foot to the other, as Madame disappeared into the pantry.

'Do you like Edith Piaf?' he asked. 'She played in Paris but I couldn't get leave to go and see her.'

'*Voila,*' Madame interrupted, before Sabine could answer. She reappeared with four eggs and a block of butter.

'*Danke, es tut mir leid*,' the soldier said as Madame handed him the food.

He nodded at Sabine again then left. Madame shut the door behind him and locked it.

'Don't look so shocked, *mademoiselle*, I don't help them because I want to but because I have to. They don't live here for free, we must pay for the privilege.'

Madame sat back down at the table and continued to knit.

'God, I'm surprised Alex hasn't killed him by now.'

'Alex can be very naïve. That boy,' she gestured towards the door with a knitting needle, 'he is just following orders.'

'But Madame, what if he discovered one of our meetings? How can you bear to let them in your house?'

'My dear friend gave me this record. I doubt I'll see him again. The Germans took him away but it was Vichy who allowed it to happen.'

Sabine reached out, laid a hand on Madame's forearm.

'I'm sorry, I didn't mean...'

'Don't be silly,' Madame pushed Sabine's hand away.

'I was in the square, I saw him being led away to the train station. A lady had her head split open because she wouldn't let go of her son. It was a *gendarme* who did it, a Frenchman.'

'I'm so sorry,' said Sabine.

Tears dripped from Madame's face, soaked into the wool she knitted.

'I'm not telling you this to make you sorry for me. Nobody is all black or all white in this war. I have as much reason as anyone to hate the Germans but to hate that German boy who is sent here by his officers, who tells me about his wife and baby back in Germany, who apologises for taking my eggs, that I cannot do. Alex likes to make speeches and play the hero, but he doesn't know anything. Alex, your friends in London, they think we're cowards for letting the Germans overrun us, but we are tired.'

'Monsieur Allard said something very similar.'

Sabine thought of the old man who angered her. The old man who shared his wine and now hung from the tree she'd parked her bike against. She poured herself another glass of water, gulped it down. Sweat dripped down her back. She stood up and fanned her blouse. Madame held up her knitting against Sabine's back, measured the pullover for size.

Madame Poirier knelt on the floor, feeding a sliver of fat to a tabby cat who rubbed itself against her and purred.

'Pas de problème,' *Sabine replied. 'now please can you go through that again. I don't want to get anything wrong.'*

'Do you need me to write it down for you?' *Alex took a pencil from behind his ear, began to write on a cigarette paper.*

'Non, monsieur. *I know what to do.'*

172

July 2008

The Wrighting's On The Wall For Hannah
Scottish swimmer to miss Beijing Olympics

Hannah Wright has lost her race for fitness and will miss out on selection for the Beijing Olympics. Hannah, who swam the Olympic qualifying time for the 100m Butterfly at the start of the year, has been suffering from a shoulder injury and has been unable to train properly.

The British record holder had been seen as one of Team GB's medal hopes for the Olympics, however will now not even make the trip to China.

'I'm absolutely devastated,' said Hannah. 'As an athlete, the Olympics are seen as the pinnacle you want to reach, and it's always been my ambition to swim at them. Unfortunately for me, it's just not worked out this time. I've still got time on my side though, and I'm determined to make the next Olympics.'

17

I THINK SOMEONE might have changed Marièle's nightie. I don't remember those little pink flowers around the neckline. It looks as though someone's combed her hair too. It's pulled back from her face and you can see the lines where the comb's run through it. Parallel through her greasy, unwashed hair.

What's the beauty regime for someone who's unconscious? Are there special hairdressers who deal only with comatose clients? Manicurists who come in to cut fingernails and toenails, because they just keep on growing?

I try to get my head in the visiting zone. I can't help it though. I'm already thinking about other things that must keep on going even if you're unconscious. Leg hair and bikini lines and underarms.

I used to shave everyday when I was in proper competition mode. Legs, pubes, pits, arms. Fuzz free.

Greg said that shaving down gave you at least a two per cent advantage in the pool. Even the boys did it.

Dad always thought that was weird. *Bunch of bloody poofs.*

But two per cent is a lot in the pool.

(Jase and I in bed together, legs scraping against each other like sandpaper)

The shave down. My pre-race ritual. I always did it the same way, down the right side of my body then back up the left side.

Stupid really.

Focus, Hannah, focus. You're here for Marièle, not to reminisce about shaving.

'Hey, how are you today?'

Her face is slack. Cheeks caved in around her mouth.

I lay my hand out flat on the white sheet covering her. My hands are bigger than hers.

(paddles)

My fingernails painted red, stolen polish from her dressing table. Her nails are discoloured, furrowed and brittle.

Her wrists are tiny, I'm scared to touch her but I want to see if…

…yes, I can. I can fit her wrist inside a loop made with my thumb and forefinger. It fits, with room to spare too. I bet there's chubby babies in the Maternity Ward who have bigger hospital bracelets than Marièle.

I let go, lay my palm on the back of her hand. Her skin's warm and papery. I expected her to be cold, which is stupid. She's not dead.

(not yet)

Her hands give her age away more than her face does, veins under tracing paper skin, liver spots. Her fingers bend slightly inwards, the knuckles knobbly with arthritis.

'Do you know I'm here?' I take her hand in mine.

I'm moved by how vulnerable she is. It took holding her hand to do that. Her skin against mine.

'Squeeze my hand if you can hear me.'

Her chest rises and falls.

Rises and falls.

Rises and falls.

I stroke her hand.

I'm here. I'm here. I'm here.

Gran was happy to have someone sit next to her. Someone to smile, to nod in all the right places. To listen while she talked, while she reminisced. It was a one-way conversation, the stories told time and time again, but it made her happy.

To have company, not to be on her own. She was lonely after Grandad died.

There it is again.

That word.

Lonely.

Alone.

It's haunting me.

Hannah Wright, failed swimmer, lived and died alone.

Would anyone even remember me enough to write the tiny obituary? The local reporters used to phone all the time for quotes, opinions, updates.

(not anymore)

What's worse? Being alone or living a lie to escape the loneliness?

I head back to her house after visiting. It feels a bit strange, not being at work this week. I don't know what to do with myself. I've always had a routine. The five am starts, the pool sessions, the gym sessions, the weights, the runs, the physio appointments, the early-to-beds to start all over again.

'Hey, fish,' I sprinkle some flakes in his bowl. He's starting to smell a bit, the water turning. A scum line rims the bowl, giving away where the water level used to be.

'You could do with a clean.'

He pecks at the coloured stones lining the bottom of his bowl, darts away from me as I dip a plastic measuring jug into it and decant some of the water. It's manky, bits of brown gunk, fish poo, float around in it. I empty the jug down the sink, run the tap at the same time to wash away the gritty silt.

I keep going until there's just enough water for the fish to swim in. He flits from side to side, his tail skimming the surface.

'Don't worry, I'm going to fill it back up.'

I scrub the line of scum with a cloth, then fill the jug with fresh water from the cold tap.

'What temperature is it supposed to be?'

I dip a finger into the bowl. The fish skims by and I pull my hand away as his tail ripples against my finger.

I add some hot water to the jug, mix until it's lukewarm, pour it into the bowl, keep going until it's full again. The fish rocks from side to side, buffeted by the waves.

'That's more like it.'

I sprinkle a few more flakes in.

'Don't look at me like that, I'm trying to help you.'

The fish nibbles at the surface, body shimmering in the fresh water.

I need to pee, so I head out into the hall.

(what's behind door number three?)

I squat above the toilet as I pee. My thighs burn, but I don't feel right touching the seat.

Her seat.

It feels weird, doing it here in her house.

The bathroom walls are painted blue and there's a china fish hanging above the bath, a picture of a blackbird in a box frame on the opposite wall.

As I wash my hands, I open the mirrored cabinet above the sink, read the prescription labels on her medicine.

BISOPROLOL	ASPIRIN	SIMVASTATIN
METFORMIN	NAPROXEN	LANSOPRAZOLE
ZOPICLONE	CO-CODAMOL	AMITRITYLINE

I wonder what's wrong with her. Just old age? Gran was on loads of pills too.

I rummage around on the shelves, moisturiser, comb, foundation, lipstick, talc, denture cleaning tablets, Savlon, cotton buds.

I close the cabinet, the mirror's smeared with fingerprints. I can't tell which are mine and which are hers. I wipe it, smudge the fingerprints together, obscure my reflection. I take out her lipstick, Mediterranean Pink, and apply it before blotting onto a sheet of toilet paper, revealing the creases and lines on my lips.

I drop the sheet of paper into the toilet, watch as it sinks under, my lip mark like a bloodstain.

I'm fidgety, can't relax, sit still. I wander into the hallway, pace up and down, up and down, up and down.

All this free time and I don't know what to do with it.

I jump at a noise outside. Someone's walking up the garden path, I see the shape of them through the frosted glass.

Closer and bigger.

Closer and bigger.

Closer and bigger.

I drop to the floor as the doorbell rings. Lie still. Don't move.

I'm trembling and my heart thumps against the carpet.

Who is it?

Who's there?

I lift my head slightly, so I can see the front door. They're still out there.

Shit, what if they look through the letterbox? They'll see me lying on the floor. I need to move.

I crawl forward along the carpet, my t-shirt rides up, catches on my belly button ring. The doorbell goes again. The shape in the glass hovers from side to side.

I move forward, reach up and push the nearest door open, then drag myself into her bedroom, the carpet burning my bare stomach. The door falls shut behind me and I sit with my back against it, hug my knees to my chest, try to stop the shaking. My stomach's red and I rub at it, pull my t-shirt back into place.

The letterbox rattles and something's pushed through. I think I hear footsteps disappearing down the path but don't want to risk moving. I sit there for a few minutes, let my breathing, my heart rate, go back to normal. Press two fingers against my neck, count my pulse. Feel it weaken and slow.

(resting pulse)

8 x 100m at pulse 180, 10 seconds rest

Eventually I stand, peer out into the hallway. There's a card lying on the mat at the front door.

WE CALLED TODAY AT 4.35PM
TO READ YOUR GAS AND ELECTRICITY METER.
UNFORTUNATELY NOBODY WAS IN. IF YOU WOULD LIKE TO SEND
US YOUR METER READINGS BEFORE YOUR NEXT BILL, YOU CAN
DO SO USING THE CONTACT DETAILS ON THE OTHER SIDE OF
THIS CARD. THANK YOU.

I dump the card with the rest of her mail, peer out through the spy hole. Nothing.

There's nobody there.

I head back into her bedroom, slump down onto the bed. Shit, what's wrong with me?

I play the last few minutes back in my head, start to laugh, can't stop myself. The doorbell, me throwing myself to the floor, crawling about on her carpet. Fuck sake, I'm such an idiot. My tummy aches from laughing but I can't stop. I lie back on her bed, tears stinging my eyes. I've lost the plot completely.

This is it. What they warned me might happen.

(meltdown)

Her photos look down on me from the shelf above the bed. I reach up, take down the one of the two women. I hold it up above my head, move it towards me so it goes out of focus then away from me so I can hardly see it.

Towards me.

Away from me.

Towards me.

Away from me.

Towards. Away. Towards. Away. Towards. Away. Towards. Away.

The more I look at it, the more I'm sure that the brown-haired girl in uniform is Marièle. There's something about her, around the eyes and the mouth. A similarity to that old woman in the hospital bed.

At first glance, the blonde girl takes all the attention. Her smile, dimpled cheeks. It's only when you look at it for a long time that you realise how beautiful the other girl, how beautiful Marièle is.

How old is she here? My age? She looks so glamorous, so sophisticated.

You should go in the boys' changing rooms with shoulders like that. Are you a swimmer or a weightlifter?

Who's the other girl in the photo? They're too different to be related. A friend?

Her best friend?

I sit up and put the photo back. It's only as I'm setting it down that I realise how gently I've been holding it. Tender. Like it might shatter in my hands if I squeezed too tight.

I push myself up off the bed, stumble over the pile of books lying on the floor, they topple over, spilling across the carpet.

I tidy them back into place. A slip of paper falls out of one.

Dear Marièle,

Thank you for all your help with my research. Please accept this copy as a small token of my
gratitude. I hope you enjoy it.

Yours, James

Women Agents of WW2 by James L Phillips.

I slip the note back inside, turn the book over and read the blurb on the back.

During World War Two, many women were selected and trained by the Special Operations Executive to work as secret agents behind enemy lines. These women were courageous and faced constant danger while working undercover. James L Phillips recounts the stories of some of these women soe agents, a number of whom made the ultimate sacrifice while working for the service of their country and the allied forces.

I open the book, scan down the chapter headings.

Fuck, there she is.

Chapter Fifteen: Marièle Downie, aka Sabine Valois, aka Blackbird.

18

SABINE WAS GLAD to be outside. It was dark, she couldn't see the others, could just hear them whispering to each other. She could smell the ploughed earth, the blossom on the hedges which lined the edge of the field.

She sat on her coat, the dew damp underneath her. In the distance she could hear the thunder of an allied air raid. It was strange to think that the people she risked her life for, the people she sat in a field in the middle of the night waiting for, were bombing France.

Madame Poirier set down a carafe of red wine in the centre of the table. It was after curfew now, the shutters were closed and they sat by candlelight.

'Out you go, Pacha,' Madame Poirier said and opened the front door briefly to let the cat out.

Sabine saw Madame hesitate before she closed the door again, her eyes dart across the courtyard outside. If they were caught together like this, they would all be arrested without question.

The Germans have outlawed all public assemblies. A gathering of three or more people is forbidden.

The candle flame flickered as Madame shut the door and locked it. When had she last sat out on the stone patio at the front of her house? A glass of wine, a book, Pacha sunning himself at her feet. Not since the invasion probably.

Maybe in peacetime she'd be able to do it again. Sit outside her own house without fear of footsteps.

A few of the *résistants* had met at Alex's hut earlier, listened out for the final signal.

Rachel Tremblay, the bicycle is unlocked.

They ate bread and cheese, had a glass of sherry as they waited for it to get dark.

'Where is Sebastian?' Alex took Sabine aside, 'he's meant to be here.'

'Maybe he's with the others, or meeting us at the rendezvous point instead?'

'He knows better than to change plans at the last minute.'

'Isn't Natalie supposed to be with him? Do you think they're okay?'

'They better be, it's too late to call it off now. Right, everyone, on your feet, *La Marseillaise*, then we leave.'

180

'You do realise we'll probably all be heard and arrested before we even leave this hut,' said Sabine.

'Sing, you are a blackbird after all.'

'Sabine, did you send the sked to London?' asked Alex.

B	L	A	C	K
I	R	D	E	F
G	H	J	M	N
O	P	S	T	U
V	W	X	Y	Z

'Oui, mais I had to cut off before the end. They should have got enough to understand though.'

'Problème?'

'Almost, I was in the cellar of that old farmhouse, you know the one that stinks of cheese…'

'We don't care about the smell, were you found out?' interrupted Alex.

'I asked Monsieur Simon to give me a signal if anyone came snooping. I was almost finished the sked when I heard him whistling our warning tune. He said he'd seen one of those detection vans drive past. I wasn't on long enough for them to pick me up properly but I can't use that cellar again. My wireless is still there though, I left it behind in case I was stopped.'

Sabine was surprised at the confidence in her voice as she told them what had happened. So matter of fact.

She felt a rush knowing that it was over, she had survived and had a tale to keep the men interested.

Sabine was happy to leave the confines of the hut. Away from the sweat and the nerves, the smells of men who lived on a diet based mainly of swede and rutabaga.

Cattle feed, before the war broke out.

Sabine had to admit that Alex was good. He led them to the field without stopping to switch on a torch or check the compass. Sabine still relied on Michelin maps.

Some of the men had argued for Alex to stay at home.

You are a wanted man, if we are found with you we're all dead men. It's not safe for you to come, you must stay in hiding. You're jeopardising everything.

Sabine had stuck up for him, even though he'd ignored her pleas to leave France.

'It doesn't matter whether Alex is seen or not. If any of us are caught after curfew then we're dead men. And women, I might add. He's our leader, we need him there.'

She'd noticed the look of surprise on his face. She meant it though. They were better with him than without him. She trusted her gut reaction and it told her that Alex must lead the drop.

```
Sand Dune 9
Drop scheduled for 22.03.44 at 01.30
43.675818 2.252197
Number of containers:11
```

Sabine jumped to her feet at the rustle of bushes, the footsteps as someone approached.

Conversation stopped.

She reached for her pistol, ready to shoot, or run, or both. Whatever was required. She didn't fancy trying to escape in the dark, if they all scattered now it would be a shambles.

She heard Alex whistle, the signal they all knew.

Nothing.
He whistled again.

Nothing.
Someone still approached them, she lifted the revolver, held it out in front of her. Alex leant in towards Sabine, whispered.

'One more chance then I shoot and we make a break for it.'

Sabine nodded then whispered '*Oui*' in reply, forgetting that he couldn't see her in the dark.

He whistled.

Sabine lowered her revolver. Someone had whistled back, given the coded reply.

She felt her legs give way beneath her, warm and aching.

'Sorry, *c'est moi*, Sebastian.'

'I almost shot you! One more second and I would have.'

'*Je suis désolé*, put the gun down. It's more likely to go off in your face than hit the target.'

'Where have you been? You're late. Where's Natalie?'

'Calm down, she's not coming.'

'What's going on, Sebastian?'

'I went to get her, we had an argument, that's all.'

'A lover's tiff,' Sabine heard one of the men whisper.

'It's not a laughing matter,' said Alex. 'Are we in danger? Sebastian, I'm talking to you, *sommes-nous en danger?*'

'*Non, non*, of course not.'

'*Amour de jeunesse*,' someone said.

'Not satisfying her needs, are we Sebastian? Tell her to come and see me, she needs a man, *pas un petit garçon*.'

'*Fermes-la*,' Sebastian replied.

'Enough,' hissed Alex. 'Do you want to draw attention to us? It's nearly time and we're one man down. Positions. Now!'

'*Une femme*.'

'Not now, Sabine.'

She hadn't felt so brave earlier. God, when she'd heard Monsieur Simon whistling that tune.

La Madelon

Her finger stopped tapping instantly. Even though her hands shook, she took off her headphones, packed the wireless away into the suitcase and hid it behind one of the wicker crates of cheese that had been left to ripen.

Her suitcase would stink of cheese now.

Monsieur Simon let her out the back door and she cycled through the woods back to Madame's, had a fit of nervous giggling on the way. Laughed so much, she hit a tree stump, fell off her bike. Then she lay on the ground laughing even more.

All that manoeuvre training: how to traverse a room without touching the floor, how to cross a pool of sulphuric acid. She couldn't even navigate her bicycle around a tree stump.

God, I'm hysterical, she thought. My first close encounter and I've had a nervous breakdown. Her stomach ached by the time she managed to compose herself and get back on her bicycle.

Madame Poirier met her at the gate, pulled leaves and twigs from her hair and cardigan.

'*Have you been rolling in the hay with Alex?*'

That set Sabine off again.

PM FC DO OA PF MU BJ BD JU PM FD BT AR UA FG

'If only you knew, Madame, if only you knew.'

Just thinking about it now, back in the safety of Madame's house, Sabine felt like she was about to lose control again. She bit the inside of her mouth, nipped her thigh under the table. Alex would send her straight back if he knew how she'd behaved.

Sabine took her place in the field. The stars were so clear out here. All around her, sinking down on either side, as if she was locked inside a snow globe.

- .... . / -.- .. .. / -... ..- .-. -. - / .- --. .- .. -. ... - / .... . .-. / -.-. --- .-.. -..
/ ... -.- .. -.

She'd never seen so many stars before, it made her dizzy and she had to look down at her feet.

She could hear the Lysander approaching, then she heard Alex's whistle.

She switched on her bicycle lamp, saw the others lighting torches around her, remembered her training. The model of a field, split up into grids with pins and string.

```
*
*
*
*
*
*
*
*       *       *       *
```

Drop here!

Sabine held the light steady, looked up as the plane came closer, closer. Saw it drop the containers, parachutes open, as they fell to earth.

The lights in the field began to sway, dissipate, as people moved towards the falling packages.

She counted the parachutes, shining in the night sky. They whistled as they fell.

Un, deux, trois, quatre, cinq, six, sept, huit, neuf.

There was a crash to the right of her.

'*Merde*,' she heard someone say, 'that one's ruined, damn parachute.'

The Lysander continued overheard, back home to Britain. Sabine listened to the hum of the engines diminish. She blew it a kiss.

- .... . / -.- .. .. / -... ..- .-. -. - / .- --. .- .. -. ... - / .... . .-. / -.-. --- .-.. -..
/ ... -.- .. -.

It made her homesick to think of it leaving her behind.

She missed Mama, Father.

Cath.

Were they being sent the carefully timed letters, written months in advance?

Did they believe what she'd written?

Hello from London, not much has changed in the last week or so. Still driving the top brass around.

Coffee dripped from the spout of the pot, staining the white tablecloth.

'I'm sorry it tastes so bad,' said Madame Poirier, 'it was the best I could do. I've had to use that ground coffee five times now, it's more like coloured water.'

'Maybe Merle could make a request in her next sked. Send more coffee vite vite,*' said Sebastian.*

B	L	A	C	K
I	R	D	E	F
G	H	J	M	N
O	P	S	T	U
V	W	X	Y	Z

TD JF GT DF BT DZ IF IY EO IY EO DY

'They have less coffee than we do, besides it's tea I miss,' said Sabine.

'Tea! You have been living in Britain too long, mademoiselle.'

Sabine smiled, sipped at her coffee, tried not to let it show on her face just how rotten it tasted. She would have preferred plain old hot water to this brown concoction, but Madame Poirier did her best with the rations she had.

'Right, lights off, containers on the transport, get rid of the parachutes.'

There was something in Alex's voice. Something that told her not to waste time. She felt it herself – tonight didn't feel right.

Madame Poirier had asked Sabine to bring her home the parachutes before they were spirited away to be sold, or made into shirts for the résistants. Sabine would have to disappoint her.

Keep your wits about you and learn to trust your gut. Usually the first hunch you have about a situation will be the right one. If something, no matter how trivial, feels wrong then it probably means that you're in danger.

She flicked off the light, put it in her pocket, ran over to the container closest to her. She took one end of the vertical cylinder while Sebastian took the other.

'Do you think Alex is mad at me?' Sebastian asked as he walked backwards towards the transport.

'Should he be?' She tried to catch the look on his face but it was too dark. She stumbled, lost her grip on the container.

'Careful,' said Sebastian.

'You need to be careful too.'

'What's that supposed to mean?'

'We need to get the field cleared.'

'Sabine.'

Alex stood behind them.

'Less talk, more work.'

They dumped the container and she ran back into the field to help with another.

Madame opened a tin of peaches, tipped them into a bowl then siphoned the syrupy juice off into a glass. She handed the glass to Sabine.

'Non, you have it Madame.'

'I'll have it,' said Sebastian, holding out his hand.

'Sabine is recovering from a terrible illness,' Madame winked. 'Besides, you boys have her running all over France on your errands.'

Sabine pushed her coffee away, put the glass of juice to her lips. It was warm and sticky, sweet against her tongue. She finished it in two gulps, then wished she'd savoured it in smaller sips, made it last longer.

'I've sent Sebastian with the containers, changed the plan though, told him to go to Monsieur Thorozan's barn,' Alex took Sabine to one side.

'*D'accord*, because of Natalie?'

'*Oui*, I'm going to see her – something doesn't add up.'

'I agree.'

'I'm worried about her motives.'

'He's a good looking boy…'

'Yes, but she's an even better looking girl.'

- .... . / -.- .. .. / -... .. -. -. -. - / .- --. .- .. -. -. ... - / .... . .-. / -.-. --- .-.. -.. / ... -.- .. -.

'You don't think she would betray us though?'

'That's what I'm going to find out.'

'I'll come with you.'

'I need you safe, just in case something is wrong. No point both of us getting caught.'

'Then I'll go, she might be more likely to speak to me, and, well… if you get caught… they know you. I can bluff my way out.'

'*Non*, I'm going, I won't argue about this.'

Alex sat in the corner of the room in an armchair, staring at a small radio balanced on his knee.

Sabine could hear the faint broadcast he listened to through the crackled reception.

ICI LONDRES

'*Ssshh*, fermez-la.' *Alex held up a hand and the room went quiet.*

ET VOICI QUELQUES MESSAGES PERSONNELS.
TP TM TP EP UI BT EF DO OS SP TD

This was the moment of truth. Had her skeds been heard by London? Had she made sense?

Sabine lit her bicycle lamp briefly, got her bearings and began the walk back to Madame's. Alex was right to send the containers to a different hiding place. Natalie knew too much about tonight. He was right about Sebastian too. He was young and romantic. Reckless.

It didn't matter if they were betrayed on purpose or by an accidental slip of the tongue. The outcome would still be the same.

Sabine pushed her way through a hedge, scratched her hand on some brambles. She was quicker following the road home, but she wanted to be out of sight. It was safer to trample along the verge. Her shoes and the hem of her skirt were covered in mud – if she was caught she'd have to come up with something good to explain the state of her clothes. Her back ached and she had blisters on the heels of her feet.

Natalie.

Was she really a traitor? That sweet girl who smelt of vanilla and whispered in Sabine's ear as she sat outside the café?

A shiver ran down Sabine's back as she remembered the way Natalie's breath had tickled her ear, her hair brushing against her face.

- .… . / -.-.. .. … … / -.… ..- .-. -. - / .- --. .- .. -. .… - / .… . .-. / -.-. --- .-.. -.. / … -.- .. -.

Une querelle d'amoureux.

That day at the café, had she missed anything?

The German soldiers sitting on the opposite side of the square, talking about Natalie. What had they said? If only Sabine's German was better, she might have picked something up.

Should she have told Alex there were German soldiers sniffing around?

Non.

Knowing Alex, he'd have suggested Natalie seduce them for secrets then kill them while they slept.

Maybe one of them got fed up looking, wanted more? Flattered her into bed? The German soldiers could offer many things that the men left in France couldn't.

A young girl, surrounded by old men, young boys, injured *résistants*. Perhaps the attentions of a man in uniform was too much to resist?

Did it mean she would talk?

Perhaps.

If she fell in love.

PM FC DO OA PF MU BJ BD JU PM FD BT AR UA FG

ANNIE LE BLANC, THE CANDLE IS LIT.

Sabine felt something tickle her ankles, looked under the table to see Pacha licking her leg.

'Come on,' she whispered under the table and patted her lap, 'up, lèves-toi.'

THE BIRTHDAY CAKE WAS STALE.

Pacha stretched, pulled back on his front paws, then sprung up into Sabine's lap. He settled himself there, purred while Sabine stroked his head and scratched him behind the ears.

THE COW HAS ESCAPED FROM THE NORTH FIELD.

Pacha was warm, she could feel him breathing, his heart beating against the inside of her thigh.

RACHEL TREMBLAY, THE BICYCLE IS CHAINED TO THE GATE.

Sabine stopped petting Pacha, he leapt from her lap and slunk away under the table.

Sabine stumbled over tufts of overgrown grass at the side of the road. Eyes glowed up ahead, then vanished as the rabbits bolted into hiding.

The drop had gone to plan. No ambush. It would have been a perfect opportunity to get them all together.

Unless of course.

They were waiting to get them on their own.

Oh God, she hoped Alex was wrong.

In a group a fight would break out, people would scatter, escape.

If they were targeted individually...

What if they were at home now, waiting for her, tired, unaware, on her own?

Do not return to your quarters if you believe you are in danger.

But she had to.

Madame Poirier.

Sabine began to run.

```
Drop report from P/O Douglas Carter —
Sand Dune 9
43.675818 2.252197
11 containers successfully dropped.
Encountered flak leaving France.
Returned at 04.32
```

Sabine felt the panic rise. She slipped and stumbled as she ran, falling onto her knees at one point. She shouldn't return to Madame's, should stay away, but she couldn't leave Madame in danger.

She hunkered down behind the garden wall. The shutters were closed, the house in darkness.

She jumped the wall, revolver ready, crept round the edge of the courtyard, keeping low, in the shadows.

Round to her bedroom window. She always left it unlatched behind the shutters, able to get in or out quickly if required.

Think ahead. Have an escape route planned, just in case you need to make a quick getaway.

She pushed the window open, hoisted herself up and into her bedroom.

She could hear music, the clack, clack, clack of Madame's sewing machine.

What was she still doing up?

Was it a warning? Letting Sabine know something was wrong, to stay away?

She knelt, peered through the keyhole, she could see Madame sitting at the big kitchen table, but couldn't tell if she was alone.

She turned the door handle, slowly, slowly, slowly, gripped the revolver in her other hand.

RACHEL TREMBLAY, THE BICYCLE IS CHAINED TO THE GATE.

'That's it, that's our signal,' Sebastian patted Sabine on the shoulder. *'Well done,* Merle.*'*

'They've agreed to the drop,' said Alex, *'we must get ready.'*

'You can't go anywhere, Alex,' said Madame Poirier. *'You are a wanted man.'*

'I am leader of this circuit and therefore in charge,' he replied and turned off the radio.

Sabine gulped down the cold dregs of coffee as Alex began to give out instructions.

'Sainte Mère de Dieu,' Madame screamed and ducked under the table, as Sabine flung the door open, pointed the revolver.

The room was empty.

Nobody else was there, nobody keeping Madame hostage.

Sabine collapsed onto her knees, dropped the revolver. She crawled forward and lifted the table cloth. Madame was curled up on the floor, holding onto a squirming Pacha.

'Madame, I'm, I'm so sorry.' Sabine was out of breath, she laid a hand on Madame's shoulder.

'What happened? What's wrong?' Madame replied. She let go of Pacha, who hissed, ran towards the front door, scraped at the wood to get out.

Sabine stood, followed him. She opened the front door, glanced around the courtyard as she let him out. It was empty. A dog barked somewhere in the distance. She shut the door, locked it.

'What is it Sabine? You're so white, *assieds-toi*, sit down,' Madame crawled out from under the table.

'Natalie didn't show, she and Sebastian had a fight, Alex was worried, he went to see her after the drop.'

'Alex is too suspicious. She's just a girl.'

'I know, but something about it didn't feel right to me either.'

'But the drop went okay?'

'*Oui, oui*, Sebastian took all the containers away.'

'You gave me such a fright,' Madame's hands trembled and Sabine squeezed them between her own.

'I'm sorry, I was worried someone was in here, I came in the window.'

'*Mon Dieu*, your hands are freezing.'

'I feel a bit sick.'

'You're some girl. What would you have done if there were a dozen soldiers in here?'

Sabine laid her head on the table, the room was spinning.

'Why aren't you in bed?' asked Sabine.

'I couldn't sleep, maybe I could sense there was something wrong too. I wanted to make sure you got home safe. I made coffee.'

Madame stood, lifted the pot from the stove.

'Something medicinal,' she said, and added brandy.

Sabine grimaced at the taste, but was revived as the warm liquid spread through her.

'Now that there's some colour in your cheeks, where are my parachutes?'

'*Je suis désolée*, sorry, Madame.'

'Sshhh, I'm only teasing you.'

Sabine took another drink of coffee, tuned into the music playing. She recognised it, George used to play that piece on the piano. It annoyed her that she couldn't remember the name, her brain was so mixed up at the moment she couldn't concentrate on anything.

'I will go to bed now though,' Madame finished her coffee and stood up.

'Goodnight, Madame. I'm sorry for scaring you.'

'Stop apologising. You came here to save me, I'm proud of you. You should get some sleep too, it's been a long night.'

'I know, I'll stay up just a bit longer, in case Alex shows.'

'I hope he remembers she's just a girl.'

Sabine nodded. Madame lifted the pistol from the floor, handed it to Sabine before disappearing into her own room.

Sabine dragged her chair over to the window, opened the shutters slightly. She sat with the gun in her lap as she finished her coffee.

Hannah Hopes Things Will Turn Out All Wright

British swimmer Hannah Wright has withdrawn from all future competitive action in a bid to recover from an on-going shoulder injury. Hannah, British record holder for the 50m and 100m Butterfly, has been suffering from the injury for the last eight months and has temporarily lost funding while she recuperates.

'It's been a really tough year for me, especially having to miss the Olympics and then being told that my funding is being cut,' said Hannah. 'I'm seeing the physio though and doing some light training to keep me ticking over. I just need to be patient.'

19

Chapter Fifteen: Marièle Downie, aka Sabine Valois, aka Blackbird.
  I sit on the edge of the bed.
  Chapter Fifteen: Marièle Downie, aka Sabine Valois, aka Blackbird.
  She's here, in a book. My old woman is in a book. I flick through the pages, inhale the crisp ink, the newness of it. No creased pages, no thumbprints, no crumbs.
  I hope you enjoy it.
  I don't think she's even opened this book, let alone read it.
  I suppose it makes sense; why read about yourself? You lived it. It's all in your head.
  Even the bad things, the things you don't want to remember.
  All those scrapbooks Dad kept about me, newspaper cuttings, photos. Shoved in a box somewhere. Sellotape cracked and brown, articles once stuck in place now falling out. A record of all my achievements. It's not as if I want to read any of them.
  I turn to the middle of the book, shiny black and white photographs. Try to find Marièle without reading the captions. Can I recognise her among all these other women?
  I flick through them, don't see her, go back to the start again. Look more carefully.
  I think that might be her.
  Yeah, I'm sure it is.
  She's looking straight at the camera, unsmiling, like a bad passport photograph or a mug shot.
  I read the caption to make sure.
  Marièle Downie, shortly before leaving for France, January 1944.
So different from the girl up on the shelf, the woman in the hospital bed. Another Marièle to add to the list. How many are there?
  I rub my finger across her face. The then and now of her tugs at my stomach.

Chapter Fifteen
Marièle Downie, aka Sabine Valois, aka Blackbird

I was lucky enough to interview Marièle in person while writing this book, one of the few not taken from us by the war or by the passing of time. I had trouble tracing her at first, believing her to be resident in France, however I eventually tracked her down to an address in Scotland.

One of the youngest to be sent to France, Marièle had not lost any of her reported 'dry sense of humour' when I met her, now aged 84. Although reluctant to talk about her experiences in detail, Marièle answered my questions candidly and spoke of her fellow agents with loyalty and affection.

She was born in 1922 to a French mother and a Scottish father. Like most of the women who went on to become agents for the SOE, Marièle was fluent in French and spent a great deal of her childhood holidaying in France while visiting relatives. She was asked to a preliminary interview in London, after answering an advert for photographs of the French coastline.

'I had no idea what I was being interviewed for – it was all very vague. They asked me questions about myself, my family, my politics. I was more confused when I came out than I was before I went in.'

Marièle was deemed to have the qualities suitable for a potential SOE agent, and, following the requisite psychiatrist's interview, she enlisted with the FANY.

She was sent to Scotland for training, sharing a room with fellow recruit Eliza Buchanan (see chapter eleven).

Eliza?

I turn back to the photographs in the middle of the book.

Marièle and Eliza are on adjoining pages.

Wavy hair piled up above her forehead, a brooch at her neck, round cheeks.

It's not her. Not the girl with the dimples.

Marièle was a good student. Existing records state: 'She possesses a dry sense of humour and gets on well with the other recruits.' She did well in training and discovered a natural aptitude for parachuting, outshining the other recruits – both men and women!

'I just turned out to be good at it, it came very naturally. I have no idea why, I'd never done anything like that in my whole life. Maybe I just didn't care about what could go wrong, I relaxed, the feeling of falling was soothing to me. I jumped from the plane without dwelling on the what-ifs.'

'Wow, pretty impressive,' I look up at the photograph on the shelf.

Marièle earned herself the nickname Merle, French for black-bird. This nickname was later used as an alias for her when she was sent to France and as the keyword in her Playfair cipher.

'It wasn't long after I finished training that I was sent to France. It was towards the end of the war, an important time, what with the run up to D-Day.'

The Sand Dune circuit, led by Alex Sylvan, was in need of a wireless operator and Marièle was chosen to fill this position.

'Sand Dune was in need of a lot of things. I was officially sent as a W/T operator, which meant that I would send messages back to London. But I did anything else required really: courier, messenger, saboteur. I was a jack of all trades.'

Going by the name Sabine Valois, Marièle was sent to France under the guise of a sickly girl from Paris, who had been sent to stay with her aunt in the country to recuperate.

Despite Marièle's obvious skill at parachuting, she travelled to France aboard the Polish manned felucca, 'Seafox.'

'It was a bitter blow to me that I was not parachuted into France. It sounds so silly, but it had been the one part of the training that I'd excelled at. It felt like a bad omen being sent in by boat. I couldn't swim, for one thing.'

'One up on you there then, Marièle.'

I can't imagine not being able to swim, don't even remember learning. It's always just felt like I was born swimming.

'I still don't know why they sent me that way. Nobody ever explained it or gave me a valid reason. You didn't ask questions of course, just followed orders. Everything was classified, you were told what you needed to know. There was a lot I was never told about Sand Dune. It was in a bit of a mess when I got there, but I suppose it was important enough to keep going rather than shut down.'

Marièle soon became an integral part of the circuit, spending long days on her bicycle, sending messages back to the UK, helping to organise drops, liaising with other members of the network and running errands as and when required.

'I was so fit back in those days – could have given that Chris Hoy a run for his money, I can tell you. Those first few days were awful though, I was so saddle sore. Everything ached, when I…'

Brrrr Brrrr

Brrrr Brrrr

The phone goes, gives me a fright. I jump and the book slips out of my lap.

I pick it up, head out into the hallway. Stand and watch the phone as it rings. Should I answer? Maybe it's the hospital? I gave them this number the last time I visited Marièle.

Brrrr Brrrr

Brrrr Brrrr

I trace my finger around a logo on one of Marièle's letters. A candle with barbed wire wound round it. My finger sweeps the curves of the wire, up and down, up and down, up and down, a backwards S.

Brrrr Brrrr

Brrrr Brrrr

Brrrr Brrrr

Brrrr Brrrr

Whoever it is, they're insistent. My hand leaves the mail, hovers over the receiver. If it's the hospital I should answer.

But if it's not…

Then I hang up and get the hell out of here.

Brrrr Brrrr

Brrrr Brrrr

(if it is the hospital, it won't be good news)

I'll give it four more rings. Four more then I answer.

Brrrr Brrrr

Brrrr Brrrr

Brrrr Brrrr

Brrrr Brrrr

Brrrr Br…

'Hello?'

There's silence on the other end.

'Hello?'

The line clicks and an automated message starts, the woman's voice slow and robotic.

'Hello, how many times have you…'

I slam the receiver down, angry and relived all at the same time. Making me get up, interrupting my reading,

(scaring me like that)

Thank fuck it wasn't the hospital.

Thank fuck it wasn't the hospital.

I take the book into the living room, it's chilly in here. I grab a fleecy blanket tucked into one of the armchairs, lie on the sofa with it draped over me.

Where was I?

'Those first few days were awful though, I was so saddle sore. Everything ached, when I got off the bicycle at the end of the day, oh it was bliss.'

Marièle hadn't been in France long before disaster struck the Sand Dune circuit, following a routine arms drop.

One of her fellow résistants, Sebastian Tholozan, arrived late. It transpired that he'd had an argument with Natalie Charron, a local waitress who was involved with the circuit.

'Sebastian wouldn't tell us what the fight was about. We knew they were having a relationship, and we hoped it was just a lover's tiff. Alex and I were concerned, but it was too late to cancel the drop.'

Unfortunately, unknown to Marièle and the rest of the network, Natalie had become involved with a German officer and had let slip about the drop.

Shit, what happened?
To Marièle?
She must have got away. I'm in her house now, I know she survived. I'm glad I know she survived. It makes it easier to keep reading.

'I don't hold any animosity for her. She was young and she fell in love. She thought he would marry her once the war was over. And she was punished, they called it a collaboration horizontale. *They shaved her head, made her parade through the village. Not the Germans, you know? The French did that...'*

There's a click, then light floods the corner where I'm sitting.
The standard lamp behind the sofa has switched itself on.
Switched itself on.
I grip the book, can feel my heart banging inside me
Thumpthumpthumpthumpthumpthumpthumpthumpthumpthump thumpthumpthump.
I lean over the back of the sofa, see the timer switch, hear it click, click, click, click as the dial works its way round.
It's just a timer, just a timer, just a timer.

(not a ghost)

I mark my place with the compliment slip. I can't concentrate now. I'm too on edge. Besides, something bad's about to happen to her, the book is working up to it, I can tell. If I read on I make it happen and I don't want to make something bad happen to her.

Not after all she's been through.

I push the blanket and the book to one side. I'll get a drink, something to eat. Come back to it after that.

My mobile's lying on the kitchen table. I bring up the internet, put Marièle's name into Google. Maybe she's really famous?

As I'm waiting for the page to load, my phone buzzes with a text.

`I'm sorry about what happened I need 2 CU`

'Fuck sake, not again. Will you leave me alone,' I switch my phone off, dump it back down on the table.

'Did you know all that stuff about Marièle?' I say to the fish.

He sits on the bottom of his bowl, tail swaying from side to side. I automatically open the fridge then remember there's no milk, make myself a black coffee, help myself to a couple of Digestives from her biscuit tin.

'Not the most nutritious meal, I know, but we don't all have flakes to keep us going.'

I switch the TV on when I go back through, turn the volume down low. It's getting dark outside and it feels a bit weird being in her house this late. The background noise makes me feel better, covers the unfamiliar creaks and strains from the walls and furniture.

The book lies next to me as I drink my coffee, dunk the Digestive biscuits. It feels wrong to read and eat at the same time. Disrespectful. I want to give her my full attention, not drop bits of soggy biscuit onto those crisp pages and treat her story like some cheap entertainment.

Her life.

I watch the images flicker across the TV screen, not really taking them in. The book lies in my lap.

I finish my coffee, toy with the idea of making another. I can't bring myself to start reading again. It's more than just making bad stuff happen to her, I feel like I'm spying on her, snooping. Which is stupid, considering I've already broken into her house. Anyway it's a book, a real book. I could get it in the library if I wanted to. It's not like I'm reading her diary.

But she's lying in the hospital and I'm skimming through her life like it's a gossip magazine. Something's not right about that.

I'm curious though, and the curiosity trumps the guilt.

I lie back, pull the blanket over my legs again. Open the book where I left off.

> '*I don't hold any animosity for her, she was young and she fell in love. She thought he would marry her once the war was over. And she was punished, they called it a* collaboration horizontale. *They shaved her head, made her parade through the village. Not the Germans, you know? The French did that to her.*'

20

Je m'appelle Sabine Valois.
Je m'appelle Sabine Valois.
She kept muddling up her cover story, getting it mixed up with other thoughts. Thoughts which pushed their way to the front, forced her alias into the background.
Je m'appelle Sabine Valois.
Where were they taking her?
*Je suis Sabi*Would they hurt her?
J'ai vingt-et-un ans.
Je suisThey'd caught her, they'd caught her, they'd caught her.
J'ai été malade.
What did they tell her in training about getting caught? Concentrate, Sabine, concentrate, get your story straight.
*Je suis Sabine Val*This is happening, this is really happening. Oh God, what would they do with her?
The part of her training she didn't want to put into action.
Wake up, wach auf, wach auf.
What had they told her? How was she to behave? What if she'd missed one vital piece of information, the piece of information that might keep her alive?
Don't let your guard down, they won't always resort to violence. Sometimes they will be gentle and persuasive.
Je m'appelle Sabine Valois Je m'appelle Sabine Valois Je m'appelle Sabine Valois Je m'appelle Sabine Valois Je m'appelle Sabine Valois Je m'appelle Sabine Valois Je m'appelle Sabine Valois
She just had to stick to her story. It would keep her safe. They'd planned it out for her, gone into great detail, made it watertight.
She had to trust it. Trust those who had created it for her.
It was designed to keep her alive.
Wasn't it? Or was it just designed to keep their secrets safe? Maybe her death was a regrettable consequence of war. To win there had to be casualties along the way.
George.
No, if she thought like that she had no chance of surviving this.
It was all very easy telling her not to speak, to stick to the story, but they weren't here now, handcuffed in the back of a Gestapo car. Where were they taking her anyway? Paris?
Je m'appelle Sabine Valois.

J'ai vingt-et-un ans.

J'ai été malade.

Try to stay strong, at least for the first twenty-four hours. This will give the other members of your network time to escape.

D'accord.

She would try and hold on for at least twenty-four hours.

Twenty-four hours.

She wouldn't allow herself to think any further ahead than that.

Just survive for one day, then we'll take a rain check. See where we are. How Sabine is holding up. Maybe Marièle will make an appearance after that.

MarieNoNoNoNoNoNo

Don't even think of that name.

Je m'appelle Sabine Valois.

Sabine Valois.

Sabine Sabine Sabine Sabine Sabine Sabine Sabine Sabine Sabine Sabine Sabine Sabine Sabine Sabine Sabine Sabine Sabine Sabine Sabine Sabine

... .⁻ ⁻... .. ⁻. .
... .⁻ ⁻... .. ⁻. .
... .⁻ ⁻... .. ⁻. .
... .⁻ ⁻... .. ⁻. .

Try to stay strong, at least for the first twenty-four hours. This will give the other members of your network time to escape.

What others? Who was left? Alive or dead.

Maybe the game was already up?

Had someone betrayed her? She had lived alongside them, thought they were her friends, but could she really trust a friendship based on lies?

No matter how tempted you may be, no matter how close you get, don't give anything away about your real life.

All that time she'd spent with Alex, Sebastian, Madame. They didn't even know her real name.

She was good, she hadn't let them in. She stuck to the rules. Even with Madame, she never let her guard down.

Madame.

Oh God, her face. Her face as she came out, as they shot her, as she lay there on the floor. Oh God, when Sabine closed her eyes she saw Madame's face.

And Sabine could have saved her. If she'd said run, told her to run. So what if it was a false alarm – at least she'd be alive. Instead of that face. That face on the floor.

And Alex. Alex lying...

Oh God, she couldn't think of them, if she did, she'd crack. She had to force the images away.

Je m'appelle Sabine Valois. Je m'appelle Sabine Valois. Je m'appelle Sabine Valois. Je m'appelle Sabine Valois. Je m'appelle Sabine Valois. Je m'appelle Sabine Valois. Je m'appelle Sabine Valois.

.. / .- -- / .... .- -... .. -. . / ...- .- .-.. --- .. ...

.. / .- -- / .... .- -... .. -. . . / ...- .- .-.. --- .. ...

It was no use though. They flickered in and out, stamping themselves on her thoughts, blocking out everything else.

Madame.

Alex.

Madame.

Alex.

Madame.   Alex.   Madame.   Alex.   Madame.   Alex.   Madame.
alexmadamealexmadamealexmadamealexmadamealexmadam

God, they were so vivid, like a scene from the pictures, she couldn't make them go away.

Madamemadamemadamemadamemadamemadamemadamemadame

She could have saved her.

Sabine's head rocked to one side, her forehead hit the car window. She slumped forward. The soldier, the one sitting next to her, he'd hit her, slapped her across the face.

She hadn't seen it coming, unaware until it had happened. She was at their mercy, but she relished the pain, the throbbing. It took her mind off Madame and Alex, brought her back to the present, the now.

'Try to control yourself,' the soldier said.

Tears prickled behind her eyes, she could feel her throat swell. She didn't want him to see her cry. She hung her head, looked down at her feet. She wouldn't give him the satisfaction. She could feel a pulse beating in her eyelid, twitching her eyelashes, sticky with dried blood. The pain spread out and she became aware of everywhere she ached. Her shoulders, arms, wrists, back. She stretched out her fingers, tried to circle her hands, loosen them off inside the handcuffs.

She breathed in and out through her nose.

In. Out. In. Out.

Calm, calm, calm.

Je m'appelle Sabine Valois.
Je m'appelle Sabine Valois.
Je m'appelle Sabine Valois.

Paris.

She hadn't been there since she was a little girl.

Mariel...

Non! Sabine. Sabine was from Paris.

.. / .- -- / .... .- -... .. -. . / ...- .- .-.. --- .. ...

She still recognised it.

Recognised it despite the changes. The twinkling café lights and tall apartment blocks, the intricate black ironwork of the balconies, the Eiffel Tower. They were all in shadow now, lights out.

The white brick buildings glimmered out from the darkness, in defiance: we are Paris, you cannot hide us.

Sandbags towered up, makeshift walls surrounding the buildings deemed to be important, the monuments. She turned her head so she could see out the window; despite the darkness she could make out shapes. Some of the buildings were in rubble. The allies, the side she was fighting on, bombing Paris.

Flags hung from windows, the black, red and yellow of the German flag. The Swastika. Yes, even in the blackout, she could make out the Swastika.

The men around her shifted, she felt their anticipation. They knew they were almost home before the car began to slow. They held the power.

The car stopped and the men got out, doors slammed around her and for a moment she was alone. She breathed in, then out, embraced the split second of calm before the door on her side was pulled open.

'*Raus!*' The man who had hit her dragged her out by the elbow. She stumbled out of the car, fell onto the pavement.

'*Komm mit, schnell.* Quickly!'

'*Je ne peux pas me lever*,' she replied, unable to push herself up without the use of her arms.

'*Steh auf!*'

She lay there, her face against the cold concrete until one of them grabbed her under the armpits, lifted her onto her feet. She felt a gun prod into her back.

She climbed the steps leading into the building. Another swastika flag draped over the doorway. She stopped at the entrance, looked up at the sky.

Stars. She could see the stars. So the blackout had its advantages. She could see the stars over Paris.

If she was going to die inside these walls, then she chose this memory as her last.

The stars over Paris.

The gun prodded her in the back, pushed her inside the doorway.

21 October 1945
    Miss Downie acted with extreme courage and
bravery under very traumatic circumstances.
She did not reveal any secrets and continu-
ously referred to her alias Sabine Valois and
the cover story created for her.

Sabine lay on the floor of the cell, a bowl of soup and a piece of bread next to her. Someone must have left them there while she'd been unconscious.

She couldn't eat.

She couldn't eat.

She was hungry but she couldn't.

Just the thought of eating made her queasy. She tried to lie as still as possible. If she moved the cramps in her stomach increased, travelling up and down her body in waves. She hadn't had a proper meal since the night of the drop. How long ago was that now? She'd lost track of time.

Her fingers throbbed, dry blood crusty on her hands. There was blood on the floor too, it had dripped from her fingers, stained the concrete. She couldn't pick up the bread or the soup; her hands didn't work anymore.

She kept her eyes closed most of the time, had done since they'd dragged her in here, dropped her onto the floor.

How long ago was that?

She'd curled up in a ball in the corner, no blanket to keep her warm, wearing the same clothes she'd had on when they picked her up. She drifted in and out of consciousness. It wasn't sleep, it didn't feel like sleep. She didn't dream. No Morse code, dot dot dashing in her head the way it had before.

- .- .--. / - .- .--. / - .- .--. / - .- .--. / - .- .--.

She tried to focus on the Morse alphabet. Run through it in her head.

.-

-...

-.-.

What was D again?

She had to get her brain working. They could break her body but she wanted to keep her brain.

-.-.

-.．
．

The monotonous running through the alphabet fixed her mind on something that wasn't pain, hunger, cold, sickness. Occasionally the repetition would send her off into one of those black-out periods, like counting sheep.

..-．

--．

Those blessed moments of release. Until she came round, automatically opened her eyes. Remembered where she was and shut them again.

.-

-...

-.-．

Someone had been in there with her for a while. At least she thought they had.

She was sure someone had spoken to her, gentle words, pulled her hair back, laid a cool hand on her clammy forehead. She wanted Mama, she'd kept her eyes closed hoping it was Mama.

Do not trust anyone if you are arrested by the Germans. It could be a stool pigeon.

Words were carved on the wall, just in front of where she lay. Someone else had crawled into this corner. The words flashed, a closed-eye hallucination.

Vive la France
Vive la France
Vive la France
Vive la France
Vive
Vive
Vive

BG YI AC ID KJ EM
BG YI AC ID KJ EM

Who had written it ? Another prisoner, like her? Were they alive or dead? They must have had the use of their hands. She couldn't pick up a piece of bread, let alone carve defiance into the crumbling plaster.

She opened one eye, felt her stomach clench, closed it again.

Vive, vive, vive, vive, vive, vive.

BG YI BG YI BG YI BG YI BG YI BG YI BG YI

The word flashed on the back of her eyelids like those other images that wouldn't go away. That haunted her.

Madame.

Alex.

Madame.

Alex.

JC JD TM CA DY JC JD TM CA DY JC JD TM CA DY
JC JD TM CA DY JC JD TM CA DY JC JD TM CA DY

Her stomach lurched and she swallowed the sickness back down, felt it burn the back of her throat.

.‑

‑...

‑.‑.

‑..

She couldn't move. It was worse if she moved. She would be fine if they just left her here, a ball on the floor.

She dreaded the sound of footsteps approaching. The clip, clip, clip, clip of those leather boots. Please, just leave me alone. Just leave me here alone. Here alone. Leave me here. Alone. Alone.

She woke later, hours, days, minutes, she didn't know. Her fingers still beat with pain, her nails were still gone. Maybe she could gauge time by her fingers? Measure it by the length of her fingernails.

What if they never grew back? When they tidied the garden, Father always told her to make sure she got the weeds out by the roots.

So they would never grow back.

Had they pulled the roots out?

The pain had to stop sometime, she could measure time by how bad the pain was.

'*Steh auf.*'

She opened her eyes, looked up, didn't move.

'Stand up! *Steh auf*!'

The soldier bent over, pulled her to her feet. She swayed from side to side, leant back against the wall to steady herself.

She noticed the German wipe his hands on his tunic after touching her. Was she that distasteful?

She looked down, felt the floor slope away, then rush towards her. Her clothes were creased and stained. She couldn't remember using the bucket recently. She must have wet herself at some point. She had a vague recollection of the shame, of the warmth spreading over her thighs. Had she imagined it?

Making the horror worse than it actually was.

The man in front of her was smart, well-presented. Pressed uniform, polished boots, slicked hair, shiny buttons and belt buckle.

MEINE EHRE HEIßT TREUE
My honour is loyalty
How to recognise the different ranks of German soldier.
Gefreiter
Leutnant
Oberleutnant
Hauptmann
SS *Hauptsturmführer*
SS *Obersturmführer*
'You are leaving us,' he said as he led her out of the cell and along a corridor. She floated alongside him.

He was new. Hadn't been there before, when they'd...

Young. Maybe he was newly promoted? Learning the ropes.

Well done, here's your lightning flashes and your pliers.

January 2009

Hannah Dives Under The Knife

British swimmer Hannah Wright is to go under the knife in a bid to save her sinking swimming career. Hannah has floundered recently due to a recurrent shoulder injury and, despite undergoing intensive physiotherapy, hasn't seen any improvement.

'The operation was always a last resort, but unfortunately the injury has turned out to be worse than we first thought,' said Hannah. 'I'm hopeful that this will sort things out though and I'll be back in the pool in no time.'

21

'I don't hold any animosity for her, she was young and she fell in love. She thought he would marry her once the war was over. And she was punished, they called it a collaboration horizontale. They shaved her head, made her parade through the village. Not the Germans, you know? The French did that to her.'

I tuck the blanket round my feet. How many times has she done the same? Snuggled up under this blanket while she read a book or watched TV. The old woman who sat on this sofa, the girl I'm reading about.

The Germans waited until the drop was over and the members of Sand Dune had returned to their respective homes before they made their move. Most of the circuit were in bed, giving the Germans the element of surprise and terror that they used so often to their advantage.

'I knew something was wrong that night, I could feel it. I ran all the way home. But when I got there, Madame was okay, everything was as it should be. I let my guard down, I went to bed. There's not a day goes by when I don't curse myself for falling asleep.'

After helping with the drop, Marièle returned to the house she lodged at with Madame Poirier. Alex went to confront Natalie.

'I told him to be careful. That was the last time I ever saw Alex. I never found out what happened when he went to see Natalie. He must have discovered we were to be rounded up. He tried to warn me. He might have escaped if he hadn't come to warn me.'

Marièle was in bed when they arrived at the house she shared with Madame Poirier.

I put the book down, try to slow my heart rate, my breathing, get it back to normal.

(resting heart rate)

I'm scared to keep reading but there's a morbid curiosity compelling me to go on. It's like watching a horror movie, I know something's coming.

Something bad. I can't look away.

She was awoken by gunshot outside her bedroom window. Realising her escape route was cut off, she tried to get out through the front door but was intercepted. She was arrested and taken to Gestapo Headquarters in Paris.

Eleven members of the Sand Dune network were killed during the raid, including Alex Sylvan and Madame Poirier. Sebastian Tholozan evaded capture and continued to work for the resistance until the end of the war. He committed suicide in 1950.

Fuck sake.

Marièle.

She must have been so scared. They killed her friends and dragged her off in the middle of the night.

Marièle. Marièle.

A complete stranger, the old woman who collapsed in the shop, my fake aunt.

This incredibly brave girl.

I know people did stuff like that in the war, acts of bravery which they never bragged about, but I didn't realise she was one of them. Her story reads like the plot of a film, not real life. It feels so far removed from my life to be real. But she did it. This was her. This was her life.

Marièle.

Marièle was held by the Gestapo in Paris, where she was beaten and tortured while being questioned. Despite being subjected to extremely brutal treatment at the hands of her captors, she maintained her story, vehemently denying all knowledge of the circuit and maintaining that she was Sabine Valois, sent to live in the country to recuperate from a bout of Rheumatic Fever.

'Apart from Alex and Madame, I didn't know what had happened to the rest of them. I was on my own most of the time I was held. I don't remember much about it, to be honest.'

A report written after Marièle's return to the UK stated that she 'acted with extreme courage and bravery under very traumatic circumstances.' During her time in captivity, she was repeatedly submerged in water, as well as having her fingernails forcibly removed.

What the fuck?

I reread the sentence.

her fingernails forcibly removed

her fingernails forcibly removed
her fingernails forcibly removed
My own fingernails, slightly too long, could do with a trim.
I grip the nail of my index finger, tug on it.
I put it between my teeth, bite down, pull, pull, pull at it, scrape the red polish. Try to imagine the force, the violence required to wrench it off completely.
And then to keep going.
On to the next one.
And the next one.
Ten fingernails.
My eyes are drawn back to that sentence. I can't look away. I'm ashamed at myself for the thrill I get when I read something so horrible.
her fingernails forcibly removed
her fingernails forcibly removed
her fingernails forcibly removed
her fingernails forcibly removed
I held her hand in the hospital. I didn't notice anything strange about her fingernails.
She definitely had them. I would have noticed otherwise.
How long did it take for them to grow back? It's painful just to cut your nails too short, down to the quick.
To have them forcibly removed. Pulled out.
What did they use to do it?
I'm disgusted at myself for wanting to know more. All the gory details, more gruesome description than James L. Phillips felt was necessary to include.
her fingernails forcibly removed
her fingernails forcibly removed
Come on, Hannah. Move on. Away from that sentence.

Marièle was transported by cattle train to a labour camp in Germany and had her head shaved upon arrival due to an infestation of lice. There she was reunited with Eliza Buchanan, her friend and roommate from basic training.

'We were so happy to see each other but we wished it was under different circumstances. Eliza had been caught sending a sked, picked up by one of the detection vans. She looked after me, made sure I made it to roll call, got my food. She kept me alive.'

As political prisoners, Marièle and Eliza wore red triangles on their clothing to distinguish them. The women were kept in cramped barracks and forced to work long days on meagre rations. Disease and dysentery spread quickly throughout the camp and the majority of inmates were exhausted and emaciated.

Towards the end of the war, when the German guards realised that defeat was inevitable, they embarked upon a policy of extermination and destruction of the camp records. All prisoners well enough to walk were led out of the camp on one of the now infamous death marches.

Marièle and Eliza were among those ordered to march. Most of the women were too weak to make it very far, and collapsed and perished at the side of the road or were shot by guards enroute.

'Eliza's death was my lowest point. To get so close to the end and still not make it... I felt like I'd failed her. She was a mother, a wife, she had so much to live for, but even with all that she couldn't hold on. I thought what hope do I have of surviving? The guards had deserted by then, too cowardly to be found with us.'

Marièle and the other survivors were picked up by American troops who transported them to a nearby Red Cross unit. They in turn were able to get word back to London and Marièle was transported back to the UK.

Marièle was awarded an MBE after the war as well as the Croix de Guerre and the Médaille de la Résistance.

'It was all a long time ago. I wasn't a hero. I just did what I thought was the right thing to do.'

That's it?
I flick through the book. There must be more. It's all so formal, so matter of fact. What did she do afterwards?
Did she fall in love?
Did she get married, have children?
Where's the rest of her story?
Fingernails ripped out, hair shaved off, death march, Eliza, home... collapses in shop? What about the missing part? The middle section?
A happy time.
I turn back to her photo. The head and shoulders shot of her in uniform. Unsmiling. Serious. Eliza on the opposite page. Smiling, beautiful. Before she died at the side of the road.
MARIÈLE DOWNIE, SHORTLY BEFORE LEAVING FOR FRANCE, JANUARY 1944.

Before…
her fingernails forcibly removed
her fingernails forcibly removed

I can't believe she did all that and still nobody cares enough to come and visit her in hospital. Nobody cares enough to even notice that she's in hospital.

But she's in a book. Someone knows who she is.

James L. Phillips knows who she is.

I thought if you were in a book, it meant you'd be remembered forever. Everyone should know about her, what she did, what she went through.

her fingernails forcibly removed
her fingernails forcibly removed

Dad has my swimming medals out on display so anyone who comes to the front door can see them. My achievements. Gold, silver and bronze collecting dust. Proof that at one time in my life I could swim fast, faster than anyone else.

Marièle's medals were given to her because she almost died for her beliefs, almost died to help others. To help future generations, to help me, a complete stranger. So that I could have a future, so that I could swim fast.

And where are her medals?

Not out on display.

If that had been me, if I'd been in her place, would I have survived?

Gran used to call me a tough cookie. Greg said I had the mental strength in me that made the difference between two swimmers of the same ability. Turned a good swimmer into a great swimmer.

But it's easy to be tough when you're the one controlling the pain. When it's a pain barrier you know you're going to come out on the other side of. It's easy to be tough when you have your family with you, when you have enough food, a warm bed.

My shoulder gave up and I fell to pieces.

Could I have gone through what she did?

And what is the life of a survivor? Was she haunted by what happened to her? Did she suffer from depression, flashbacks, bad dreams? I had all those from the death of a swimming career. They gave me a sports psychologist to speak to and all I'd done was hurt my shoulder and give up racing.

What happened to her after the war?

Just because she made it home doesn't mean she made it.

Marièle was transported back to the UK

Marièle was transported back to the UK

Her story ends there. Back to the UK. Nothing further to say. Real life, the getting on with it, just isn't as interesting.

22

ONE FOOT IN front of the other. One foot in front of the other. One step, One step. One step. One step. One step.

Step.

Step.

Step.

Step.

Sabine looked at her feet as she walked. Concentrated on putting one foot in front of the other.

Step.

Step.

Step.

Step.

She didn't look up, didn't want to see how far they had to go, to see the other women in front of her, struggling, dragging themselves forward. They all concentrated on the same thing. Putting one foot in front of the other.

If anyone tries something you're not happy with, hit him between the legs.

That wasn't going to work, not here.

Sabine could still feel the sensation of the train, the ground moving underneath her. In the dark for most of the journey, the only light coming from chinks in the walls of the wagon, as trees, houses, stations, German signposts flickered past.

She thought she was blind when they finally let her off the train. All she could see were shapes, shadows, her eyes adjusting to the light.

'Out! Raus!'

'Du bist mir zum kotzen, disgusting!' A female officer shouted at them after they'd been stripped and given different clothes to put on. The shoes were too small, pinched her toes and cut into the heels of her feet, while the skirt and blouse were covered in stains. They all had coloured triangles on their clothes. She'd been given a red one, sewn on the sleeve of her blouse.

Communist?

Resistor?

Political prisoner?

It didn't really matter, they were all enemies of the Reich.

They sat her in a seat and she let them cut off her hair, hacking at it with scissors first before taking a razor to her head, shaving right down until her scalp buzzed and tingled. She could still feel her hair on her ears, the back of her neck, even after it was gone. Swept up from the floor by a woman with a broom.

She ran a hand across her head, felt it bristle and prickle.

'Quarantäne, *new arrivals to quarantine.*'

Step.

Step.

Step.

Step.

Breaking the miles down into one step at a time. There were guards on either side, forcing them to keep going, keep moving forward. To keep putting one foot in front of the other. All Sabine wanted to do was stop, collapse to the ground, to never move again.

But no, she couldn't. If she stopped, if she faltered, they would stop too. They'd beat her, kick her.

Shoot her.

Leave her lying in the ditch. As much as she wanted to lie still, she didn't want to die. She had a stubborn streak which forced her to keep going. To stumble onwards. To. Put. One. Foot. In. Front. Of. The. Other. Foot.

Step.

Step.

Step.

Step.

'Marièle, Marièle is that you?'

Sabine ignored the woman, carried on walking.

'Marièle, it is you.'

The woman grabbed her arm, held onto her. Sabine recognised the voice but not the person speaking to her.

'That's not my name. Je suis Sabine.'

'Sabine, I'm sorry,' the woman gripped her forearms, kissed her. 'Although it doesn't matter what name you go by in here.'

- .... . / -.- .. .. / -... .- -.-. -. - / .- --. .- .. -. ... - / .... . .-. / -.-. --- .-.. -..
/ ... -.- .. -.

Sabine flinched as the woman's lips touched her, as the smell caught in her nose. The woman let go, took a step back. She was like the others, the ones who had been there for a while. Thin, bony. Her hair had grown back but not fully, she had bald patches all over her scalp.

Sabine looked at the woman's face, her eyes. She wore the same red triangle on her sleeve. The same category as Sabine.

'It's me, Eliza.'

'Eliza, I'm sorry, I didn't recognise...'

As soon as she said the words, she regretted it. It didn't help to draw attention to how bad Eliza looked, how much she'd changed. The ample bosom flat under a shapeless blouse, darkness shadowing her eyes

'Don't be silly, I know I've changed since I last saw you. You've obviously just arrived, you've still got some meat on your bones,' Eliza patted Sabine on the bottom and smiled.

'I've just left quarantine, I'm a bit disorientated.'

Sabine's mouth was waxy, she needed a drink.

'Come with me.'

Eliza took Sabine's hand, squeezed it. Sabine winced, pulled away.

'What is it?' Eliza said, 'Oh darling, what have they done to you? They're cruel bastards.'

She gripped Sabine by the wrist.

'Come on, we're roommates again.'

Step.

   Step.

      Step.

         Step.

Eliza stumbled and Sabine tried to hold her upright. They walked with linked arms, helped each other to keep going.

One foot in front of the other.

'Schnell, schnell.'

Where were they being taken? Sabine doubted if she'd ever get to find out. They'd lost so many since they'd left the camp. When was that? Days? Weeks?

Maybe this was the plan. Just keep walking them until they all eventually dropped. For all she knew, they were going round and round in circles.

Sabine and Eliza had been deemed 'fit to walk.' That was a joke. Nobody was fit here. They were all marching skeletons. Simply putting one foot in front of the other in the hope of surviving.

They were told they were being moved to another camp, but who believed a word they said? As usual the rumours hissed up and down the line of women.

They're taking us to be shot.

The Russians will find us then we'll all be raped and murdered.

Everyone left behind is dead, they killed them all.

Sabine was tired and disorientated. In training they'd showed her how to use the position of the sun, the moon, the stars. She couldn't remember any of it. Couldn't find the energy to lift her head to look up at the sky, let alone use it to work out which direction she was going in. She didn't even know what country she was in anymore.

Step. Step. Step. Step. Step. Step.

.-

-...

-.-.

-..

She ran through her memory exercises, tried to keep her brain active and alert. Tried not to think of the weeping abscess on her leg, of how weak Eliza was, of her hunger.

.

..-.

--.

--.

.-

Everything she'd learnt slipped away from her, she couldn't retain it. It took all the concentration she had to keep putting one foot in front of the other.

Madame.
Alex.
Madame.
Alex.
Madame. Alex. Madame. Alex. Madame. Alex. Madame. Alex. Madame.
JC JD TM CA DY JC JD TM CA DY JC JD TM CA DY
Sabine woke, sweating. Her hair stuck to her forehead. She felt Eliza next to her, squeezing her, they were both shaking. They lay side by side in the bunk, the thin blanket pulled up over their chins, damp and

*woolly and covered in lice. It scratched Sabine's skin, made it break out
in a rash. It didn't keep them all that warm, but they huddled under it
all the same. Sabine had an abscess on her leg and the blanket tugged at
the open wound, the wool sticking to the raw skin.*

'Ssshhh, are you okay?'

'Yes, I'm sorry, it was a bad dream.'

*Eliza's hand reached up, brushed across the chain Sabine still wore
around her neck.*

'What's that?'

'My cross,' *Sabine answered.*

'How did you get that in here?'

'I hid it on me when I was on the train. I was scared someone would
steal it. They didn't search me all that thoroughly.'

'That training came in handy then?'

'I was lucky, if you can call it luck. They'd have found it if they'd
looked properly.'

'They've given up doing things properly round here. It's too crowded,
they've lost control.'

*Sabine didn't think she could bear it if she lost the cross now. She felt
as if she spoke to George when she held it.*

George rather than God.

*Eliza pulled Sabine in close to her, her legs curled around Sabine's
back and bottom. Sabine felt Eliza's bare feet, cold against her thighs.
Rough skin, brittle toenails, so different from those soft feet she'd
massaged back in training.*

'Remember that story your dad told us? About his kilt during the
war?' *Sabine said.*

'You've never met my dad, darling, he died before we even met.'

'Oh, of course, sorry. I'm half asleep, thinking of someone else.'

- .... . / -.- .. .. / -... ..- .-. -. - / .- --. .- .. -. ... - / .... . .-. / -.-. --- .-.. -..
/ ... -.- .. -.

'Tell me the story.'

'They wore kilts in the trenches, he would slide a fingernail up each
pleat of the kilt and it would come away covered in lice.'

'Oh, that's horrible.' *Eliza whispered. Her breath was hot and sticky
on the back of Sabine's neck. It smelt musky and fetid. Neither of them
had brushed their teeth in weeks.*

*And to think she'd thought the men had smelt bad, cooped up in
Alex's hut.*

*That was nothing compared to here. Hundreds of them to one tap.
The water brown and putrid. Their toilet a hole in the ground, you had*

to wade through excrement to even get close. They were all ill. Most of them never even made it to the hole in the ground. Didn't even try.

Sabine's sense of smell had adapted, her nose had got used to the stench. The odours she'd found so offensive when she first arrived. The odours that caught in the back of her throat, made her gag, made her want to step away from people, not get too close, not have them touch her. All that had changed. She was one of them now. She saw the new arrivals grimace and shy away from her.

There was something different about lying here in the dark though, huddled in bunks together, their breath visible in the cold air. She could smell the sweet rot of Eliza's breath when she spoke, felt it coat the back of her neck.

- .... . / -.- .. .. / -... .. .- .-. -. - / .- --. .- .. -. -. ... - / .... . .-. / -.-. --- .-.. -.. / ... -.- .. -.

'I think you have a story to outdo his now.' Eliza said.

'Do you think they're still sending our letters?'

'I don't know. Maybe they'll tell them the truth now?'

'I hope not. Mama couldn't cope with another telegram. You know, I found those notes so hard to write. I ran out of things to say.'

'There's only so many times you can say you drove an officer around.'

'Ssshhhhh, I'm trying to sleep here.' The woman lying next to Sabine and Eliza spoke up.

Did anyone actually sleep here? It wasn't possible. Collapse with exhaustion, yes, but sleep?

Mama would always say 'I'm having a physical collapse,' whenever she was tired or had a busy day.

Un effondrement physique.

Father would shake his head, physical collapse, good God woman, stop exaggerating. Sabine barely dozed in here. Kept awake by snoring, moans of pain, other women sobbing in the dark, the movement and creaks of the wooden bunks, the scuttling of rats. It wasn't sleep. It was the same unconscious feeling she'd had in the cell back in Paris.

'Your turn,' Sabine whispered.

They rolled over, Sabine put an arm over Eliza, pulled her close, heard the woman next to them tut.

'Will you tell your wee boy?' Sabine whispered in Eliza's ear. Her lips were crusty, stuck together when she spoke. She tried to lick them but she had no saliva.

'Tell him what?'

'Our lice story?'

Sabine felt Eliza tense. She didn't reply.

'*You will see him again.*'

Eliza's tears dropped warm onto her hand. It still surprised her, how much they could cry in here when they were so dehydrated, wasting away from lack of food and water.

'*I'm sorry, I shouldn't have…*'

'*SSSHHHH.*'

Sabine felt a bony elbow dig into her side. She closed her eyes, cradled Eliza until the bell rang for roll call.

Step. Step.
   Step.
      Step. Step.
     Step.
         Step. Step.
         Step.

They'd been told to march but it was barely a shuffle. A march was supposed to be regimented, in time, in rhythm. They had marched in training. Rows of them, arms and legs in step, backs straight, heads proud. Polished shoes and spick span uniform.

No, this wasn't marching. This was a shambles. Women stumbling, tripping, falling, barely able to lift their feet from the ground. No regimentation. They dragged themselves forward.

Step.
  Step.
   Step.
   Step.

Sabine and Eliza hadn't spoken for hours now. No words of encouragement, of hope. Eliza walked with her eyes closed. She was struggling. Her breath stuttered and gasping.

There were less of them now. Even the number of German soldiers seemed to have deteriorated.

Two of them walked to the left of her and Eliza. They whispered to each other.

'*Aus der traum.*'

Sabine's shoulders and back ached from standing. It was still dark, the middle of the night when they called them for roll call. Every morning there were less of them. Sabine felt herself sway from side to side, teeth chattering. Black dots fuzzed her eyes. She had to stay alert, remain standing. If she toppled, she would never get up again.

The Aufseherin *blew her whistle and Sabine felt the women around her relax. She did the same, shuffled closer to Eliza, ready to walk back to the barracks for the brown water the guards called coffee, drunk*

from old tin cans like the ones she'd used to bail water out of the Seafox.

Eliza had found a lump of potato in her soup the other day, had tried to share it with Sabine, but Sabine refused. Eliza had been there longer. Was so much thinner.

TD JF GT DF BT DZ IF IY EO IY EO DY

Madame and her coffee pot warming on the stove. To think Sabine had thought that coffee was bad. That was pure Parisian luxury compared to what they were served here.

JC JD TM CA DY JC JD TM CA DY JC JD TM CA DY

Was Madame still lying on the floor of her kitchen or had someone moved her?

No, she couldn't think of Madame. Her spirits were low enough already.

Eliza took Sabine's hand, led her across the camp. The Aufseherin *had let them away earlier than normal, usually made them stand for hours, swaying and shivering in their rows. She'd already had her fun for the day though. One of the other women had fainted, lain in the mud as the* Aufseherin *set the Alsatian on her. Sabine had tried not to look but she couldn't ignore the cries, the screams, the growls, the sound of the dog worrying the woman from side to side. She kept her eyes focused on the barbed wire fence in the distance, kept them there until the woman went quiet.*

Step.
 Step.
  Step.
   Step.

Sabine could feel Eliza, heavier, heavier, heavier against her arm.

She opened her mouth, then stopped herself. What was the point in asking Eliza if she was alright? None of them were alright. And Eliza was too exhausted to answer anyway.

The women in front had stopped walking. Was this another stop? Would they get something to eat? She heard the whispers.

They've gone.

White flags.

We're on our own.

They've left us, they've run away.

'Come on, darling,' Sabine led Eliza to the side of the track, lent her against a tree, 'I think they've deserted. The rumours about us winning must be true.'

Eliza's face was grey. She didn't answer, couldn't hold herself up. She slid down the tree. Sabine sat next to her, used her weight to prop them both up. Other women were doing the same now, sitting, lying down, collapsing where they stood.

Eliza slumped to the side. Sabine caught her, lowered her, placed her head in her lap. She stroked Eliza's face, whispered to her.

'It's okay, we're almost there, darling. Stay strong. You'll be home soon, with Adam and with Bill.'

She still cradled Eliza when she heard the rumble of the approaching lorries. A few of the women stood up, began to scream.

It's the Germans, they're back, with machine guns.

It's the Russians, quick, hide.

Sabine stayed where she was. She couldn't move Eliza, they would just have to sit here and wait for whoever it was to arrive.

'Ma'am, can I help you into the transport?'

A GI held out his hand. She saw the disgust and pity flit across his face, he didn't want to touch her.

She must have fallen asleep. Other women were already in the back of the lorry. They had blankets, food, water.

'Take Eliza first, she's so poorly.'

The soldier knelt down.

'I'm very sorry, Ma'am, but I'm afraid your friend hasn't made it.'

'No, you're wrong. Eliza, Eliza, wake up, darling, wake up. Please wake up. They're here. They're here.'

Sabine's legs were numb, Eliza's head heavy in her lap. She tried to lift her, but she couldn't do it. She was so heavy. So heavy for someone so tiny.

'Eliza, wake up, wake up, we're safe now.'

'I'm very sorry for your loss, Ma'am.'

Ma'am.

Ma'am.

Why did he keep calling her that?

Did she look like an old woman to him?

'Please, Ma'am, let me help you into the transport. The Red Cross are nearby, they're expecting...'

'Stop calling me Ma'am. I can't leave her, I can't leave her here.'

The GI stood up, waved over two other soldiers. They lifted Eliza, helped Sabine to her feet. She wanted to fight them off, hit them, struggle, she wasn't leaving without Eliza. But she was so tired, too weak to fight back.

And she knew.

She knew they were right.

Eliza was dead.

She let the men carry her to the lorry, lift her in beside the other women. The ones who had made it. The lucky few.

They handed her a blanket and a square of chocolate. She let the chocolate melt on her tongue as she watched the men. Men carrying spades.

They lifted Eliza, put her in a pile with the other bodies.

There were so many of them.

So many who hadn't survived the

Step.

   Step.

      Step.

         Step.

           Step.

              Step.

224

Swimming Star Sunk by Shoulder Injury

Scottish swimming star and British record holder Hannah Wright yesterday announced her retirement from the sport.

Hannah, 20, has been suffering from a shoulder injury for the past eighteen months and has had to endure painful surgery and weeks of rehabilitation.

'The operation was my final chance,' said Hannah, 'and unfortunately it hasn't worked out the way I'd hoped. I'm absolutely devastated to give up my swimming career.

I thought I'd have a few more years to enjoy it. The decision to retire hasn't been easy, but it's been taken out of my hands. I've been in pain for months and the doctors have told me I risk permanent damage and disability if I continue with the intensive training that I need to do to compete at my best. I'm struggling to come to terms with it and it's going to take me a while to get my head around things. I'd like to thank my coach, Greg Candy, for everything he's done for me.'

23

THE WHISTLE BLOWS, signalling the start of the race.

_____   _____   _____   _____

    Three short blasts followed by one long.

    Only I'm not ready.

    Not ready to get up on the starting block.

    I don't have my cap and goggles on yet. I've still got my tracksuit on over my costume. I'm not ready.

    They're going to start without me. I'm not ready.

_____   _____   _____   _____

    I'm not ready, my goggles have snapped, I try to unzip my tracksuit top but the zip's stuck.

    I'm not ready.

_____   _____   _____   _____

notreadynotreadynotreadynotreadynotreadynotreadynotreadynotreadynot

    I sit upright. Where am I? It's dark, takes my eyes a while to get accustomed.

    I'm still on Marièle's sofa, the blanket's tangled around me, I can't get my arms free. The wool itchy and hot.

    The book lies open on the carpet, must have fallen. One of the pages is bent and I smooth it down. Slide the author's note back inside.

    What time is it?

    It's dark outside. It must be late.

_____   _____   _____   _____

    Why can I still hear the whistle from my dream?

_____   _____   _____   _____

    I'm disorientated, half asleep, trying to catch up with what's going on.

_____   _____   _____   _____

    Idiot, it's not the whistle, it's the phone.

_____   _____   _____   _____   _____

    I put my hands out in front of me, shuffle towards the ringing.

    It's dark and it's not my house, I can't see where the fuck I'm going.

    'Shit.'

    I bash my shin off the coffee table. That was sore. I rub at it.

226

I'm never going to get to the phone on time.

———— ————   ———— ————   ———— ————
———— ————   ———— ————   ———— ————

Wait.

Why am I going to answer the phone? It's not my house, it could be anyone. Who the hell's ringing at this time anyway? Whatever time it is.

Foggy, middle-of-the-night brain. Doesn't work properly, makes decisions that don't make sense to wide-awake-middle-of-the-day brain.

I reach for the living room door, pull it open. I can see shapes and shadows now. Street light shines in through the frosted glass of the front door.

The phone stops.

The clock on the wall ticks, ticks, ticks, ticks, ticks, ticks.

I flick the hall light on.

Half three.

Shit, half three. I should have gone home hours ago.

———— ————   ———— ————   ———— ————
———— ————   ———— ————   ———— ————

I jump as the phone starts to ring again.

———— ————   ———— ————   ———— ————
———— ————   ———— ————   ———— ————

Half three.

Nobody rings at half three in the morning with good news.

I'm still holding the book. Why am I still holding the book?

I put it down, stand with my hand over the phone, grip the receiver, but don't lift.

It buzzes against my palm, the ring vibrating up my arm.

———— ————   ———— ————   ———— ————
———— ————   ———— ————   ———— ————

I don't want to pick up. I know who's on the other end. I know what they're going to say to me.

If I pick up.

———— ————   ———— ————   ———— ————
———— ————   ———— ————   ———— ————

It's so loud. I look for a volume control. An off switch.

What if I pull the cord out of the wall?

Just ignore the ringing. If I don't answer then…

Then what?

(she's not really dead)

'Hello?'

My voice is a croak, a whisper. My mouth's dry. I cough, clear my throat.

'Hello?' I repeat.

My hand's shaking and I have to squeeze tight on the receiver to keep it steady against my ear.

'I'm phoning from the PRI, it's about Marièle Downie.'

I nod my head, remember I'm on the phone.

'Yes.'

'I'm sorry to call you so late, but I'm afraid I have some bad news.'

'Uh-huh.'

I'm not pretending anymore. My throat's thick and I can't speak. I don't want her to be dead. She can't be. Not now.

'I'm very sorry, but Marièle passed away this morning. It was very peaceful. She never regained consciousness.'

'Oh,' I try to say okay but only manage the first part.

Peaceful.

her fingernails forcibly removed

The pressure builds, builds, builds in my chest.

Erupts.

Why am I crying? I didn't know her. We weren't friends.

'I'm very sorry for your...'

I put the phone down. I can't speak. There's no point trying to continue the conversation. I sink to the floor, lean my head between my knees, dig in my jeans for a tissue but can't find one, so I wipe my sleeve across my nose and eyes.

'I'm sorry. I'm sorry I'm in your house and I'm sorry for what happened to you and I'm sorry you died.'

Saying the word out loud makes it worse.

Died.

Died.

Died.

I force myself to stand, into her bedroom, take down the photo of her from the shelf.

My tears drip onto the frame, smear the glass as I try to wipe them away.

I make my way along the hall towards the kitchen. The fish is swimming back and forth, back and forth, back and forth. Having one of his mad half hours, zipping from one side of the bowl to the other.

I sit at the kitchen table, stand the photo in front of me. Angle it so the fish can see it.

'It's bad...'

That sets me off again and I can't speak, I can't speak, I can't speak. My breath comes in short gasps, shuddering and painful.

What the fuck am I doing? I need to get out of here, go home.

But what about the fish? What'll happen to him if I leave him here? On his own.

'I could take you with me?'

No, Hannah, wake up. Middle-of-the night-brain doesn't talk sense. Stop listening to it and just go home. You shouldn't be here. You should never have come here in the first place.

Someone needs to organise the funeral. And it can't be her fake niece. Too many lies. Too much breaking and entering.

Ex-swimmer, Hannah Wright, was arrested today...

'I'd better feed you before I go,' I reach for the tub of flakes, catch a flash of red.

The lottery ticket.

It could be you.

(it could be me)

The lottery ticket. I could take it. Cash it in. Nobody would ever know.

(it's not as if I haven't thought of it before)

£100, 000

£100, 000

Give Dad something to be happy about, make him proud of me again.

What if she'd died straight away? If she'd died before she reached the hospital? If I'd never come to her house, never looked at her photos, visited her, read about her.

I could have taken the ticket.

She would still be the old woman lying on the shop floor, the one I didn't want to touch, to go near.

She wouldn't be Marièle and I wouldn't be this upset.

Jesus, the world is fucked up.

announced her retirement from the sport

her fingernails forcibly removed

Me and her just haven't caught a break.

(except I almost have)

It could be you.

Maybe this is the universe's way of making it up to me. Sorry we fucked around with your swimming career, but here's something to make up for it. No hard feelings, eh?

I pull the ticket out from behind the bowl. Walk to the phone table in the hall.

Pick up the pen that's lying there. Write the name and address on the ticket before I change my mind.

NAME: Marièle Downie
ADDRESS: Douglas Crescent, Kinross

The book's still lying next to the phone. I carry it through to the kitchen.

'I've got to go, fish. Don't worry, they'll come here first when they can't get in touch with me. You'll be okay.' I try to convince myself that I'm doing the right thing. That someone will find him, look after him, that he won't end up floating on the top of his bowl or flushed down the toilet.

I put the book down on the kitchen table next to her photo, mark the right page with the author's note, place the lottery ticket on top, pocket my mobile.

Chapter Fifteen: Marièle Downie, aka Sabine Valois, aka Blackbird.

Something stops me and I head back to the phone table again, tear a blank piece of paper from the notebook lying there. Leave a note beside the book and the photo.

She wasn't just an old woman who died.
Please look after her fish.
Thank you

'Who knows, maybe she left everything to you?' I kneel in front of the fish bowl. I can feel tears coming again. Fuck sake, what's wrong with me?

Saying goodbye to a goldfish has me sobbing.

I've got quite attached to that wee fish though.

'Goodbye, look after yourself.'

I stand at the back door for a moment, take in Marièle's kitchen. Exactly how she left it that day she went out and never came back.

I wave.

Close the door.

No, I can't do it. I can't leave him. She can have the lottery ticket, but I'm taking her fish.

I push the door open.

'You're coming with me, fish.'

Please look after her fish.

I lift the bowl, water sloshes over me. I decant some of it into the sink, carry the bowl towards the back door, set it down on the step as I leave Marièle's house. Close her back door. Lock it. Drop the spare key back inside the flowerpot.

I wheel my bike out onto the street, tie it up against a lamppost. I can pick it up in the morning. I need both hands for the bowl, have to walk slowly. The fish is rocked from side to side with the movement of the water.

The streets are deserted. Nobody about except me and the fish. We could be the only two left. The survivors of some zombie apocalypse.

'That's what you and me are, fish. We're survivors.'

The lights are on when I get home. Dad must be up. He'll be wondering where I am.

I balance the fish bowl against my hip, cradle it with an arm, while I search in my pocket for my house key.

Dad's sitting on the stairs when I open the door, Shirley's behind him, one step up, her hand on his shoulder.

'Whereve you been? I've been tryingphone you. I senyou messages,' he says as he stands.

'What messages?'

'Yourmobile,' he replies.

'Sorry, my phone's been switched off.'

He stumbles down the stairs, knocks over an ashtray. Fag ends and ash tip out onto the carpet. I can smell the whiskey coming off him as he grabs me.

'Careful, Dad,' I step back as water splashes from the bowl.

'Whathe hellave you gothere?'

'It's a goldfish.'

'I cansee isssa bloody goldfish.'

'Everything okay?' Shirley asks from where she's sitting on the stairs. She doesn't look very happy with me.

Does she know I shagged her son? Did she tell Dad?

Shit.

I nod, put the fish bowl down on the carpet, out of the way of Dad who sways in front of me, whiskey breath on my face.

Shirley stands, grabs her jacket which is slung over the banister.

'I'll push off then.'

'Ohokay, thankshiry.' He looks like he's forgotten she was even there.

'No bother,' she squeezes past us both, gives me a look as she lets herself out the front door.

Dad stumbles to one side, clatters into the glass medal cabinet. The medals and cups rattle about inside, one hits the sliding door, cracks the glass panel. Dad sinks back onto the stairs, holds his head in his hands.

'Dad, I'm sorry.'

He looks up at me. He's crying. Shit, my dad's crying. I kneel in front of him.

'Dad, are you okay?'

'I wassso worried, Hannah, thoughyoudone something daft.'

'What? I wouldn't do that. Of course I wouldn't.'

'Butyou've been solow, sossad, I know you missswimming.'

Tears run down his cheeks, glisten on his beard. He wipes his eyes, takes my hand, his fingers are damp.'

'Sno fair, Hannah, it's jussno fair.'

He lets go of me, takes a hankie from his pocket and blows his nose.

'I'm jussssilly old duffer,' he rubs his eyes and cheeks with his hanky. His skin wrinkles, doesn't spring back, folds up under his eyes. He picks up the fag ends, puts them back in the ashtray, wipes the ash into the carpet with his hand.

He's getting old.

I haven't really thought about it until now. Now that I'm at face level with him. I see the grey hair, the lines on his forehead, around his mouth. He's always just been Dad to me, but now I look at him, realise that one day he won't be here anymore.

Like Mum. Like Gran. Like Marièle.

My swimming.

Pressure builds in my chest, in the back of my throat.

My mouth hurts, my tongue hurts, my teeth hurt. I can't swallow it down. It rises and rises and rises and rises and…

I lean my head on his legs. He strokes my hair as I cry all over his jeans.

'We'recouplea idiots arenwe.'

I nod. I can't speak. I can't speak. I can't speak.

'Where were you tonight?'

I swallow, the lump's too big though, sticks in my chest. I swallow again, try to compose myself.

'Iwentforacyclethatoldwomandied,' I say it quickly so I can get the words out.

'Whaollwoman?' Dad stops hugging me and I lean back, gulp air into my lungs.

'Collapsedatwork.'

Short, fast sentences, that's all I can manage.

'Jesus, I forgoabou her. Howdyou finout?'

'Phonedthehospital.'

'Poor olllssoul, Jesus, whaawaytogo. Collapsingin bloody Shirley'sshitey wee shop. That'sa bit of a tongue twister. Shirley'sshiteyweeshop, Shirley's chiteyweeshop, Shirley'sshiteywechop. Give it a go.'

'Shirley's shitey wee shop. Shirley's shitey wee shop.'

'No, no, you have to say it faster than that. 'Shirley'sshiteyweeshopS hirley'schiteyweechop.'

'Shirley'sshiteyweeshop, Shirley'sshiteyweechop, Shirley'schiteyweechop, Shirleyshitey.'

'I don't know whatwas thinking, letting you work in Shirley'schiteywee shop. I've told her, yourno going back. You'reso like your mum, no wonder she left.'

'Don't say that.'

'Ach, it's true.'

He leans forward and kisses me on the forehead. His lips leave a sticky whiskey mark on my head, but I resist the urge to wipe it away.

'Asmuchas I'll miss you, you need to get out of here, away from Shirley'sshitey wee shop. Don't get stuck here.'

'Okay,' I nod.

'No, donjust say okay, I really mean it, promiseme. There'still so much you can do. Swimming's not the beall and enall.'

He squeezes me, tight, painful, his fingertips bruising my upper arms.

'I promise, Dad, I promise.'

He just stares at me, like he's working out if I'm telling him the truth or not then he stands, groans as his knees creak.

'Look, look,' he gestures at the cracked medal cabinet, stumbles off-balance, 'so you had to stop, but look what you did before that. Thasmore than a lot of people ever do.'

I nod.

'Righ, olduffer needsis bed. Where did that come from?' He asks, noticing the fish again. He doesn't wait for an answer though, sways past me up the stairs.

I put my hand out, the carpet's warm from where he's been sitting. I curl up on the stairs, rest my face against the warmth of him, watch the fish as he swims from side to side.

24

SHE HAD JUST put a pot of soup on to heat up when the phone rang.

Ring Ring

Ring Ring

'*Zut*! Who's that?'

She took a wooden spoon from the cutlery drawer, stirred her soup, decided to ignore the phone for the moment.

Ring Ring

Ring Ring

'Someone's persistent,' she said to the fish.

Marièle lay on her bed, looking up at the ceiling. She couldn't face leaving her bedroom, going out there into the rest of the house.

The atmosphere was thick, oppressive. She could feel it, even in here. They were stuck in it, it was all around them, squeezing them tight, tight, tight, tight. Like those jam traps Father left outside for wasps. The stickiness caught them, sucked them under into the water, drowning, drowning, drowning them.

'*Marie,*' *there was a knock on her bedroom door.*

She hesitated before replying. Maybe she should pretend to be asleep? Mama seemed happy to sink into the jam.

What was it she said at dinnertimes?

You can have bread and butter or bread and jam, but you can't have bread and butter and jam.

'*Marie,* chérie.'

You can have bread and butter or bread and jam, but you can't have bread and butter and jam.

'*Yes, Mama.*'

'*I think you should see this.*'

'*What is it?*'

Marièle tried to keep the frustration out of her voice. What did she want? Marièle just wanted to lie there, lie there still, not sink any deeper into the jam.

'*Please,* chérie, *come here.*'

Marièle sat up, swung her legs off the bed, could feel the stickiness cling at her as she opened the door onto the hallway.

'*Where are you, Mama?*'

'*In here,*' *her voice came from George's room.*

Oh God.

The jam was stickiest in there. Marièle didn't want to see his bed, his clothes, his books.

'Mama, what is it?'

'Mon Dieu, stop being silly, just come and see this.'

Marièle felt the jam clamp around her middle the moment she stepped into George's room, it sucked the air out of her.

She could smell him, smell him in here. The blankets on the bed, the jumper slung over the armchair, the dressing gown hanging up on the back of the door. The scent of Aqua Velva, the pomade he sometimes used on his hair, tobacco, boot polish, those cinnamon boiled sweets he liked to suck on after smoking.

It was a safe smell, comforting, but, God, it made her ache.

She had to get out of here.

Marièle had sat on the bed, watched George polishing his boots before he left for the last time.

Were his boots still shining? Still sparkling somewhere, while the rest of him...

God, she couldn't bring herself to think about the rest of him.

Mama stood at the window.

'What is it, Mama?'

'Is that Cath out there?'

'Cath?' Marièle took a step forward, 'why would she be out there?' She stood behind Mama, followed her gaze.

'Yes, that's Cath? What's she doing?'

'She must be freezing, go and get her. Bring her in, I'll make tea.'

Marièle felt the jam begin to release her. She followed Mama downstairs, put on her coat hanging at the back door, slipped on her shoes.

God, it was bitter out.

Your carriage, m'ladies.

Marièle pulled her coat tight, stuffed her hands in the pockets, walked towards Cath, who sat on a wall at the back of the house.

'Cath, dear, what are you doing? You'll catch your death.'

The word death hung in the air between them.

'Oh, Marièle, I'm sorry, you weren't supposed to see... what I mean is, I didn't want to...' Cath looked down, her face flushed pink while her dimples shone out white against her cheeks.

'Cath, your hands are like ice, you can't stay out here. Come inside, Mama's making tea.'

'Oh no, I don't want to intrude.'

'You're a daftie,' Marièle rubbed Cath's hands.

'I miss him dreadfully,' Cath said, still looking down. Tears dripped off the end of her nose.

'Me too.'

'I just wanted to be close to him.'

On bad days you needed somewhere to go, a grave to visit. But there was nowhere like that for George. At least not in this country. Had they even found all of him to...

No, she stopped herself. Wouldn't let the jam thicken. They didn't have a grave they could visit, but they had a wall. A wall outside his bedroom, where they could sit for a while and feel close to him.

Ring Ring
Ring Ring

'I'd better answer it, I suppose.'

Ring Ring
Ring Ring

She turned off the heat, moved the pot to one side, before she made her way along the hall towards the telephone.

Ring Ring
Ring Ring

'Hello?'

'Hello, is that Marièle?'

'Who wants to know?'

There was a knock at the door. Marièle pulled the tartan rug around her, she didn't want to see anyone. Why did people keep turning up? Did they just want to look at her? See if the rumours were really true.

The Downie girl's come home. Prisoner of war. What she was doing out there in the first place I don't know. Imagine doing that to her parents after all they've been through. Yes, she's brave, but it's not the same for women as it is for men.

She tucked the rug into the neck of her pullover, hid her hands underneath. If she could she would hide her face too. If they couldn't see her then she wasn't really there.

She heard Mama open the front door, whisper to someone out in the hallway. Maybe it was another doctor? The psychiatrist back to check up on her?

The door to the sitting room opened. Mama stood in the doorway, someone hovered behind her.

'Cath's come to see you, ma chérie, isn't that nice?'

Marièle nodded. Mama had taken to speaking to her like that since *she'd come home. Like she was a child. Needed everything explained slowly and loudly.*

She was physically damaged, but she'd kept her mental abilities. She'd held on to them, by God, fought hard to keep them.

.-

-...

-.-.

-..

Cath stepped out from behind Mama. She looked terrified. Marièle had to stop herself from laughing. *Was she that monstrous now?*

Cath's cheeks were white, no smile to show off those dimples.

'I heard you were home and I wanted to come sooner, but your father said you were sick. But then, today of all days, I thought...'

Everyone wanted to stare at the freak. With her boy's haircut and her gaunt face. Good job she'd thought to hide her hands. One glimpse of those fingertips and Cath would run screaming for the door.

It's all true, it's true. I've seen her for myself.

No.

Stop Marièle.

Stop it.

So hateful and cruel.

So unfair to her best friend.

To her (almost) sister.

To her...

- .... . / -.- .. .. / -... ..- .-. -. - / .- --. .- .. -. ... - / .... . .-. / -.-. --- .-.. -..
/ ... -.- .. -.

Cath wasn't there to stare, or to gossip about what she'd seen.

But then, today of all days, I thought...

Today?

What was today?

Marièle had lost track of time in France, in the camp, on the

step   step   step   step   step   step

She'd not managed to find it again.

'Cath, what's today?'

Her words stuck in her throat, came out as a croak.

'It's George's birthday, remember?' Cath took a step forward.

Marièle felt herself sink deeper into the armchair.

Oh God.

She'd been sitting there all day. Getting annoyed with Mama. Snapping at her for not bringing soup when it was lunchtime. Wondering why Father had gone out so early.

Oh, God.

She was so arrogant. So selfish. She thought they were upset because of what had happened to her. How could she have forgotten today?

Forgotten George.

What was wrong with her? Was she ever going to get better?

She thought she'd kept her brain active, she'd tried, tried so hard.

.-

-...

-.-.

-..

But she'd forgotten, she'd forgotten what day it was.

'*Darling, are you okay? You've gone so white.*'

Cath knelt in front of the armchair. She reached in under the blanket, took Marièle's hand. Stroked it. Didn't flinch at the deformed fingernails which scratched and grew at a strange angle.

'*I forgot. I forgot what day it was.*'

'*But you know now, dear, and now you know what today is, then you know what yesterday was and what tomorrow is and the day after that and the day after that.*'

'I'm sorry to bother you, I'm Lee Webster, Lucy's husband.'

Marièle was caught off guard. Lucy Webster?

Who was Lucy Webster?

Then she remembered.

'*Oui*, of course.'

'I'm afraid I have some bad news. It's Cath. I'm afraid she passed away this morning. Lucy said you and her mum were good friends, went back a long way.'

Marièle felt the air rush out of her and she steadied herself against the telephone table.

Oh Cath, her Cath.

- .... . / -.- .. .. / -.... ..- .-. -. . - / .- --. .- .. -. -. ... - / .... . .-. / -.-. --- .-.. -.. / ... -.- .. -.

'*I brought you something. Remember I said I would, you thought I'd been ripped off, ye of little faith.*'

Cath opened her handbag, took out a brown envelope and handed it to Marièle.

'*What it is?*' *Marièle slid a finger into the opening of the envelope.*

She could control her fingers again. Could grip the contents between thumb and forefinger, slip it out. Her nails were still shorter than they should be, came about halfway up the tips of her fingers. Dimples had formed in the base of them, down near the cuticle. If she held her hand vertically at eye level and looked along the line of fingernails, she could see the clear depression in each one.

They'll fade but never disappear, the doctor said, like a scar.

Marièle preferred to think of them as dimples. That's what Cath called them.

George always called me dimples, but now you're the one with that nickname.

A photograph.

'God, I'd forgotten about this,' Marièle said, holding the photo of them both.

Caught as they walked along the pavement, arm in arm. Marièle in uniform. Cath in her polka-dot sundress, smiling, dimples on display. Not for the photographer though.

For her, Marièle.

What had she said to make Cath smile like that?

Marièle couldn't remember.

Home on leave. Hair intact. Nails intact.

Sanity intact.

Pre-France.

'God, that feels like such a long time ago now.'

'I know.'

'It's a good photo, I like it.' Marièle slipped it back inside the envelope, handed it to Cath.

'No, it's yours. I want you to have it. I said I'd give it to you when you came back and, well, here you are, dear. You came back.'

Also published by **LUATH PRESS**

Trackman
Catriona Child
ISBN 9781908373434 PBK £7.99

Trackman Trackman Trackman
Trackman Trackman Trackman
Trackman

Davie was about to leave the MP3 player lying on the pavement when something stopped him. A voice in his head. You'll regret it if you leave it. You'll only come back for it later.

Can a song change your life? Can a song bring people, places and moments in time alive again? Davie Watts is the Trackman. He knows what song to play to you and he knows exactly when you need to hear it. Davie seeks out strangers in need and helps them using the power of music.

In her debut novel, Catriona Child has all the makings of a cult hit... She handles the tension between the fantastical premise and the raw and sensitive matter of a dead schoolboy tastefully, and the book's sense of place makes it a delight for lovers of Edinburgh. THE HERALD

Details of this and other books published by Luath Press can be found at
www.luath.co.uk

Luath Press Limited

committed to publishing well written books worth reading

LUATH PRESS takes its name from Robert Burns, whose little collie Luath (*Gael.*, swift or nimble) tripped up Jean Armour at a wedding and gave him the chance to speak to the woman who was to be his wife and the abiding love of his life. Burns called one of the 'Twa Dogs' Luath after Cuchullin's hunting dog in Ossian's *Fingal*. Luath Press was established in 1981 in the heart of Burns country, and is now based a few steps up the road from Burns' first lodgings on Edinburgh's Royal Mile. Luath offers you distinctive writing with a hint of unexpected pleasures.

Most bookshops in the UK, the US, Canada, Australia, New Zealand and parts of Europe, either carry our books in stock or can order them for you. To order direct from us, please send a £sterling cheque, postal order, international money order or your credit card details (number, address of cardholder and expiry date) to us at the address below. Please add post and packing as follows: UK – £1.00 per delivery address; overseas surface mail – £2.50 per delivery address; overseas airmail – £3.50 for the first book to each delivery address, plus £1.00 for each additional book by airmail to the same address. If your order is a gift, we will happily enclose your card or message at no extra charge.

Luath Press Limited
543/2 Castlehill
The Royal Mile
Edinburgh EH1 2ND
Scotland
Telephone: +44 (0)131 225 4326 (24 hours)
email: sales@luath. co.uk
Website: www. luath.co.uk